Utherrian

Part One of the Blood & Dragons Trilogy

by
M. S. Lewis

Published by XanderCat Productions

Cover design by Mike Lees
Interior design by M. S. Lewis

ISBN 979-8-9931377-1-1

First Edition: November 2025

For Carol, Rebecca, and Sandy.

Thank you for teaching me to love the written word.

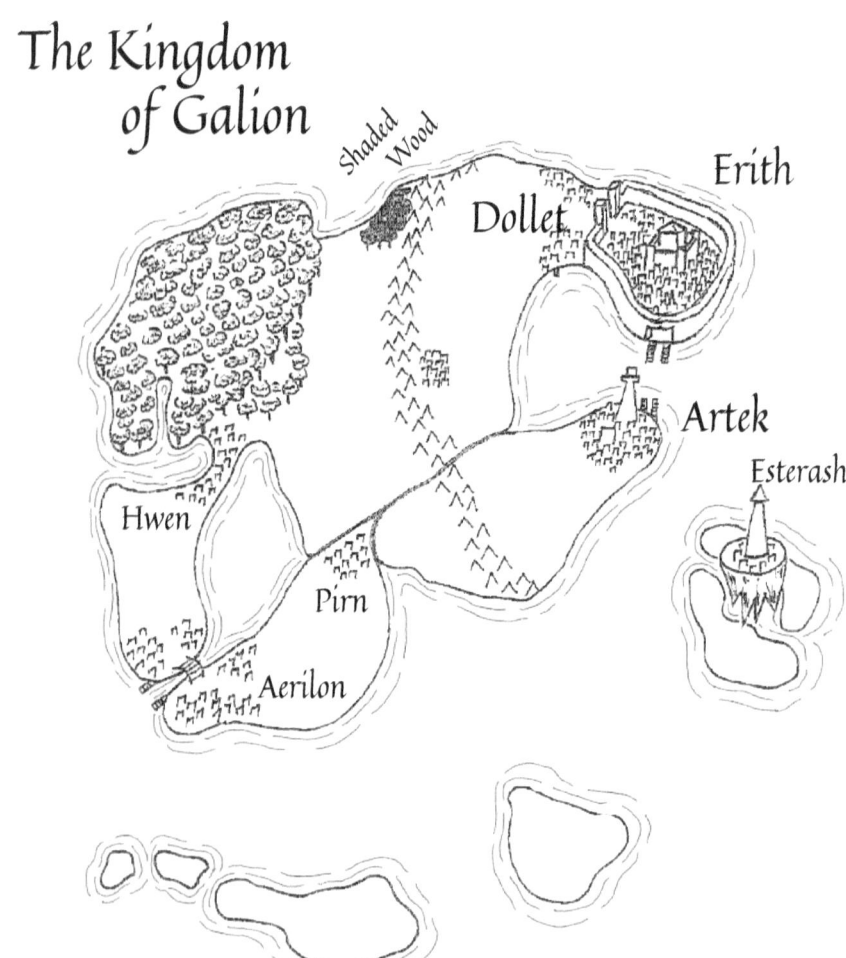

The Kingdom
of Galion

Shaded Wood

Dollet

Erith

Artek

Esterash

Hwen

Pirn

Aerilon

The Known World of
Camledor

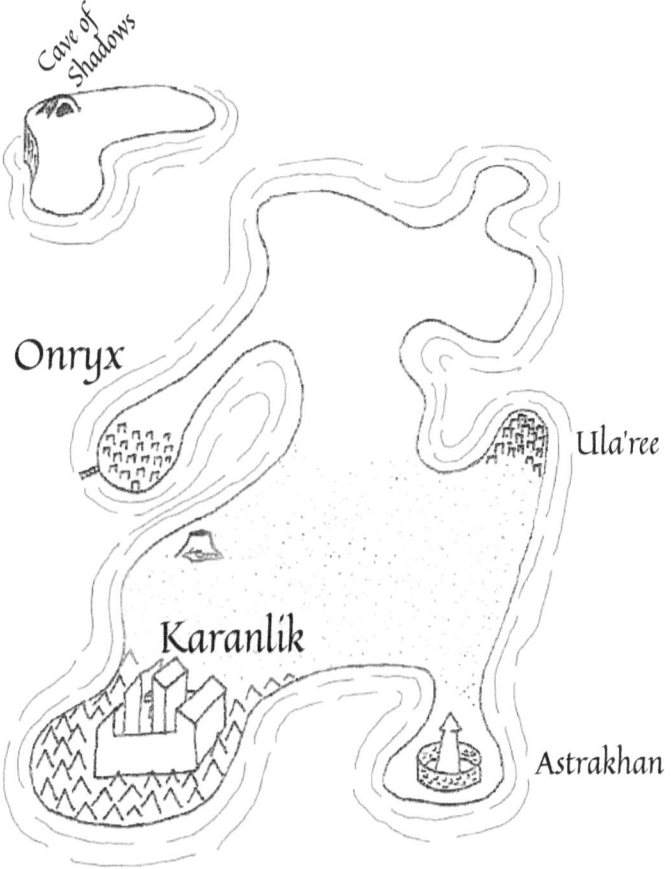

Cave of Shadows

Onryx

Ula'ree

Karanlik

Astrakhan

The Kingdom
of Ska'ell

Prologue

"All men must die in the end. If my time is now, so be it," the knight said, dropping his shield and taking his sword in both hands. The enemy was all around him, a band of vampire servants loyal to Logan Lacrym, King of Ska'ell. The knight's kingdom lacked a true king, but he was still sworn to protect the realm and its steward.

The vampires were advancing slowly, confident in their greater numbers. The six vampires that had already fallen to the knight's blade lay around the stone chamber. There were two doors, one leading inward, the other back out into the night. The knight rolled backwards towards the door to the keep's interior, dodging a swipe from the vampire nearest the door. His blade sang as it slid through the vampire's chest, puncturing its heart. When he withdrew the blade the vampire slumped to its knees, its hands reaching up to the wound in its chest. The knight swung the blade in a sharp arc and removed the creature's head. He turned towards the chamber again, his back now to the inner door.

Nine remaining.

The vampires were all glaring at him, saliva dripping from their fangs. Hisses erupted from their mouths as they all charged the knight. He kicked the first one to reach him, then spun with his blade extended, severing the head of one vampire and burying into the shoulder of another. When the knight tried to pull the blade back he found it was stuck, so he dropped it and grabbed for his dagger, a plain piece of steel the length of his forearm. He ducked under the attack of one vampire, buried the knife in the heart of another one, and shoved through their line, receiving a gash along his arm for his efforts. He grabbed at his fallen sword on the way through, but it was still lodged deep in the vampire's bone.

The knight now had his back to the outer door, with the vampires between him and his steward. He knew the vampires would not turn from him until he was dead and dry; the smell of his blood was too much for them to ignore. The knight stood weaponless, facing the seven remaining vampires. He clutched at a small pouch that hung from his neck and yanked, breaking the leather strap that held it in place. He dumped a small glass orb from inside into his hand, closing his fist around it.

The vampires were still advancing, and the knight took a deep breath before charging them. "For Galion!" he screamed as he advanced. The vampires fell on him quickly, biting and clawing and tearing at his skin. The knight howled in pain as the weight of the vampires brought him to his knees. He closed his eyes and whispered: "Utherrian," before slamming the glass orb into the stone floor.

A white mist erupted from the shattered glass, filling the room almost instantly. The vampires stopped their feeding and began to move for the outer door, forgetting their meal in their haste. Before they made it even two steps the mist exploded into a burst of sunlight, searing the flesh on vampire and human alike. The vampires fell one by one, their skin blackened and burnt. The knight was still on his knees when the light vanished, his skin burnt and cracked. Blood poured from a dozen wounds, pooling on the floor around him.

"Utherrian," the knight whispered again, closing his eyes. He fell forward as the final bits of strength left his body. Strong arms caught him before he hit the floor, and he felt himself being turned over onto his back. He opened his eyes and gazed up into a man's face, surrounded by silver hair.

"Utherrian!" the knight exclaimed, his voice rough but joyous. A cough racked the knight's body, and when it ended blood poured from his mouth.

"Rest now, you have done well," Utherrian said, his voice a deep rumble in the quiet stone chamber. Utherrian looked around the room. "You have done well indeed. You have earned your rest, and for your protection and your service I thank you. You have served both Galion and I faithfully."

"Thank you...steward," the knight wheezed. "But what...what if more come?"

"I am leaving this keep tonight; it does not contain what I'm searching for. But I am getting close," Utherrian said, his gray eyes blazing in the pale light of the room. "And once I do, young knight, all will be put right. Our King is still out there, and I will find him. The day that he stands with us will be the day that this war begins to end. He will win us through to the end, and Galion will rise from the ashes of Lacrym's bloody conflict."

The knight smiled, showing teeth stained red with blood. Utherrian smiled back.

"Now, young knight, look for the door. And once you've found it, walk through it into eternal peace. We shall all meet up there in the end, and I fear that many more will follow you before this fight is done. Rest, knight."

The knight's smile remained bright as the light faded from his eyes. Utherrian rested the knight's body on the ground before standing; he deserved a burial, but there was no time. More of Lacrym's vampires would arrive any minute, and Utherrian was now alone. He pulled his cloak around him and moved through the outer door, emerging into a night illuminated by a full moon. Utherrian looked up into the brightness before moving off. He was in search of a way to bring the true King over into his world. He knew who the King was, but the King was trapped in the world called Earth, and Utherrian must draw him to Camledor before it was too late...

1

The Drawing

Joshua Reese woke suddenly, sweat rolling from his pores. The small bits of his dreams that he could remember after waking were awkward, like glimpses of another world. Tonight he had dreamed of vampires, a guy with a sword, and another guy with silver hair and gray eyes. None of the people were Joshua in the dream, which was what had made it so weird.

Shaking his head to clear the grogginess, Joshua climbed out of his bed and walked to the bathroom to take care of his morning needs. Showered, teeth brushed, stubble shaved, he felt more himself. He dressed in a black t-shirt, jeans, and a corduroy jacket before grabbing his keys. He pet his cat, Cleo, before putting on his coat and heading out the door.

It was January in Pennsylvania, and the air was crisp and cold. A layer of frost covered the grass and his car's windshield. It was going to be another cold day, and the weather channel was calling for a late snowfall. As was his luck, he had classes throughout the day, and it would be late by the time he arrived home again.

Joshua unlocked his car, leaned inside, and started the ignition, hitting the buttons for the defroster and heat before grabbing the ice scraper from the backseat. He cleaned off his car's windows and tossed the scraper into the backseat, then turned up the radio for the drive to school.

He wound up parking in one of the furthest lots from his first class. No matter how early he tried to get to school, it always seemed like the commuter lots were full before he arrived. He walked through the bustling paths towards his first class of the day, Statistics, and got inside just as class was starting. He hadn't even gotten his coffee on the way in thanks to traffic.

It's going to be a long day, he thought.

Joshua's final class let out at 9pm. He was tired after a twelve hour day of nearly solid classes, with just enough time in the middle for lunch. Snow had started to fall halfway through his last class, and by the time he swung his car onto the highway there was already three inches on the ground. The worst part was the patches of black ice, but they were few and far between. Joshua turned up the radio and started singing along as he drove, trying to forget about how exhausted he felt.

Fifteen minutes after getting onto the highway he was reaching his exit, and he was thankful to be close to home. The entire drive he felt like he had been hearing things, voices. He assumed it was just the fatigue and exhaustion, but he kept hearing his name being called, as if from far away.

Joshua merged into the right lane to exit, and as he did the car behind him hit a patch of ice in the road and began to spin.

Joshua saw the lights swinging wildly behind him.

Saw the red taillights as the car spun around completely, and then the headlights again, just as the out-of-control vehicle hit him.

The first contact was the other car's front bumper tangling with his rear bumper. Metal squealed as the two cars began to slide together, then began to scream as they started to rip apart. Just as the cars disentangled, the right side of Joshua's car hit the guardrail, bouncing him back into the middle of the road.

This time it was Joshua's car that slammed into the other, all the while skating across ice and snow with no way to slow down. Both cars were spinning now and, just when it seemed like it was about to end, Joshua saw a tractor-trailer in the opposite lane lose control and blast through the center divider. The truck's headlights were bright in Joshua's eyes, and the sound of metal was a massive explosion in his ears as his car slammed into the front of the tractor-trailer. Glass rained down on Joshua's head as his airbags finally deployed, knocking his head backwards.

He heard the voice again: "Joshua, to me!" it called.

Then there was only darkness.

2

Transitions

Joshua opened his eyes to darkness. There was nothing else, nothing but the thick black. It clung to him, fitting like a second skin. He tried to call out, to beg for help, but he made no sound. He tried to draw in air, to catch his breath, but there was no air, just the thick blackness. He tried to move his arms, but they wouldn't budge; and when he tried to move his head it was held in place by the dark.

Time passed in that place, how much Joshua didn't know. It could have been five minutes, but to Joshua it felt like an eternity. Just when he felt like time had stopped completely and left him behind, Joshua glimpsed a small speck of light in the distance. He wondered if it had always been there, or if it had just appeared. He tried to move toward it, but the speck of light receded every time that he pushed himself forward. He was beginning to tire from the effort of trying to reach the light.

Just as he began to lose energy, will, and hope, Joshua began to hear an odd noise. The noise was quiet, but it sounded like drums. He struggled to make sense of the noise, and as he did it began to sound closer, more distinct.

"Joshua..." it called, as if across a great distance.

Joshua struggled towards it, forcing every ounce of his being to swim. The more he struggled, the more he felt the darkness closing in, threatening to snuff out the bit of light that he knew. He resigned himself to the dark, began to welcome its embrace. He drifted back into the dark, closing his eyes and giving in to his fate.

"To me Joshua..."

His closed eyes burned red, bright as daylight. He squinted his eyes open and was blinded by a bright white light. It was overwhelming, all encompassing, devouring. He tried to see through the light, tried to find its source.

"Joshua!"

That voice again. Louder, more clear. Joshua thought it was coming from the light. Whether good or bad, he saw no other option. He pushed. The grip of the darkness seemed to slip and Joshua launched forward. He felt himself flying through the space, the darkness receding behind him, the light enveloping him.

"JOSHUA!" The voice boomed through the darkness. His name. Someone calling out to him through the space.

"TO ME JOSHUA!!!" the voice demanded.

Joshua complied, moving his arms, moving through the space faster now. He didn't know the voice, but some part of his mind found it familiar, and nothing could be worse than the darkness. The blinding light seemed to get brighter. It grew in intensity, overtook him. There was nothing but light, and after the darkness it was overwhelming.

Just as he thought that it would destroy him, the light began to steady out, ease in intensity. The light changed from intense white to a swirl of purple and silver, forming a tunnel. Joshua moved into the tunnel willingly, happy to escape the eternity of darkness.

The tunnel became smaller and smaller, tighter and tighter, until there was nowhere else to go. Just as he thought that there was no way to move forward, the tunnel pulsed outward, taking him with it. Pressure built up around him, pressing him from every direction. The pressure built, compressing his lungs. The air whooshed from his body, abandoning him completely. His chest heaved with effort, and just as the blackness overtook him again he felt the tunnel explode, throwing Joshua out.

Just before his eyes fell shut he saw a burst of light and the sound of birds chirping in the distance. The last thing he noticed was a blue sky, marred by a thin pillar of smoke in the distance. Then blackness.

3

The Captain of the Guard

"I see you have taken your sweet time in your dreams," said a strange voice with a thick accent that Joshua couldn't place. It was not the one that had been calling him.

Joshua's eyes fluttered open, the light slowly flooding in. He recognized the sound of the birds chirping in the trees, but as he opened his eyes and sat up he was greeted by a landscape that he had never seen before. Trees, larger than any he had ever experienced, grew around the open grove of grass that he laid in. He stood, rubbing his sore legs. He looked around, taking in the surrounding forest that seemed too big to be real, when his eyes were caught by the source of the voice sitting on a rock nearby.

The man had black hair that fell straight down his back, and he wore a cloak of black lined with silver that draped across his shoulders. Around his waist was a long curved blade in a crimson sheath, but in his hands he held a dagger and a whetstone, absently sharpening the blade. His eyes were a vibrant purple, though the color shone and rippled with some inner light. He wore an easy smile, and his posture was that of a man who felt no threat.

"Who..." Joshua croaked, coughing. He cleared his throat. "Who are you?"

The man chuckled before setting aside the whetstone. He

raised the dagger to point at Joshua and stepped down from the rock. He walked towards Joshua in an arc, keeping a couple of feet between Joshua and himself the whole time.

"So you are supposed to be it?" the man said, chuckling again. The light in his eyes flared, and he charged at Joshua.

Joshua dove to his right, landing hard in the grass. The man moved past him, whirling on the balls of his feet. He flipped the dagger that he held, grasping the blade in his fingers. He flung the dagger at Joshua, arcing it blade-over-hilt, only for it to bury itself in the ground at Joshua's feet.

"Quick reflexes at least," the man said. "That is a start."

The man raised his hand and spread his fingers. He mumbled a couple of words, flipped his hands, and flame sprouted from his fingertips. Joshua crawled backwards at the sight of the fire. The man spun his hand around and held his palm to the sky. The flame from his fingertips moved inward, forming a ball of fire that floated just above his flesh.

"So how quick are you?" the man whispered. He flicked his hand forward and the ball of fire launched towards Joshua.

Joshua cringed, shrinking back. The ball of fire flew through the air, and just as Joshua thought that he was about to be incinerated by it he heard a familiar voice boom through the field: "Martin! ENOUGH!"

The fireball exploded against a shimmering wall of light that had appeared inches in front of Joshua's face. He expected to feel heat, but nothing penetrated the barrier. He scrambled to his feet as the flame dissipated in the air around him. He looked around when he was vertical, but he couldn't locate the source of the voice and protection. He turned and saw the man who had launched the fireball at him, Martin.

"He will not always be around to protect you, young one," Martin said. "Better you learn to defend yourself."

Martin turned and began to walk away. Joshua hesitated for just a moment, but instinct took over. He sprinted towards Martin, scooping the dagger from the ground as he ran. He closed the distance quickly, but instead of slowing he used the momentum to launch himself forward. He flew through the air, his feet straight out behind him, the dagger clutched in his right hand, the blade held tight against his forearm. Martin whirled just before Joshua collided with him. Joshua's arms flew out, wrapping around Martin's neck. As they crashed to the ground together Joshua fought to stay on top of Martin, and when they finally came to a rest Martin was flat on his back with Joshua straddling him, holding Martin's knife to his throat.

"You were saying Martin?" the familiar voice said, an edge of laughter in his words. Martin stared up at Joshua, his face a mask. As Joshua looked down at him Martin's mouth quivered, then broke into a broad grin. He laughed and clapped Joshua on the shoulder.

"Not bad, young one, not bad at all," Martin said.

Joshua relaxed and dropped the knife next to Martin. Martin picked it up as he stood. Joshua was turning around, trying to find the source of the strange voice, but there was no one in the field other than Martin and him. Martin tapped him on the shoulder, and when Joshua turned around Martin was holding the dagger out to him, hilt first.

"You should keep this, you do well with it," Martin said. "You will need something you are comfortable with in this place."

Joshua reached out and took the blade. "What place is that?" he asked.

Martin opened his mouth to respond, but it was the familiar voice that answered.

"Galion," the voice boomed. Joshua spun and scanned the field again. As he looked a man appeared, seeming to walk out of thin air. Silver hair fell past his shoulders, framing a broad face that was dominated by bright gray eyes. The man wore a flowing silver cloak that sparkled in the sunlight over a dark gray robe. "You are standing in Galion. Welcome."

Martin walked back to his rock and took his seat again. He drew his feet up under him and sat atop the rock, tossing flashes of lightning from one hand to the other.

Joshua had eyes only for this new figure. Martin's dagger was still clutched in his right hand. "Galion?" Joshua asked.

The stranger walked forward, his hands clasped together in front of him. He looked Joshua over and smiled. "Yes, Joshua, Galion, the Eastern Kingdom of Camledor, the last bastion of light in a world quickly being overrun by darkness." The stranger walked around Joshua, smirking at his clothing. Joshua was still wearing the corduroy jacket, jeans, and black t-shirt, and almost every piece was ripped and torn. Bits of broken glass clung to his jacket. Grass stains covered his entire right side. "You have already met Martin Witt. I will admit that he can be a bit difficult to get along with, but there is no better wizard in Galion. He will serve you well through the coming campaign-"

"What the hell is going on?" Joshua interrupted. "The last thing that I remember is being..." Joshua struggled to find some memory, but was unable to remember anything but darkness before waking up in the field. He felt his composure slipping away from him and turned and met the stranger eye to eye. "Who...the fuck...are you?" Joshua asked.

The stranger smiled gently, his entire demeanor shifting into one more welcoming. "I am sorry Joshua, I am. I did anticipate that Martin would welcome you the way he did," the stranger said. "As for who I am. My name is Utherrian, steward of Galion, protector of the kingdom. I am at your disposal, and I will answer any questions that you may have. I warn you though, our time here is short. The others are coming, and when they arrive we must be off."

"Off to where?" Joshua asked.

"Erith. Or, more specifically, Eringhall, the royal castle within the capital city."

"How long do we have?".

"As long as we have," Utherrian responded. "Shall we move somewhere a bit more comfortable? Martin can watch for the others."

Joshua hesitated a moment, looking around at Martin, who still sat on his rock. He turned back towards Utherrian and nodded. Utherrian led Joshua towards the trees, sitting down on a fallen log a few paces past the tree line. Joshua sat on a stump nearby and looked at Utherrian.

"Joshua, ask your questions. You will understand more once we are on our way, but I will do my best to explain as much as I can to you now."

Joshua thought for a moment, trying to figure out where to start. "Okay. So, we're in Galion...what is Galion?"

"Galion is the kingdom that I serve, the kingdom that I have served for over 60 years. It is the bastion of light in a world going dark, the last port in the storm, and we are quickly being overwhelmed by Ska'ell."

"Ska'ell?" Joshua asked.

"Yes, the Western Kingdom of Camledor, the source of the spreading darkness, the storm that threatens to overtake us all."

"And what does Ska'ell or Galion have to do with me?" Joshua asked.

"Ska'ell is currently winning the war. Their forces hold the entire western continent, nearly all of the islands between, and they are beginning to land on the shores of Galion. Not since the Dragon Wars has Galion faced a threat such as this."

"Dragon Wars?" Joshua interjected.

"That is a story for another day, one that you will hear on the road. For now just know that Galion is under threat and is in dire need of a leader."

"What do you want with me?" Joshua asked.

Utherrian looked at him for what seemed like an eternity before answering. "What I want with you, what we all want with you, is for you to take your place in our kingdom."

"My place?"

"As king," Utherrian said, his face a neutral mask.

Shock hit Joshua like a hammer to the chest. His face fell, his brow furrowed, confusion sketched across his features. "King?" he asked.

"Yes," Utherrian said. "I have searched for years, but it was not until just now that I was able to find you. The search has cost many great knights their lives."

"What makes me so special?" Joshua asked.

"That is a story for another day. What matters is that leadership is within you. The ability to be king, to save the people of Galion, and to bring glory back to the throne of Light." As Utherrian finished speaking they heard a horn blow in the distance.

"What was that?" Joshua asked.

Utherrian looked towards the field, towards Martin. "That marks your last question for the moment. I apologize, but it is time for you to meet your guard." Utherrian stood, brushing the leaves from his robe and cloak.

Joshua stood to follow him. "My guard?" he asked.

"Enough questions for now, we need to move," Utherrian said, his voice stern, leaving no room for additional questions. "Follow me."

Joshua followed.

4

The King's Guard

Utherrian led Joshua back to the clearing where Martin waited, levitating a small horn above his outstretched hand. Without shifting the horn sounded again.

"Yes, Martin, I heard the horn the first time," Utherrian said. "Where are they?"

"They are here," Martin said. "Look down the hill."

Joshua and Utherrian turned at the same time to look down the hill that Martin had gestured to. Joshua saw a small group of people walking towards them. They were dressed in an array of outfits, and every one of them carried a weapon of some sort. Most had swords, there was one with a bow, and a large man carried what appeared to be a massive hammer across his back.

When they reached the top of the hill the five new people spread out in a loose line in front of Joshua and Utherrian. Martin jumped down from his rock, picked up a staff that had been hiding in the tall grass around the rock, and joined the line.

"Meet your guard," Utherrian said to Joshua. "They can introduce themselves, but do it quickly; we need to be off soon." His eyes scanned the sky as he said the last, and Joshua followed his gaze to find a flock of birds circling over the forest in the distance.

When Joshua turned back to the line, Martin had stepped

forward. "We have met, but not formally. My name is Martin Witt," he took a deep bow, sweeping his arm out to the side. "Dragon slayer, sorcerer, and the captain of this merry guard, may the Light help us all," he said, laughing at the end. The others in the group smiled or laughed with him. All but the person at the end of the line, dressed all in black with a hood pulled so far forward that it completely hid the individual's features. Joshua felt a chill run down his spine as he looked at the figure, but it passed as he turned back to the others.

The man with the massive hammer slung across his back stepped forward. He stood towering over the others, easily a head and a half taller. He wore a darkened steel breastplate over his large chest, along with dark steel arm and leg guards. Layered chainmail peeked out through every small gap in the armor. A crude helm, darkened like the rest of the armor, hung from a leather strap at his side. "My name is Ryland," the man said in an extremely deep voice. "Ryland DeFeo. Utherrian picked me up in a bar outside of Erith-"

"Erith?" Joshua asked.

"The seat of the king in Galion," Utherrian explained. "A vast city in the northwest, surrounded by a great wall protecting it from sea and land. You will see it in time, and sooner than you may think."

Ryland waited for Utherrian and Joshua to look back to him, then continued. "I was drunk, had been for days, but Utherrian dried me out and gave me a purpose. That was, what, twelve years ago now?" He looked towards Utherrian, who nodded. "Yes, twelve years. I have been with him ever since."

Ryland stepped back into the line. Another armored man stepped forward, but where Ryland's armor was dark and dull, this man's armor shone in the sunlight. Silver and gold colors danced across it, and the helm that hung from his side seemed to have light blue and sparkling white jewels set into it. A great sword, over 5 feet long and a foot wide, hung from the man's hip. His hand rested on the hilt, holding the tip of the blade off the ground behind him. Joshua had no idea how anyone could possibly swing such a weapon in any controlled way.

"I am Alaric Lado," the man said, holding his head high. "I found my way to Erith from Onryx, a city across the sea where I was posted with my fellow paladins of the Lightguard. I went to the king's seat when my men were killed, and there I pledged my sword to the protection of the realm. Utherrian looked into me and named me the First Sword of his Steward's Guard, the King's Guard to be."

Alaric stepped back into line and the man next to him stepped forward. This man wore a white robe with a scarlet sash around his waist. From the sash hung countless pouches, a large book on a silver chain, and a short sword. The left sleeve of the robe was rolled and pinned up to cover a missing arm.

"Corwin Whitefell," the man said, his voice soft and quiet. "For many years I have acted as an advisor to the Guard, as well as a healer, but as you can see I am not really up for much battle anymore. Utherrian came to Artek a week ago and found me in the tower, poring over my books. He convinced me to come along on this journey by telling me that it was time to draw the new King. I could not pass up that kind of opportunity, so I followed him here."

When Corwin stepped back a woman stepped forward. She was the one with the bow. She wore a leather tunic, dyed a deep purple, which hugged her form tightly. The sleeves ran all the way to her wrists, flaring out there. The hilt of small daggers peeked out from the flare in each sleeve. Her legs were covered by a leather skirt that split just below her waist and brushed the ground around her boots. She wore dark pants under the skirt that clung as tightly as a second skin and disappeared into the top of her boots. Joshua finished looking over her gear and looked up to her face. Her eyes were bright green. Her hair was a dark brown that was pulled into a tight bun behind her head.

"Rainira," she said, her voice sweet. "Rainira Manda. I have been with Utherrian for a little over three years now, ever since winning the archery tournament in Erith." She stepped back into line, dropping her eyes to adjust the flares in her sleeves.

Joshua looked down the line to the individual in the black robe. The figure stepped forward, but made no move to remove the hood. "I apologize for my appearance, but there is nothing that can be done," the figure said, and Joshua realized with surprise that it was a woman. "I am Nitika. I came to this guard as..." she trailed off. She stood so still that Joshua wasn't even sure that she was breathing. When she remained silent Joshua turned to Utherrian.

Utherrian was looking at Nitika. He walked to her slowly, placed his hands on her shoulders, and leaned down to whisper into her ear. Nitika sagged as Utherrian spoke, but when he walked back to Joshua's side she held her head high again.

The hood turned back towards Joshua, and when she began to speak again her voice was steadier, stronger. "I came to this guard under orders of the dark King, Lacrym. I was to kill Utherrian. I entered the throne room through a high window and he was standing there, looking right at me, waiting for me. He...he forgave me. He offered me a position in his guard, a chance for salvation. Then he held his throat to me so that the decision would be mine. I gave him my dagger and fell to his feet. That was eleven years ago, and I have been his shadow guard ever since."

Joshua was intrigued, but asked "So why can't I see your face?"

Nitika hesitated a moment. "Because I am a vampire, and the sunlight would burn the flesh from my bones before I could finish dropping my hood."

Joshua was stunned, but before he could respond Utherrian called "To the trees, now!" Joshua whirled and looked at Utherrian, then followed his eyes to the sky. The flock of birds was closer, only a quarter mile away now. Joshua stood still as the guard sprang to motion. When he didn't move to follow, Ryland scooped him up and ran with the others into the woods. Moments after the last of them made it into the woods the birds broke into the clearing, swarming over the grass and the stone, only for the flock to break and spread out over the surrounding forest.

5

Setting Camp

They had entered the woods in late afternoon, and Ryland had set Joshua down once they were under the cover of the trees. They hiked through the dense forest until the sun had set in the west. They were heading north with Ryland leading, Alaric guarding the rear, Rainira and Corwin guarding the sides. Utherrian and Martin walked with Joshua, but no words were shared. Martin's staff emitted a soft light that lit the path in front of them. Nitika had vanished soon after they had hit the tree line, but when Joshua had asked about her Utherrian had merely laughed and told him not to worry.

Utherrian called a halt not long after sunset. The group spread out in all directions, going one hundred paces before returning. While they searched Utherrian produced a bag the size of Joshua's head and opened it. From inside he began to pull blankets and bed rolls; bread and water; and finally a plump, fully plucked chicken. Joshua watched, mouth agape.

Utherrian laughed. "Not everything is as it seems," he said. "This bag is much larger on the inside, while other things may be smaller on the inside than they are on the out. The thing to keep in mind is that nothing is infinite, and there is always a balance. I packed this bag full before we left, and already it is half used. We will have plenty for the return journey, assuming we do not get sidetracked. Sit.

Rest. You have had a trying day, and I must say that you are handling it very well."

Joshua obeyed and sat on the carpet of fallen needles, waiting for the others to return. It was only a moment before they began to trickle into the clearing, all of them carrying either wood or food.

Rainira held her tunic like a bowl in front of her, filled with berries and nuts. Corwin returned with a small net filled with mushrooms. The others returned with wood, which Martin took and began to lay for a fire. He built a tall cabin from the largest logs, filling the inside with the smallest twigs. On the outside he leaned thicker sticks against the cabin, creating a teepee around the center support. He looked to the sky when he was finished. The night was clear, with a full moon that dimly lit the small clearing. Martin closed his eyes.

After five minutes passed in this way, Joshua asked, "What are you doing?"

"Looking," Martin responded, eyes still shut tight.

"But your eyes are closed."

Martin opened his eyes and looked at Joshua. "Sometimes we must close our eyes in order to see."

Joshua just looked at Martin, puzzled. Before he could respond Martin quietly muttered something guttural and a flame bloomed in the base of the fire. Within minutes the small clearing was filled with light and heat.

Joshua watched as the group set about making the night's meal. Utherrian spit the chicken on a long, thick branch and handed it to Martin to turn over the fire. Corwin cleaned the mushrooms he had returned with before handing them out. Joshua took a bite of one and found the flavor surprisingly sweet. He ate the rest of the mushrooms he had been handed and was given a skin full of water. He drank deeply of water that tasted of rich minerals. The chicken came next, and everyone sat around the fire eating ravenously. Finally, Utherrian produced a handful of greens for each of them, and the end of the meal was marked by a healthy belch from Ryland, who looked at Joshua and smiled.

Joshua returned the smile and leaned back on his hands, looking up at the sky. The group was quiet, though a few spoke in hushed tones. Corwin sat on the edge of the clearing, his large book open in his lap. Joshua looked around and saw Nitika at the very edge of the light, her hood still up. On the ground behind her lay the shriveled husk of a small deer.

The fire began to burn low and Martin stood, walking off into the night and returning quickly with his arms full of wood. He laid the wood into the fire and blew new life into the flames, which soon began to eat the new fuel provided and the fire burned bright once again.

"I feel like I've been awake for days, but I don't feel tired," Joshua said to Martin. "I should feel exhausted..."

"Time is funny, and stretches out as needed to accommodate us this night," Martin replied.

Joshua looked at him inquisitively. "What do you mean time stretches out?"

Martin laughed, "It is something that I do not even understand, but for as long as I remember the days have never been the same. Some days nothing important happens and time flashes by in a blink. Other days are filled with work and the time stretches on. Yet others require conversation, and time seems to stop altogether until the conversation is complete. This day, this night, is critical, filled with work and the need for conversation. I have a feeling that this night could last forever if needed."

"What's so important about tonight?" Joshua asked.

"Our King has arrived," Martin said, his eyes locked on Joshua.

6

Sleeping Memories

Martin sat down by Joshua after stacking more wood by the fire. Utherrian sat across from them, watching through the flames. The others sat in a small group nearby, but away from the flames. Apparently this time was for the three of them alone.

"What do you remember?" Martin asked Joshua.

"I remember you running at me, then throwing a dagger and fire at me in the clearing," Joshua responded, his voice quiet and distant.

Martin laughed. "Yes, I am sorry about that, my actions sometimes run ahead of conscious thought. What do you remember before that?"

Joshua thought back, trying to remember. "Darkness," he said. "I was lost in darkness and someone was calling my name."

"That was me, calling to you across the void," Utherrian said.

"What about before the darkness?" Martin asked.

Joshua struggled with his thoughts, trying to remember, to push backwards. "Nothing, I...I don't...I can't remember..."

Martin placed a hand on Joshua's shoulder. "It is all right if you cannot, but try."

Joshua closed his eyes and tried to remember. There was the darkness, yes, that thick darkness that enveloped him and made him feel like hope had disappeared from the world. There was something before that, he knew that there must be, and it was right there, so close, but just out of reach. He began to tremble in his effort to force his mind back. Lights flashed across his mind, red and white. The sound of metal, the sound of an explosion. Then the accident flashed through his mind.

"I was in a car accident," he said finally, his voice trembling.

"Good, that is good. Can you remember anything else?" Martin asked, still grasping Joshua's shoulder.

Joshua thought back, and the memories came easier now. He remembered going to classes during the day, he remembered saying goodbye to his cat, and even the odd dream he had had the night before. He rarely remembered dreams this vividly, but with this one he recalled every detail. He told Martin and Utherrian about the dream, every detail he could remember. When he was finished he opened his eyes again and looked from Martin to Utherrian. "It was you in the dream, comforting the dying knight. You were talking about a King; you said that you were close to finding him..."

Utherrian smiled. "That is how I found you. I sent the vision of that night into the void, then followed it myself to find the one who would receive it. When you received it I knew I had found you, and I was presented with the chance to bring you across to our world that very night. This is no coincidence, Joshua; the stars have aligned and the fates have conspired to bring you here to us."

Joshua was silent for a moment. "You think I'm the king that you were searching for?"

"I do not think it, Joshua," Utherrian said. "I know it, with every fiber of my being."

"But...how can I be the king of a world I never knew existed? How can I be a king worthy of leading people when I don't even know how to fight?"

"I believe that you know more than you think, and that your skills will prove more substantial than even you believe. We have time, and in that time we will teach you all the rest that you need to know; that is our sworn duty. I will teach you to lead the kingdom, as steward of Galion it is my responsibility to see that you are fit to lead and to assist you as you take the throne. Your guard will teach you to fight, to wield magic, to care for those less than yourself. You do not need to bear this burden alone; your entire guard will stand by your side through it all."

Joshua hugged his knees to his chest and fought back the urge to scream. This was ridiculous. Him, a king? Let alone a world full of magic and people with strange accents wielding weapons out of fantasy novels?

Martin gently touched Joshua's shoulder again, and warmth spread from the spot that he touched. It calmed Joshua, and he realized that Martin had been doing this throughout the day. Any time that Martin had touched him he felt calm, like there was power flowing through him.

"What are you doing?" Joshua asked.

Martin smiled. "I am helping to ease you through this. We have fought too long and too hard against the darkness. We need you, you must understand that. I know that this is quite a bit to take in, and even without my aid you are handling it like a true king. I will admit that I still have my doubts, but soon you will understand why we need you, and who you truly are."

Joshua closed his eyes and breathed deeply in and out, concentrating on the warmth of the magic that Martin was spreading through him. As he relaxed he realized that it was more than just warmth spreading through him; it was also images and words, sensations and emotions.

"I am giving you glimpses of our world, memories that I have from our long battle," Martin whispered. "The magic of our world will help to fill in the things I cannot directly recall. Be calm and concentrate, allow the magic to carry you on its current."

Joshua continued to breathe deeply as Martin's memories flowed through him...

7

The Dragonslayer

He stood on top of a high tower, looking out over a rich, blue ocean. Ships filled the water, and overhead large creatures flew through the air.

"Dragons," a voice whispered, seemingly from all around him. It was Martin's voice, speaking to Joshua by the fire as Joshua stood in Martin's place within the memory.

As he watched, the dragons dove, blowing waves of flame before them, flames so hot that the ships exploded in fire before quickly falling apart and sinking. He heard men screaming in the distance as the flames consumed them.

"This is the beginning of the end of the Dragon Wars, eleven hundred years ago."

The world turned to smoke around him, swirling around in a haze of color. The haze collapsed in on itself and solidified, and he found himself standing in the middle of a field, surrounded by men in armor. There were massive machines all around, firing bolts into the air. He followed the course of one bolt as it slid through the air and collided with a dragon. The bolt struck the dragon in the chest, burying itself completely in the dragon's body. The creature fell from the sky and landed with a crash on top of another ballista, crushing the machine and the men standing around it.

He ran forward, lunging and burying his katana to the hilt in the fallen dragon's skull. As he removed the blade the dragon's blood burst from the wound, showering him in fragments of bone and brains. Power swirled from the dragon's body and into him, making him feel as though he had just consumed lightning. He looked up, spotted a dragon diving in for a kill, and pointed his staff. He screamed words that were at once reflexive and incomprehensible to him, and a white lance burst from the end of his staff, flying through the air with a crackle before slamming into the dragon's head. The head disappeared in an explosion of white light and the dragon crashed harmlessly to the ground. Another swirl of power rushed into his body and he felt his control weaken.

"The Wars were brutal. I was one of the few dragon hunters left in the world, and I slaughtered dozens of dragons in those bloody battles. The power was addictive, and even after the Wars ended I searched for more…"

The battlefield turned to smoke again and solidified to find him standing on the bank of a lake. Before he could take in the surroundings, he was diving into the lake, his staff and katana held tight to his body. He found that he had no trouble breathing in the water, and there was power flowing through him, propelling him forward. At the bottom of the lake there was a dragon, curled up and sleeping. As he approached the sleeping beast lifted its head. Before it could fully stir, his katana was buried in the creature's head, the hilt flat on the top of its skull and the point sticking out below its jaw. Power crashed into him again.

"I consumed so much power that it began to drive me mad. I spent the three years after the Dragon Wars hunting the remaining dragons to the point of extinction. I longed for the power they held, the magic, but I could not control it. Before it could drive me completely into darkness I disappeared into the woods…"

The lake blew into smoke and he found himself in a dense forest, very similar to the one where they had built their fire. The staff was still in his hand, but the katana was sheathed at his side. He walked deeper into the forest, guided by the light emanating from his staff. He came to a tree that was easily twenty feet wide, planted his staff at its base, and spoke more strange words. The tree opened before him, unfurling like a blooming flower, to reveal a small space the size of a coffin within its core. He walked into the center of the tree and leaned against the soft, damp inner wood. He hugged his staff to his chest and uttered more words. He closed his eyes as the tree folded shut around him, and there was only darkness. The darkness swirled and he was suspended, floating in that swirling mist.

"I put myself to sleep, deep inside an ancient tree. I stayed that way for nearly one thousand years until Utherrian found me. He woke me..."

Smoke blossomed around him, and when he opened his eyes he noticed a familiar figure standing before him.

"Come, Martin, the time has come to awaken," the figure said.

"I cannot...I cannot control it. The voices...you must let me sleep," he responded desperately.

"I will teach you to calm the voices, to control the power. Take my hand and we will usher in a new age for this world, together."

Martin hesitated before taking the outstretched hand. As soon as their fingers touched, the voices calmed to a dull whisper and relief burst through his mind. He stepped from inside the tree and fell to his knees before the figure.

"My life for you, always for you," he cried out.

The figure helped him to his feet. "I am Utherrian, and I am only Steward of Galion. But if your pledge is heartfelt, I will accept it gladly. You will be the captain of the King's Guard, and when the King arrives your pledge will be to him."

The smoke returned, blocking out the scene. This time the smoke did not solidify, but rather faded away. Joshua opened his eyes as himself and saw the fire still burning fully. He saw Utherrian watching him through the flames, and felt Martin's hand fall away from his shoulder.

Joshua tried to find the words to respond to everything that he had just seen, but words failed him. Instead he looked at Martin, whose head was cast down, staring at the base of the flame. Joshua reached out and took hold of Martin's arm. When Martin looked up Joshua embraced him. Martin was surprised, but put his arms around Joshua.

"To go through all that..." Joshua said, trailing off since there were no words to describe the full breadth of empathy and sadness coursing through him. Joshua released Martin and smiled at him. Martin returned the smile.

"Do you believe it now Martin?" Utherrian asked.

Martin hesitated only a moment, looking at Joshua. He turned and met Utherrian's gaze. "Yes," he said.

"Believe what?" Joshua asked.

Martin only stared into the fire in response.

8

Twisted Through Darkness

"It is time to get some rest, we still have a long journey ahead of us," Utherrian said. "There will be time for you to hear the rest of the Guard's tales along the road, but for now, sleep."

"Where are we heading in the morning?" Martin asked.

"North, to the Shaded Wood. There is something there that Joshua must get...and something that he alone must see."

With that cryptic statement hanging in the air Martin and Utherrian took bedrolls and joined the already sleeping Guard. Joshua followed, and Utherrian directed Joshua to set his bedroll next to his own.

"Nitika will keep the watch through the night as she always has. Rest easy, for vampires have no need of sleep or light," Utherrian said.

Joshua laid down on his bedroll, pulled a blanket over himself, and fell asleep almost instantly. That warm power was coursing through his body again, and he knew that Martin was helping him fall asleep. Joshua was grateful for the help.

No dreams came that night, and Joshua woke in the morning to the sound of activity around him. The rest of the Guard was already up and had the camp packed. Rainira handed him a green leaf with a smile. Joshua took a bite and found that it was filled with the remaining chicken from the night before, and even cold the food was delicious.

"Thank you," he said.

"You are welcome," Rainira said. Joshua bent and rolled up his blanket and bedroll before handing them to Utherrian, who slipped the long roll into his bag before cinching it shut.

They began to move, hiking north again. The Guard spread out the same as the day before, and again Nitika disappeared almost instantly. They hiked through the morning. The sun was out and Joshua could see clear blue skies through the occasional gaps in the roof of the forest, but otherwise it was like twilight under the thick layer of foliage. As they approached midday Joshua could see brighter light up ahead, and just before they reached it Utherrian called a halt. They sat and ate more of the leaves filled with the meat from the night before. Joshua ate quietly, watching the others joke and laugh as they ate. Their easy camaraderie gave him a sense of comfort and security for the moment, despite his aching feet.

The meal was over quickly and Utherrian led them back to the path. They soon emerged from the forest and into a rolling plain. Off in the distance Joshua could see more trees, and beyond them mountains at the edge of his view. The day was so clear that the trees could have been a mile away or thirty, Joshua didn't know.

"That is where we are heading," Utherrian said, pointing to the trees. "The Shaded Wood. Just beyond those woods are the Galation Mountains. Beyond them sits Erith, our final destination for this part of our journey. We should reach the Wood before nightfall. If we do not we will have to set up camp in the clearing, and that is something best avoided."

Utherrian called them forward and they hiked across the open plain. The Guard kept scanning the skies, watching, Joshua assumed, for the birds to return. He could faintly see a dark figure far ahead of them. Nitika. She stayed ahead of them, and as they hiked they came across her kills. The first was a wolf, completely drained and shriveled. About a mile after that they found a pig, still whole, with its throat slit. Ryland fell out of the Guard to carve the meat from the pig and place it in his net. Within half a mile he had caught back up and resumed his place amongst the Guard's formation. Joshua could not keep track of how far they had gone or how long they had marched, but every time that he felt his strength begin to fade Martin would grasp his shoulder and that warmth would flow through him, refreshing him.

"I can keep you refreshed, but you will sleep like the dead tonight," Martin said, laughing.

Joshua smiled and Utherrian picked up their pace, leading them at a jog. After three more miles he called a brief rest as they came upon a dead creature that Joshua couldn't recognize. It was small, maybe the size of a child. The skin was a dark brown and bumpy, like a lizard's. The face was longer, but seemed smashed inward on itself. Two small black eyes peered out from under a large brow, glassy with death. The nose was a small protrusion in the center of the face, and below that was a mouth, twisted into a snarl, a row of sharp teeth showing through the torn lips. The creature wore blackish-brown rags, and a short twisted bit of metal lay beside it.

Martin bent and picked up the piece of metal carefully, examining it. "Sharp," he said, gesturing to the twisted part. "This would do some serious damage if thrust...and these markings at the bottom...Ska'ell?" He handed the blade to Utherrian.

"Yes," Utherrian said after examining the marks. "Lacrym's sigil." He held the blade out to Joshua.

The markings were rough: three lines forming a triangle, running through each other at the points. In the center was a swirl of lines, seemingly a vortex or an eye of some kind. The sigil sent a chill down Joshua's spine, as did the twisted creature lying on the ground before him. "What is it?" Joshua asked.

"A goblin, formed by Lacrym," Utherrian explained. "This creature was once a human child, though its soul has been crushed and its form twisted through Darkness. Lacrym uses them as scouts, or as a front line in his army to distract from his true power."

Joshua shuddered and dropped the blade to the ground by the goblin. Utherrian touched his shoulder and Joshua looked up to meet his gaze.

"This is just one example of the Darkness that creeps from the west," Utherrian said. "This is what we fight to stop, lest the entire world be consumed." He looked around at the others. "We must hurry, the woods are close now. When we reach them, Joshua and I will enter alone. The rest of you are to continue to the foot of the mountains and make camp."

"Understood Steward," Martin responded. Utherrian handed Martin the bag containing their camp gear. They set off again, leaving the goblin behind them.

They reached the Wood in less than an hour, just as the sun was beginning to set. Martin led the Guard towards the mountains as Utherrian led Joshua to the edge of the woods.

"The Shaded Wood is a place of magic," Utherrian said. "Inside you will hear many voices, but you are to listen to none but my own. The creatures will try to distract you, to pull you from the path, but do not listen. Keep hold of my hand and do exactly as I say. Understood?"

"Yes," Joshua said, trying and failing to swallow the lump rising in his throat. Utherrian nodded and took Joshua's hand before leading him into the darkness of the woods.

9
The Shaded Wood

The light was blocked out the moment that Joshua and Utherrian entered under the dense canopy of foliage that was the Shaded Wood. A thin layer of mist hung over the ground, hiding the Wood's underbrush from sight. Joshua was comforted by the strong pressure of Utherrian's hand around his own. That sensation of pressure was the only thing that gave him the will to walk further into the black.

The air in the Wood was thick with the smell of decay. The ground beneath their feet was soft with a carpet of dried leaves, but Joshua didn't know for sure whether the occasional snaps he heard were twigs or dried bones breaking beneath his feet. He wasn't sure that he wanted to know. He held tight to Utherrian's hand as they drew deeper into the Wood's blackness. Soon the light had vanished so completely that Joshua could no longer see the back of Utherrian's gray robe, or even his own hand outstretched before him. Sounds began to emanate around them: the call of an owl, the chirruping of insects, the growl of something wild and hungry...

Utherrian showed no sign of worry, or even of having noticed the sounds around them. He pushed onward with unrelenting spirit, keeping the same steady pace that he had while leading the group on the march. Joshua had no choice but to surrender his senses and force his feet to keep pace with Utherrian, guided by their intertwined hands.

Fear continued to creep in from all sides, and Joshua continued to fight back with all his will. He was so concentrated on his internal battle that he walked directly into Utherrian's back when the man stopped. Only Utherrian's grip on Joshua's hand kept him from falling to the ground.

"Are you all right?" Utherrian asked, his voice a whisper.

Joshua nodded, then realized he couldn't be seen and said "Yes, I'm fine," in the same soft tone.

Joshua heard Utherrian take a breath.

"Are you ready?" Utherrian asked.

Joshua hesitated before saying "Yes."

Joshua heard a thump and a dim light filled the path. The light grew brighter, washing over him, spreading out. He soon realized that he stood in a large clearing, despite the dense branches still intertwined far above his head. The light reached the first tree's trunk and stopped, slowly growing in intensity. The clearing became as bright as a cloudy afternoon. Joshua saw shapes just beyond the edge of the light, low shapes hunched and backing into the darkness, away from the light.

Utherrian followed Joshua's eyes to the creatures. "There will always be twisted creatures that fear the light," he explained. "It is the natural order of things. As long as there is life and light there must be death and darkness. There is no trust without lies, no love without hate, no strength without weakness."

Joshua looked after the creatures for a moment longer, feeling a strange mix of anger and pity twisting through him. He shook his head and turned his attention back to the clearing. His instincts had been right; the ground was completely covered with leaves halfway through decay. The light pushed between two trees and he noticed light colored branches on the ground. Above them the branches of the massive trees that bordered the clearing intertwined into a ceiling so solid that not a single point of sky could be seen. It could be midnight or midday and one would never know under the canopy. When he had finished surveying the entire clearing he turned back to Utherrian.

"You said I was supposed to get something here, but there's nothing here," Joshua said.

Utherrian smiled. "Look again, but this time open your eyes and see everything," he said.

Joshua gave him an inquisitive look before closing his eyes and taking a deep breath. That smell of decay filled his nose and he almost gagged, but he exhaled deeply and opened his eyes slowly. He swept them over the clearing quickly, then back across more slowly. After the fifth pass he was about to tell Utherrian that he still didn't see anything when his eye caught a twinkle off to the right, near the center of the clearing. Joshua walked towards it and brushed away the leaves.

It was a white stone that he had seen, one with flecks of crystal that seemed to shine with their own light. He reached down to pick up the stone and felt a jolt jump through his hand as his fingers brushed its smooth surface. Joshua snapped his hand back and looked at it, but when he saw no mark he reached out and snatched the stone from the ground.

Light exploded in his head, washing out all vision, feeling, and thought. He fell to his knees in the clearing, clasping the stone to his chest, as images flashed through his mind:

Mountains blocking out the sky...

A plain stretching to the horizon...

A small village tucked against a towering stone wall...

Gates, larger than life, swinging open against a clear blue sky...

A castle of polished stone shining in the sunlight...

Safety, weapons, a ship...

The open ocean, fraught with peril...

An island and a cave...

Fear in the darkness...

More water before a vast sea of sand...

Hunger that consumed all thought...

A tower of dark stone, filled with blood...

Darkness overwhelming...

Death...

The images whirled through his mind until suddenly he was back in the clearing under the canopy of leaves, looking at Utherrian. Utherrian stood with his hands behind his back, seemingly unworried. As Joshua looked at him, Utherrian began to smile. When Joshua got to his feet Utherrian walked towards him and fell to one knee.

"You are my King," Utherrian said, his voice full of relief. "My search is over. You are Galion's King."

10

The Sigil of the King

"What is it?" Joshua asked, turning the stone over in his hands. It was perfectly smooth; the flecks of crystal he had seen were actually in the center of the stone, the rest was a translucent pearly white. The flecks pulsed with light, and as Joshua held it he felt power flowing through his arm.

"It is the Sigil of the King. I placed it here when the last King of Galion passed, and only the next true King would have the ability to wield its true power," Utherrian explained.

"So because I'm able to hold this stone I'm the new King?"

"Not only hold it, but use it. If you were a normal person, a pretender, or a false king, the stone would have struck you dead as soon as you touched it. For you, the true King of Light, the stone will be your armor, your weapon, and will grant you the power you need to rule in dignity and truth."

"My armor and weapon?"

"Yes. Observe."

Utherrian bent and lifted a branch from the ground and held it in front of him like a sword. Without waiting he leapt towards Joshua and swung the branch towards Joshua's head. Joshua raised his hands in reflex. He felt a surge of power from the stone and looked up to see a shield of light between his hands and Utherrian's branch. The shield was small, but it had blocked the blow. Utherrian stepped back with the branch in his hand. As soon as Joshua lowered his hands the shield vanished.

"It will block any blow that you anticipate," Utherrian said. "It is not, however, a perfect shield, for a king must be strong as well as blessed. If someone strikes you from behind or before you can react they will still draw blood."

"You said it was also my weapon?" Joshua asked.

"Yes. Strike the branch."

Utherrian held the branch out to his side. Joshua lifted the hand holding the stone and swung it at the thick chunk of wood. The stone flashed and the top half of the branch fell to the ground, cleanly cut in two, yet Joshua's hand still seemed empty except for the stone.

"...how?" Joshua asked.

"Hold the stone in front of you and think of the perfect weapon," Utherrian instructed.

Joshua held the stone up in front of him and thought. The only weapon he knew how to use was the rapier from his fencing classes back at school. As soon as the weapon entered his mind the stone shone brighter and the sword materialized in his hand. It was a basic looking weapon, with a curved guard and a long, thin blade. It weighed nothing, and Joshua swung it back and forth with ease. He raised his other hand and thought of a shield. In an instant the small curve of light surrounded his hand again.

"Very good!" Utherrian exclaimed. "Few kings have been able to harness the power of the Sigil so quickly. There may yet be hope."

Joshua dropped his hands and the sword and shield disappeared. He slipped the stone into his pocket and lifted his hands again. The sword and shield appeared again.

"I don't need to be holding the stone?" Joshua asked.

"No, as long as it is in your possession you can wield its power. When we reach Erith I will have a chain made for you, that way you will never need to be without it."

Joshua allowed the blade and shield to disappear and looked at Utherrian. "This is what I needed to get...what did I need to see?"

Utherrian smiled. "Not distracted from your purpose, are you? Very well, you have earned the truth, and I will show you. First: what have you been told about the history of our world?"

"Martin told me...showed me...about the Dragon Wars," Joshua said. "He also told me that he hunted the dragons to extinction after the wars were complete before hiding himself away in a tree...I know a little about Logan Lacrym, the king of Ska'ell, who serves the Darkness. That's it, other than knowing that Erith is the capital of Galion."

"Good, that is a start. There is only one thing that you misunderstood. Martin did not hunt the dragons to extinction, only to the point of. There are three left in the world.

"Lillith is the first, a red dragon with no allegiance to either side of the current conflict. She is filled with hatred, but it is neither dark nor light, simply red and twisting. She will fight and manipulate the realms of men until she has satisfied her bloodlust, her thirst for vengeance. She cannot be trusted, though very few are able to stand against her control.

"Droven is the second, an obsidian dragon that stands with Lacrym in the west. Which one is truly in control is something I do not yet know, but it is likely that Lacrym's power has been given to him by Droven. Killing one will weaken the other, but they will both be powerful foes to best."

Utherrian began to walk away from Joshua, but when Joshua tried to follow he held up his hand.

"Who's the third?" Joshua called to Utherrian.

There was no answer from Utherrian, but when he reached the tree line he spun and leapt into the air. Silver light exploded through the clearing. Joshua gasped for breath as the air rushed towards the swirl of silver light. The light swirled tighter and tighter in on itself before exploding outward, pushing the air back in a gust strong enough to knock Joshua on his back. A tremor shook the ground, and when Joshua sat up he found himself looking into the eyes of a massive silver dragon.

11

The Silver Dragon

Despite the fact that Utherrian had vanished and the dragon was staring at him, Joshua felt oddly calm. Whether it was a lingering element of Martin's magic or some property of the stone in his pocket he didn't know, but he welcomed it. He knew that he should be afraid, he just...wasn't.

The dragon stood perfectly still, looking directly at Joshua. Joshua got to his feet slowly and looked back at the dragon. When it still didn't move Joshua approached it slowly. His mind tried to make sense of the creature's size, but in the enclosed area of the Shaded Wood it felt too large to be real. As Joshua approached he could feel the hot breath from the dragon's nostrils rhythmically washing over him. When he got within reach the dragon raised its head and stood to its full height, the top of its head brushing the canopy of branches above them.

The dragon's scales were a brilliant silver, and even in the soft light of the woods they shimmered. Joshua imagined that in the open sunlight those scales would shine like mirrors. Its legs were as large as old trees, ending in feet the size of small cars. Joshua looked between the feet and saw a long tail slowly swaying back and forth and tipped with a large plate that looked like steel. Joshua looked up at the dragon's head high above him. He reached out a hand and the dragon lowered its head again. Joshua laid his hand cautiously on the dragon's nose and felt the hard scales, like heated steel. He looked into the dragon's eye and understanding hit him.

"Utherrian?" he whispered.

"Yes, Joshua," the dragon said. Its mouth didn't move, but Joshua heard the words clearly, almost as if they were spoken directly into his mind. "I am the third, the last of the silver dragons."

Joshua was at a loss for words. He stepped back and looked at the dragon. "So that's why you refused to become king...you were worried about your secret being discovered?"

"Partly out of concern for my own safety, but mostly because I am not the true King of Galion, no matter how much I wish I could be. Only the true King can lead Galion through the coming darkness. I knew that the people would destroy me as soon as my secret was discovered. I am the only remaining dragon who harbors no ill-will towards mankind, for I merely wish to see them grow, to give them a chance at the greatness they have within them. The Darkness spreading from the west will snuff out the Light that is barely holding in Galion, and the only way to fan the flames is to bring them their King. You, Joshua, you are the only one that can restore the Light and shine it into the darkness."

Joshua thought about that, wondering how exactly to be a king. After a moment he took a breath to calm his nerves, hoping that the answers would come in time. "What now?" Joshua asked.

"Now, we rejoin the others and make our way through the mountains. Once on the other side it is only a two day journey to Erith, where you will have to gather the people to you. All hope hangs on that, you *must* have the support of the people. But fear not, I will be by your side the entire way, and you have already begun to win over your Guard."

Joshua nodded and pulled the stone from his pocket. He looked at it, trying to fully accept the role that had been thrust upon him. As he looked at the stone it began to shine again. He began to think that he may actually be able to accept this.

It wasn't so different from the fantasies he had lived his entire life, whether in books or movies or games. He had always felt like an outcast in his world, so didn't it make sense that it was because he belonged here? He had just been born in the wrong place, in the wrong world, but thankfully at the right time. As his mind raced onwards through the possibilities, the light from the stone grew brighter, pulsing in time with his heart, the light gaining clarity in time with his mind.

When Joshua looked up again Utherrian was standing in front of him, back to his human form. Joshua was shocked to see tears running down his face.

"What is it?" Joshua asked.

"Relief," Utherrian responded. "Relief and joy. I have been searching a long time for you. That stone will continue to shine brighter and more clearly as you accept your kingship. I can see that you have already begun to, and it is more than I could ever have hoped."

Joshua slipped the stone back into his pocket. "Let's go back to the others."

"Yes...my King," Utherrian said.

12
Wielding the Stone

Joshua and Utherrian made it to the camp just before the sun had fully set. The Guard had set up in a small copse of trees that stood at the base of the mountain. The entire guard stood at their approach, Ryland holding his great hammer while the others simply kept their hands near their weapons. When Utherrian called a greeting they all relaxed and called greetings back. Everyone returned to the fire together. When they were all seated Martin lit the wood that had been piled with an outstretched hand and a few guttural words. Joshua smiled at the display of magic, enjoying the simplicity of it.

"How did you fare in the Shaded Wood?" Martin asked. "What did you see?"

Joshua looked to Utherrian, who simply shrugged. Joshua understood the gesture perfectly: it's up to you.

"I found what Utherrian wanted me to find, and saw what he needed to show me," Joshua responded, deciding to keep Utherrian's secret for the moment.

Alaric laughed from across the fire. "You sound as cryptic as Martin and Utherrian," he said. "There is no need for secrets with us, we are sworn to you. Your secrets will be protected, and even a king needs those he can trust. You need not carry the burdens of a kingdom alone."

Joshua thought for a moment. He had only met these people a day ago, but Alaric was right: despite the seeming improbability of it all, the ground he currently stood on was as real as any back on Earth. He was clearly not dreaming, and if he was going to trust them and try to be the king they were claiming he was, then he couldn't do it alone. He needed them as much as Utherrian said they needed him. He reached into his pocket slowly and wrapped his hand around the smooth stone. He looked to Utherrian for guidance and found only the hint of a smile on the face of the man who was actually a dragon. Joshua pulled the stone out and stood up.

"Like I said, I found what I was supposed to find, and saw what I was supposed to see," he said, looking around the fire at the guard. All but Nitika was present, though Joshua knew that she was watching.

"What did you find?" Rainira asked.

Joshua met her gaze and held out his hand, the stone laying in his palm. It was glowing faintly, reflecting the fire's light.

"The Sigil," Corwin whispered, his voice filled with awe. Joshua noticed that the entire guard was staring at the stone.

"So it is true...you really are the King," Rainira whispered.

Joshua smiled. "It would seem so," he said. The stone flared with light, filling the clearing. The entire guard jumped to their feet with the exception of Utherrian, who stood slowly. Joshua felt power running through his arm from the stone, filling him. He thought of armor, and light swirled from the stone, surrounding his arm as it spread towards his chest. The light washed over him, forming plates as it went. He thought of the rapier again and the stone obeyed, forming a long slim blade in his hand. He wrapped his hand around its hilt, with the stone caught in the middle. Within seconds he had gone from wearing the torn clothing he had come into this world with to being covered in armor made of pure light, wielding a sword that outshone the fire.

The guard stood still, shocked. Even Nitika dropped from her watch-place in the trees and stood staring at him. Her hood was down, and Joshua noticed that she was beautiful, her pale skin shining with reflected light.

"My King," Ryland said, dropping to one knee.

Corwin went to one knee as well, followed quickly by the rest.

Utherrian and Martin both went to a knee, leaving Nitika as the only one still standing. She approached Joshua slowly, staring at him oddly. Joshua let the sword vanish and stood wearing only the armor. Nitika reached out and touched the breastplate, slowly running her finger down the solid light. Joshua noticed smoke coming from her skin and let the gauntlets disappear, catching Nitika's hand in both of his. He turned it over and saw the raw flesh where she had touched the armor. As he looked, the flesh began knitting itself back together.

"A creature of darkness cannot stand against true Light," Nitika whispered. "I am unworthy to stand with you." She looked down, unwilling to meet Joshua's gaze.

"But will you?" Joshua asked. He reached up and touched her cheek. "Will you stand with me? I cannot do this alone."

Nitika looked up and smiled, revealing her sharp teeth and elongated fangs. Joshua returned the smile.

"If you ask it of me, yes," Nitika said, dropping to one knee in front of him.

Joshua looked around at the guard, all kneeling. "Will you all stand with me? I will do my best to be King, to help Galion, but I cannot do it alone. Will you help me?"

Everyone looked up at Joshua.

"You will have my knowledge," Corwin said, laying his book at Joshua's feet.

"You have my magic," Martin followed, tossing his staff forward.

"You have my hammer," Ryland said, heaving the giant hammer to Joshua's feet.

"And my sword!" Alaric called, his voice full of joy. His great sword sailed through the air and stuck in the ground in front of Joshua.

"My bow is yours," Rainira said, her voice sweet. She slid her bow across the ground to Joshua.

"All that I am, all of it, is yours," Utherrian said.

"Then stand, all of you," Joshua said. He began to return the weapons to the Guard, offering each a hand to pull them to their feet. The Guard stood around him in a loose circle, all watching him. Joshua let the armor vanish and looked at each of them. "I am yours," he said, his voice low and soft, the words seeming to come from some unknown depth within himself, flowing through him as the Sigil glowed more brightly in his hand. "I will do all that I can, and I will lead where you will follow. Utherrian has told me that our first stop is Erith, where we will gather the people and form our plan." He smiled and looked back at his Guard, turning in circles to look at all of them. His voice grew louder and more confident as he continued, the words strange and familiar at the same time. "Our first stop may be Erith, but it will not be our last. From Erith we will do what is necessary to take the fight to Ska'ell, to bring the destruction and chaos that Lacrym has wrought back to his door. We will rekindle the fire and fan the flames of Light, and we will shine the Light into the darkest corners of Camledor. We will stand together and burn the Darkness from this world!"

A call went up from the Guard, a joyous yell that filled the night. Cheers of "Our King has arrived!" filled the night, and for just a moment there was no doubt in Joshua's mind that he could be the King that they were seeking, as long as he had these people by his side.

13
Practice with the Guard

Joshua was woken by Corwin, and as he opened his eyes he noticed that the sun still hadn't crested the mountains. Corwin followed Joshua's gaze and seemed to give the mountains a wary look, then turn back to Joshua.

"Today could be dangerous," he said quietly. The morning was cold, and Joshua could see steam flowing with every word Corwin spoke.

Joshua looked at Corwin, waiting for him to go on. Corwin gestured to Joshua's pocket, where Joshua had slid the Sigil of the King.

"Do you know how to use that?" Corwin asked.

Joshua slid the stone from his pocket and looked at it. In an instant he was holding a long, thin blade.

"Very good," Corwin said. "What I meant, however, is do you know how to use *that*." He gestured to the blade in Joshua's hand.

"I took some classes where I came from," Joshua said, still groggy.

Corwin stood and tapped the short sword that hung at his side. "Come with me."

Joshua stood, stretching as he did. He followed Corwin towards the base of the mountains, away from the sleeping group.

Joshua felt like he was being watched and scanned the area, spotting Nitika sitting between two large rocks that sat aside an old, crumpled road leading into the mountains. Joshua raised his hand in greeting, but Nitika didn't even shift. Joshua shrugged and continued forward until Corwin stopped in front of him.

"Let us see what you can do," Corwin said, drawing his short sword. Joshua held up his hand, the rapier appearing there again. He lifted his left arm and a glowing curve surrounded it. He looked at Corwin, who simply smiled.

They stood for a moment, looking at each other. The wind blew through the mountains high above, making a whistling sound. Joshua was about to ask how Corwin wanted to start when Corwin leapt forward, striking downward with his blade. Joshua raised his left arm, blocking the blow out of reflex. Corwin spun and brought his blade swinging in on a horizontal strike, only to be blocked by Joshua's rapier. Corwin continued to throw blows at Joshua while Joshua parried or blocked each one. When their blades met there was the sound of metal on metal, and the noise of it drowned out the sound of the wind. As they sparred Joshua felt an odd calm fall over him. He saw Corwin move and attack even before the blows came, moving into position to block easily. After a time Corwin stepped back and lowered his sword.

"Very good," Corwin said, breathing a bit heavy. "The Sigil will continue to help you see more than most in battle, making your reflexes faster. It will not, however, take over for you. You must observe and react. Now show me your offense."

Joshua stepped forward and then quickly to the side, thrusting in towards Corwin. Corwin raised his sword to block, but Joshua was already rolling to his left, the thrust having been a feint. Joshua was up and sidestepping behind Corwin while Corwin spun to track him, only to find Joshua's blade resting on his shoulder.

Corwin looked stunned, but quickly recovered and laughed. "I would have expected no more from the King. Again."

This time Joshua attacked with a thrust, followed by two quick slashes. Corwin attempted to counter, but Joshua pushed the blow aside with his shield. With a thought the shield changed into a dagger, which Joshua flipped backhand so that the blade was laid across his forearm. He bent his knees and went at Corwin low, thrusting with his rapier again. This time, when Corwin parried, Joshua spun and held the dagger to that man's throat.

Off to his left Joshua heard approaching footsteps, accompanied by clapping and laughter. He turned and saw Martin approaching, smiling and laughing. The source of the clapping was Rainira, walking with Martin and smiling as well.

"Very well done, Joshua, very well done," Martin said. "But for a true test you should probably go against someone a bit more efficient with a blade than our noble one-armed cleric here." Martin clapped Corwin on the shoulder and smiled at him. "No offense Corwin, but you are much better at healing wounds than inflicting them."

Corwin laughed. "That is very true, Martin. I leave the King in your hands." Corwin moved to stand next to Rainira and Martin.

Martin looked to Rainira and said, "Rainira, how about you face the King?"

Rainira smiled "With pleasure, Martin."

She set her bow on the ground and dropped her quiver next to it, drawing a long sword from a sheath attached to its side. She walked towards Joshua and nodded at him. Joshua returned the nod, and before he even knew what had happened he was on his back with the tip of Rainira's blade at his throat.

Martin and Corwin laughed as Rainira offered Joshua a hand up. He took it and stood, brushing the dust from his pants.

"Never let the beauty of a woman disarm you," Martin said through bellows of laughter.

Joshua blushed and looked at Rainira. "What happened?" he asked.

"I tackled you in a roll," she answered, "allowing myself to regain my feet quicker and, had you been a foe, slide my sword through your throat."

Joshua nodded and took a step back. He inhaled deeply, and with the exhale his blade and shield appeared in his hands. Rainira smiled at him and leapt forward, striking so quickly that her sword became a blur. This time Joshua was ready and blocked or parried every blow. Rainira jumped into the air, flipping over Joshua's head. Instead of tracking her jump, Joshua turned and struck out, his blade stopping just before Rainira's neck. Rainira looked at him in shock. Martin laughed again and Corwin cheered "My King, my King!"

Joshua lowered his weapon and smiled at Rainira. She nodded to him and walked back towards Martin. "So you excel in one on one, that is good," Martin said. He walked towards Joshua. "The Sigil of the King has granted you amazing insight into battle. For today that will be enough, but as we drive further west you will need to hone your abilities, or else we shall all certainly fall."

Rainira had already sheathed her sword and was putting her quiver back on. Joshua walked towards her and touched her arm. She turned and smiled at him.

"Are you all right?" Joshua asked.

"Of course," Rainira responded. "I was just surprised; no one has ever countered that move, let alone bested me with it. You fight well, my King."

"Sure, he does not ask if *I* am all right," Corwin said with a laugh. "If you were wondering, yes, I am. But it does look like you could use some help."

Joshua looked at Corwin with confusion, then followed Corwin's gaze to his own shoulder. A thin line had been sliced through his shirt and blood seeped slowly from it. Corwin approached and placed his hands over the wound. The hands glowed white, and Joshua felt heat radiating into his arm. When Corwin removed his hands the blood remained, but the cut had healed as though it had never been.

"The power of the Light," Corwin said, looking skyward. "It has granted me great healing abilities, but even I have my limits. Wounds I can heal, but the loss of a limb, death, these things are beyond any man to heal..." Corwin absently touched the folded sleeve where his left arm had been, then turned and walked back towards their camp.

"Do not worry about him, he gets a bit melodramatic after a fight," Rainira said. She touched Joshua's shoulder. "Let us go help the others break camp."

Rainira walked off and Joshua looked at Martin. Martin just smiled at the young king and walked away. Joshua followed.

14
Ascending the Mountain

With the camp packed the group set off into the mountains. The path that Martin led them to began where they had sparred, its entrance marked by two crumbling pillars. The path itself may have once been a road, but time and the elements had worn the stones down, and nature had begun to reclaim the area.

"The path is still clear here, but as we go it will be worse," Martin said, looking off down the road. "The top of the mountains is covered in snow, and this time of year there could be rockslides, avalanches, or any number of obstacles. Not to mention that Lacrym's forces could be anywhere. Stay vigilant."

The Guard took their usual positions as they started into the mountains. After a mile the path began to narrow, forcing Rainira and Corwin to take up new positions. Soon the Guard was moving in single file, with Ryland leading, followed by Rainira, Martin, Joshua, Utherrian, and Corwin, while Alaric covered the rear. Nitika was, as always, out of sight. They moved steadily through the morning, and when Martin called a halt at midday Joshua turned to see the plains they had crossed spreading away behind him.

They were nearly halfway up the mountain, and Joshua shielded his eyes against the sun as he looked. He could easily make out the Shaded Wood, and, off in the distance, the large forest where he had started, a faint silhouette on the horizon. Utherrian walked up to him, scanned the horizon, and laid a hand on Joshua's shoulder.

"We have come a long way in only a couple of days. How are you doing?" Utherrian asked.

"Actually, I feel great. It was just a bit of a shock to see how far we walked. I don't remember the last time I walked a mile, let alone this," Joshua laughed. "How far is it to Erith?"

"After the mountains it is a day to the coast, then two more to the outskirts of Erith where we will rest in the town of Dollet." Utherrian looked at Joshua and saw surprise on his face. "You have come a long way, my King, but there is much further to go. The path winds ever onward, until one day the door will open. Every man comes to the door in the end, and everyone must open it."

"The door?" Joshua asked, but Utherrian had grown silent and walked away. Joshua looked around and saw Alaric. "Alaric, what's the door?"

"The door, my King, is the end of our life. I know not what they believe in the world you came from, but in Galion we believe that at the end of our lives we all come to a door. It looks different for everyone, but we all must open it and step through. No one knows what lies on the other side. Perhaps it is another life, perhaps salvation, or perhaps nothing but darkness." Alaric laughed, and his voice instantly shifted from a sullen tone into a jovial one. "It matters not, my King, we shall not see the door for many years. Not until long after we have sent Lacrym himself through it!" The Guard all laughed at that, and with the tension broken Corwin passed around the remaining wraps of mushrooms and meat.

They continued their climb through the afternoon, and by the time the sun began to set they found a small cave on the side of the mountain. The opening was large, but the cave itself was shallow, only going into the mountain a couple of paces. The Guard set camp inside the cave, with Joshua positioned at the back. Alaric and Ryland were assigned the night's watches, and after they had eaten they all settled in for the night. Joshua fell asleep quickly, grateful for the help of Martin's magic.

Joshua woke to find the camp already broken down. He quickly packed his bedroll and joined the others, all of whom were standing just outside the cave, looking at something off the mountain. Joshua followed their gaze to see storm clouds around a distant peak. Lightning flashed from inside it, and a rumble echoed out, causing snow to rush down the side of a nearby peak.

"The storm complicates things, but does not change our direction," Utherrian said. "We must move quickly, I want to be on the other side of the mountain by nightfall."

The Guard moved in the same single file formation as the day before, but the pace that Ryland set was much different. They moved at a near run, slowing only when the path had crumbled away or they approached a blind turn. The storm continued to move towards them all the while.

At midday Corwin passed out more of the wraps, but their rest lasted only long enough to eat the food quickly. The storm had reached the closest peak, and as he ate Joshua watched lightning strike a tree, setting it on fire. The following thunderclap caused the already loosened snow on the peak to break apart, and the ensuing avalanche took the burning tree with it. Joshua could only stare at the mixture of snow and fire as it ran down the mountain. As they finished their meals and began to move out, snowflakes began to fall on them.

15

A Dark Storm

Martin called for a faster pace as they began to climb again. The snow was falling faster every second, and the peak was in sight. Lightning flashed inside the clouds, and the thunder was like an explosion, shaking the ground beneath them.

"We must move faster!" Martin called. Ryland began to run over the smooth parts of the path, only slowing to a jog over the looser sections. To Joshua's amazement, he could faintly hear Ryland singing as he ran. It wasn't long before they reached the peak at this pace, and Martin called out again "Slow a bit, down the mountain is just as treacherous!"

Ryland slowed their pace to a jog, yet they only made it a dozen paces before the storm hit them fully. The sky above them turned black from the clouds, and when Joshua looked up he could see the lightning rippling through those dark clouds, turning the world into a constant rumble. A bolt of lightning broke loose, and Joshua felt the air around him electrify. Ahead of him, Martin raised his staff and shouted something guttural into the air. A light flashed out and met the bolt, causing it to explode outward just above their heads.

The resulting explosion shook the ground violently. Joshua watched as Ryland went down, sliding down the mountain's path. Ryland struck out with his hammer, catching a jag of rock in the mountain wall and stopping his slide. Behind him, Rainira began to fall, and Joshua saw that she had nothing to catch hold of. Joshua leapt around Martin as Rainira lost her feet completely, pushing off of the mountain wall with his feet. He flew forward, his hand outstretched. Rainira reached her hand out as she fell backward. Joshua's hand caught hold of her wrist, and as he hit the ground he held tight.

Rainira dangled from his hand, and when Joshua looked he saw the vast drop behind her. Another rumble shook the ground, and Joshua slipped forward. Ryland had regained his feet and dove on Joshua, grabbing his feet. The air above them began to crackle again, and as Martin raised his staff he was thrown back by a falling rock. Joshua looked back for aid, but Utherrian was already occupied with Corwin. He could see Alaric just beyond. The air continued to crackle, and a bolt of lightning hit the rock wall mere feet from Rainira. She yelled out, but her cry was swallowed by the rolls of thunder.

As the air crackled again Joshua saw Alaric and Utherrian carrying Corwin between them. Joshua looked up to see a bright spot forming in the clouds above them. He tried to pull Rainira up, but he wasn't able to lift her from his stomach.

"Rainira!" Joshua bellowed. She looked up at him, his voice breaking through the fear that had frozen her. She reached up with her free arm and took hold of Joshua's to pull herself up. Joshua screamed with effort, and when Rainira's hand touched the path Ryland took hold of it, pulling her the rest of the way up. The entire Guard was crouched by the mountain wall, battered, but in one piece.

Joshua looked up again at the electricity gathering above them. The center point exploded, and a massive bolt of lightning struck out towards them. Without thinking, Joshua stood and raised both of his hands above his head. Just as the bolt hit, white light exploded out around him. The bolt struck the light and exploded outward in a deafening cacophony.

When the Guard was able to see again they found themselves surrounded by a dome of light, emanating out from Joshua's raised hands. Martin finally regained his feet, raised his staff, yelling more guttural words that rose above the storm. When he finished the incantation an arc of light flew from its tip into the clouds. The light spread outwards, breaking the clouds from the inside. When the light faded, the black storm clouds had vanished, leaving behind nothing but a gentle snow.

Rainira stood up, breathing heavily. Joshua looked around to find the entire Guard staring at him. When his eyes met Rainira's, she threw her arms around him, burying her head in his shoulder.

"Thank you," she whispered. Joshua responded by wrapping his arms around her. He looked over her shoulder at the rest of the Guard, all of whom bowed their heads to him. Rainira stepped back from the embrace and bowed hers as well.

"Stand tall, all of you," Joshua said. He looked to Utherrian. "How did I do that? The dome that covered all of us?"

"The Sigil, when combined with the heart of the King, cannot be matched, not even by the power of darkness," Utherrian responded. He looked at Martin. "That was no ordinary storm, was it?"

"A creation of Lacrym's dark magic," Martin responded. "We need to get off the peak immediately, and off this mountain as soon as possible."

16
Doubt

Alaric led the Guard down the mountain while Martin scanned the skies, looking for any potential signs of a second enemy attack. Joshua kept pace in the middle of the group, ready to use the power of the Sigil as a shield again if needed. His mind was all but blank, filled with only the task at hand and nothing else.

The Guard made their way down the mountain, and as they reached the halfway point Joshua noticed that the sun was beginning to set. Still Utherrian called on them to continue forward. Four hours passed at the same pace, with Martin infusing the Guard with extra energy whenever fatigue began to set in and Utherrian lighting the way with his own staff. They reached the foot of the mountain just after midnight and Utherrian directed them towards a thick copse of trees about a mile out. The group made the trek in minutes, and once inside Utherrian called a full halt. Despite their exhaustion the Guard fanned out instantly, securing the area and gathering any food they found along the way. Everyone gathered back around Joshua and Utherrian in the center of the trees.

"We will sleep here tonight. Thank you all for keeping the speed up today, you have earned the rest," Utherrian said. "We had a close call on the top of the mountain, but you all handled it admirably. Especially you, my king," Utherrian said, turning to face Joshua. "Your faith in not only your Guard but your own position saved us all in a time when we would have perished without you."

Joshua shifted uncomfortably as Utherrian praised him. As he looked around he noticed that the entire Guard was looking at him, seeming to inspect him. He tried to ignore it, looking towards the food that the group had returned with: more mushrooms, some nuts, and a heaping pile of leaves that seemed to have been roughly stripped from branches as someone walked by. He closed his eyes and took a breath, but when he returned his gaze to the Guard he was yet again met with those inquisitive, admiring eyes. He felt his heart begin to race, his breath became shallow. Before the panic could completely overtake him, Joshua turned from the group and ran.

Utherrian held his hand out to the Guard, allowing Joshua to leave.

Joshua cleared the trees at a sprint, relishing the pain in his body as he pushed it further than he ever had. His breath burned in his lungs, his heart pounded against his chest. He pulled in gulps of air that felt like icicles stabbing his insides, but he didn't care, the pain was centering him, bringing him back to himself. By the time he stopped running and looked around, the trees and mountains were far behind him. He fell backwards onto the ground and stared into the sky. What he saw there didn't help to calm his panic at all.

Far above him in the night sky the stars circled, but they were stars unlike any Joshua had ever seen. There seemed to be more of them, and they all held different patterns in the sky. The dippers were gone, and Orion no longer stood in the sky. His father had taught him the constellations when he was a child, but none of them hung above him now. Cassiopea, Aries, Gemini, Leo...all of them were gone. Instead the sky seemed an amalgamation of random patterns, like someone had swirled the sky he had once known with a spoon. Yet it all seemed vaguely familiar, and his panic deepened at the realization.

Joshua heard a noise and was back on his feet in a moment, his vision a blur in the darkness and panic. He saw something move to his right and struck out, the Sigil forming a blade in his hand. Something to his left. He struck again, the blade appearing and sliding through empty air. He spun as the shape disappeared, trying to find it again in the darkness. His heart raced, his temples throbbed, and his throat pulsed with the heat of bile that threatened to overcome him. Just as Joshua felt that he couldn't take any more, something hit him from the front, tackling him. He felt himself flip backwards, rolling through the long grass with another. When they came to a stop Joshua was on his back with his arms pinned, but when he opened his eyes he saw nothing above him.

Joshua closed his eyes again and tried to take a breath, choking on the cold air. He kept his eyes clenched shut, knowing that if it was an enemy above him he would surely be dead already. Once he had regained his breath and reduced his panic he slowly opened his eyes and looked up. The figure was nothing but a black shape outlined against the starry night.

"My King," the figure said. "Are you alright? Did I hurt you?"

Joshua shook his head. The figure moved off of him, kneeling in the grass beside him. Joshua sat up slowly, watching the figure the entire time. They sat there watching each other, the figure still as a statue while Joshua struggled to catch his breath. When Joshua finally began to calm down the figure pulled back its hood and Joshua saw Nitika sitting on her knees beside him, her face illuminated by the moonlight.

"My King, did you see something? You were striking out as if under attack. I saw you from the trees, but could not spot any of Lacrym's forces. I came as fast as I could, and when I still saw nothing I tackled you, worried that you may hurt yourself. My King I...I am sorry for that transgression. I understand if you are angry, if punishment is required. I accept whatever fate you decide for me." Nitika lowered her head, offering Joshua the back of her neck.

Joshua just stared at her for a moment, struck speechless by her shame and her willingness to give up her life. He felt compassion and a need to protect Nitika swell from deep within himself, though he didn't understand why. He reached over and gently touched her chin, lifting her face towards his.

"You don't owe me any apology," Joshua said. "Fuck...you don't owe me anything. None of you do. I don't know what I was thinking, I can't do this, I was never meant to be here. None of this is right. I was driving home...I was just heading home to sleep after a day in class...I can't be a king...Utherrian...he sounded so convincing, he made me believe. But I'm not who you think I am, any of you. I'm just a random guy..." Joshua fell silent and looked away from Nitika towards the vast open expanse of the plain.

Nitika just stared at Joshua, not moving at all. "My King..." she began, but Joshua cut her off as he jumped to his feet.

"Don't call me that!" he yelled. "I'm not a King, I'm not even a soldier. I'm just a guy from Pennsylvania."

"My King -" Nitika began again.

"STOP!" Joshua screamed. Nitika flinched at the admonition, and Joshua frowned. "I'm sorry, I didn't mean to upset you. Just please stop calling me your King. Just call me Joshua."

"My...Joshua," Nitika said. "I do not know what Pennsylvania is."

Joshua chuckled. "Pennsylvania is the place I'm from. It's not important."

Nitika nodded, seeming to find the information important. "Joshua. I do not know what brought on this sudden idea that you are not our King, but I am not worried about that for the moment. All that concerns me right now is your safety. Are you alright sir?"

Joshua laughed again at the use of sir. "You just can't help but treat me like I deserve some ultimate respect, can you? Yes Nitika, I'm fine. I just panicked. I hope the others don't take it personally, I didn't mean to worry them." He paused and looked at Nitika. "Thank you for knocking some sense back into me."

Joshua was barely able to make out the trace of a smile that appeared on Nitika's lips at that. "I am sorry if I caused you any physical pain my...Joshua."

"I'll probably have a bruise or six, but I'm sure Corwin can fix me up once I get back to camp."

Joshua stood and held his hand out to Nitika. She reached out tentatively and Joshua took her hand and helped her to her feet. Joshua turned to start back towards camp, but Nitika held her ground, and her grip held Joshua in place.

"Joshua, I..." she began before falling silent. When Joshua turned around Nitika was looking up at the stars.

"What is it?" he asked.

"I believe that you are in fact our King, the King of all of

Galion. It is all right if you have doubts for now, but we will need you to accept it soon."

"What is it that makes you believe?"

"A number of things really. You wield the Sigil, for one. And not only wield it, but in a way that even the stories do not explain."

"The stories?"

"Of the old Kings. There are plenty of great feats in those stories, but none that rival what I saw atop the mountain. Some part of you must not only believe but *know* that you are King for anything that powerful to have come out of the Sigil. Maybe it is because the stories all involve the Kings using the power of the Sigil to conquer lands and defeat foes rather than defending those around him, but what I saw up there surpassed anything I thought possible."

Joshua listened and remained silent, but when Nitika kept quiet he asked "What was the other thing?"

Nitika looked at him for a long time before answering, staring into his eyes and seeming to look into him. "I feel some connection to you, some feeling that I cannot explain. There is something connecting us, but I do not know what it is or where it comes from. I am feeling things that I did not know that I could still feel."

"What do you mean?"

Nitika hesitated before answering. "Love," she said. "I feel love. I did not know that I still could, but there is a burning in my chest that I cannot explain except by love for you."

Joshua was shocked by the admission, but did his best not to show it. Some flicker of his reaction must have flashed across his face however, because Nitika cast her eyes down again, her face falling. Joshua stepped towards her and wrapped his arms around her.

"I'm sorry Nitika, I didn't mean to insult you. You just took me off guard is all."

"It is all right. But in recompense, will you please allow me to call you my King? I cannot keep calling you Joshua when I know in my heart that you are more."

Joshua chuckled at the request, then smiled as he released Nitika. "I guess if it makes you feel better that's fine." He lifted Nitika's face to look at him again. "I am trying to accept it all, it's just proving harder than before, especially with everyone else so completely convinced."

"I can understand that my King, but they have been waiting and searching for you for a very long time. Please do not give up on them, or on yourself. At least give us the benefit of belief until we reach Erith. If you are not convinced by the time we reach the throne room, I will do all that I can to convince Utherrian to send you back to your world...your 'Pennsylvania'."

Joshua smiled at Nitika and tugged on her hand.

"Thank you for the offer. I think that deal is fair enough. I'll act the part until we reach the throne room. Who knows, maybe something will happen along the way to make me want to stay. For now though, let's go back to camp, I'm starving."

Nitika smiled and disappeared into the night. Joshua looked around for her and laughed at the empty field before jogging back to camp, knowing that Nitika was watching and would keep him safe.

17

Leading from Within

Joshua re-entered the camp and looked around as the Guard all stood. He could tell that they were all concerned, and wondered briefly why none of them had attempted to chase him down. He walked to Utherrian and looked up into the man's silver eyes before shifting his gaze uncomfortably to the ground.

"Utherrian, I'm sorry," Joshua said. He turned to the rest of the Guard and continued. "I'm sorry to all of you, for any worry I may have caused you."

The Guard stood still for a moment, giving Utherrian the chance to voice the first response. When no response came it was Alaric who stepped forward first, placing one massive hand on Joshua's shoulder. "It is alright my King. A lot has happened in just a few days, and I am sure that it has shaken your world to the core. It is understandable that you should have doubts. You are only just beginning to build your strength, and at times it will flag and sometimes fail." Alaric turned in a circle, scanning the Guard for approval or support. Each nodded in turn, and Alaric continued. "In those times, when all seems darkest, that is what we are for. We kneel before you and stand by you so that you must never do the same to the darkness that threatens us all. You shall never be alone on this road that you have been thrust onto, and by all the strength that I possess you shall never need to carry the burden of the Light alone. I stand by your side, always. Your Guard stands by your side. Each of them will follow you wherever you lead, holding your council and sharing the load of your burdens, as long as there is strength in our bodies. Until our last breath, we will be with you."

Alaric paused, looking around at the Guard for confirmation. Corwin was the first to kneel. Nitika dropped into the clearing from the trees and fell directly to her knee. Martin came next, followed by Utherrian. One by one the rest of the Guard knelt before Alaric and Joshua. Once the last of them had taken a knee Alaric turned back to Joshua and knelt.

After a moment Alaric looked up to Joshua. "I know that this is all new, that your place amongst us is overwhelming, that your role in this world is frightening. I can only ask that you do not try to bear this alone, that you accept us and rely on us. That you seek our council. Each of us has something to offer, or else Utherrian never would have accepted our oath to the Guard. Each of us can help you along this path, but only you can lead us and conquer the dark. Only you, Joshua, are the true King of Galion and her people. If you ever doubt, merely look to the stone you possess, or to each and every one of us who has pledged unending fealty to you. We acknowledge you as our King, we know it in our hearts to be true. We can only hope that you will join us in that belief."

Alaric fell silent, lowering his head. Joshua looked around and saw that each member of the Guard had lowered their heads to him. He closed his eyes, fighting back the myriad of emotions that threatened to overwhelm him. Sadness, fear, joy, pride...all swirled within him, fighting for control. He knew that he couldn't let any one of the emotions settle into him, or else the panic would rise again.

He took a breath...released it.

He took another breath, as deep as he could, and as he exhaled he opened his eyes. Not a single member of the Guard had shifted, all still knelt with the back of their necks exposed to him.

"Stand up," Joshua choked, his voice cracking. One by one the Guard looked up and stood. "I don't know what I did to gain such admiration, or affection, or...what did you call it Alaric? Fealty? I don't know what I did to gain any of it, but I know that I don't deserve it. I haven't earned it. I tried, I really did. I tried to act the part, but I just don't feel it the way that you all apparently do. I don't feel like I'm a king, like I'm some powerful ruler. I don't feel like I have any special power to lead Galion to victory, even if I can wield some stone." Joshua raised his arm and thought of the sword, but only a slim, faintly lit blade appeared in his hand, and before he could think of putting it away the sword disappeared into the night. He was taken aback for a moment, but regathered himself.

"There was a part of me that bought it, that truly thought I could be what you needed. But that's not who I am. I'm just a guy from Pennsylvania, trying to get through college. I'm not the savior you need. I'm not like Martin with his magic, or Rainira with her bow. I don't have Nitika's speed, and I surely don't have Corwin's faith. I don't have the strength of Ryland or Alaric, and I certainly can't rival Utherrian. Any one of you could make a better ruler than me."

As Joshua watched, the Guard all shifted. Joshua looked down at his feet, then struggled to lift his eyes to look at each of them, even though they weren't looking back at him. "I am not what you want me to be. I'm sorry, but I'm just not the guy you need, or the man I wanted to be. I'm weak, I have more than my share of flaws. I really don't know what to do." Joshua fell silent at this, turning his gaze to his feet again. In the quiet that followed he noticed that his Oxford shoes had nearly worn through their soles during the hiking and climbing. He looked at the rest of his clothing from there and noticed rips and tears throughout, including a large split in the shoulder seam of his blazer.

Joshua was so consumed by the state of his clothing that he didn't notice Nitika approaching until her arms wrapped around his chest. He looked up suddenly, surprised by the sudden gesture. When he looked up he noticed the rest of the Guard approaching. Rainira was the next to embrace him, followed by an awkward half hug from Corwin's only arm. Ryland and Alaric came next, their strong arms lifting all of them off the ground for a moment. Joshua, caught in the middle of the embrace, laughed at the sight. The rest joined his laughter, and the somber feeling that had consumed him a moment ago passed in an instant. As the Guard set him back on the ground and stepped back Joshua felt comfort wash over him. In an instant he was enveloped in a shining suit of armor. Nitika jumped back behind the others quickly, almost as if shocked, but Alaric clapped Joshua on the back hard enough that he would have gone sprawling into the dirt if not for Ryland's outstretched arms.

In the midst of the laughter Joshua saw a space open in front of him. Utherrian, with Martin close behind, stepped into the gap. Utherrian looked at Joshua's armor and said, "The strength of a King does not come only from within. Without a strong fellowship even the strongest in the world would fall. If not for the strength of your Guard, we never would have succeeded in drawing you to our world. If not for the strength of the kingdom that you will lead, the Light would have died long ago."

Utherrian's face turned stern, his eyes drawing tight. The Guard all fell silent and stepped back. "Never make the fatal mistake of thinking that you have more power than another merely because you rule. The highest among us have the furthest to fall. You are our *true* King not because you are high above us, but because you rule among us. Look how your armor shines as you revel with your Guard. Look at each of them, look into their eyes. Look...and know that each and every one of them would die for you, would fight for you. Because you are their King? Yes, but only partly because of that. The main reason they would fight and die for you is because you are one of us, you are an equal taking the mantle of King and leading us against the dark. Without someone to lead, we would all fall. But with someone leading who thinks they are above the rest we would suffer a fate worse than death; we would suffer as a nation succumbing to the darkness, becoming its minions. You are our true King simply because you *do not* think that you deserve it. In time you will earn the admiration of the people, but never forget that you are one of us. You lead from within. You will embody the strength we already have. You are the sharpened blade forged by the master blacksmith and wielded by our most experienced knight. We do not expect you to do anything alone. We ask only that you lead us, act as the point of the blade, and help us strike to the heart of Lacrym's kingdom of darkness."

When Utherrian stopped talking the clearing was silent except for the insects. Joshua looked to each of his Guard, and each nodded in agreement with Utherrian's words. In the end Joshua returned his eyes to Utherrian. "Utherrian...Steward of Galion...what if I fail?" Joshua asked. "What if I fall?"

Utherrian's face softened as he placed a hand on Joshua's shoulder.

"Then we all fall," he said. A smile spread across his face as he finished by saying "But we will all fall together."

A cheer erupted in response, one coming from soldiers who have sworn a pact that they find pride in. It was simultaneously a battle cry and a cry of passionate relief. It was Alaric who led the cheer, a sound of jubilation loud enough to silence the insects and send the sleeping birds into the air. It was a sound that lit the darkness and drove back the night. The Guard moved back in to embrace Joshua, this time sweeping Martin and Utherrian into the mix. For the moment Joshua's armor shone bright enough to light the clearing like the midday sun. For a moment Utherrian was able to believe that it all may yet be possible.

18
Last of the Lightguard

The rest of the night was substantially more light-hearted. Martin set and lit the fire while Corwin and Rainira prepared the night's meal. Nitika vanished again, but reappeared moments later with the carcass of a doe, completely drained of blood. Rainira moved to carve the meat from the animal, mixing it with the vegetables they had gathered in a pot that Utherrian produced from his bottomless bag. Once the pot was placed in the fire the scent of cooking meat filled the clearing, making Joshua's mouth water.

The Guard mingled around the fire, discussing trivial things that Joshua was barely able to understand. He picked up bits and pieces, mostly based around places that he had been told about: Camledor, Galion, Dollet, and Erith. He overheard Utherrian discussing the state of Erith, the capital, with Martin; he heard mention of Galion and the Lightguard that Alaric was telling Ryland about; and he heard a brief mention of Camledor from Rainira as she spoke with Corwin. Despite the mixed conversation, or perhaps because of its aimlessness in his mind, Joshua felt at ease, relaxed. To Joshua it felt like he was back in one of the novels he read at home, something by Tolkien or Martin, maybe King, some rambling adventure that went on and on.

After a while Corwin stood up from his conversation and announced that the meal was ready. Utherrian produced rough wooden bowls and spoons for the group from his bag and passed them around as Corwin ladled out the stew. The guard all found a space on the ground to sit and dug into the meal. Everyone went for seconds, while Ryland and Alaric seemed to be in a competition to see who could eat the most. In the end Alaric finished off four bowls while Ryland finished five. The end of the meal was signalled by another hearty belch from Ryland, accompanied by a smile to Corwin and Rainira signifying a job well done. Joshua laughed at the exchange.

Utherrian gathered everyone's bowls and disappeared to clean them, returning a few minutes later with the cookware safely stored within his bag. Joshua assumed that magic must have been involved in the cleaning, since he had neither seen nor heard any evidence of a stream nearby.

The members of the Guard spread out after the meal, with Corwin and Ryland heading to different edges of the woods to keep watch. Rainira laid out her bedroll and laid down to sleep, while Utherrian and Martin moved a distance away and sat in the fallen leaves to discuss something Joshua couldn't hear. Alaric stayed to tend the fire, and Joshua leaned back on his hands to enjoy the warmth it cast.

For a while Joshua merely watched Alaric tend to the fire. The man's large hands moved deftly, taking wood from the stockpile and using it to build a new structure over the embers of the original one. Within minutes the dwindling fire had roared back to life. Alaric looked up and met Joshua's eye, giving him a smile that spread from ear to ear. Alaric laughed at Joshua's apparent wonder.

"Tending a fire is not a difficult task, my King. 'Tis only a matter of giving fuel to that which is already well lit," Alaric said.

Joshua smiled in return. "I know Alaric, I was just impressed with how easily you moved in the small space."

"I am a bit large," Alaric responded with a laugh. "My mother once said she did not know how one as large as I ever came from her. She was a small woman, you see, and my father was not much larger. I took my size from my grandfather, who was nearly a giant compared to the rest of the family."

Joshua chuckled. "I'd like to hear more about you, about all of you. I know Martin's story, and some of Utherrian's, but I don't really know much of anything about the rest of you. How did you end up as part of the Guard?"

"That is a long story, my King, one that I doubt we will have time for tonight."

"Then just tell me the short version," Joshua said. "I honestly want to know."

"All right," Alaric said. He stood up from the fire that he had brought back to life. "But there is a better way than just telling you. One that you have experience with if I am not mistaken. If you are amenable to a trip down memory lane, I would like to do it justice. If you have no objections, of course, my King."

"No objections at all," Joshua said. Before Alaric could speak again Joshua turned around and looked towards Martin. "Martin!" he yelled.

The wizard looked up from his palaver with Utherrian. "Yes sir?"

"If you have a moment we could use your help," Joshua said.

Martin stood and walked towards Joshua and Alaric. "It looks like the fire is burning fine. What is it that you need?"

"Alaric was just about to tell me how he came to be a part of the Guard, but we agreed it would be better for me to experience the story. Would you mind helping us out?" Joshua asked.

Martin sat down next to Joshua. "Your wish is my command, my King. Take my hand and I will lead you into Alaric's memories."

Joshua took Martin's outstretched hand. Martin extended a hand to Alaric, who sat down next to the wizard and enveloped Martin's hand with his.

As soon as the connection between the three was complete Joshua felt the world fade into mist. He felt himself adrift in a cloud, with nothing but swirling grays.

The grays slowly came into focus, and eventually Joshua found himself standing in a dark stone room, surrounded by weapons and armor. He had to look up to see the man standing in front of him: a tall man wearing shining plate mail and wielding a greatsword. The man smiled down at Joshua.

"Thank you Alaric, you have done a fine job thus far as my squire. Shall we move ahead to the tourney?" the man asked.

"*Yes, m'lord,*" Alaric said. *When he looked down he saw a young man's hands, and as he looked around he caught a reflection of himself in the shining armor nearby. He was a boy, maybe thirteen. He wore a simple cloth tunic and high leather boots. A mop of unruly blond hair sat on top of his head, strands poking out in every direction.*

"*Then let us go,*" *the man said.*

"I was a squire in my younger years," Alaric explained. "I served three of the greatest tourney knights that Galion has ever seen. But I believe that this is too far back Martin. May we move forward to my days in the Lightguard?"

The scene swirled into smoke as the small boy followed the large knight. When the smoke reformed he stood atop a crenelated tower overlooking a sparse field. The grass below him looked yellow, and in the distance he thought that he could see the land transitioning into nothing but sand. A desert.

"At eighteen I was anointed as a knight of the Lightguard. Seven years later I was stationed in Onryx, a town across the sea. A year later the dark creatures began to appear out of Ska'ell. Two years after that the war had fully begun."

He watched from the tower as something appeared in the distance, moving quickly towards his position. He yelled, "Archers to the ready!"

He looked to his left and saw a row of men drawing bows, and when he turned to his right he saw another long row of men with bows drawn.

"*Up thirty degrees,*" *he called. The men on both sides raised their bows into the air.*

"*On my mark...FIRE!*"

All at once the men to both sides of him released their bowstrings. Arrows flew through the sky, enough to darken a strip ahead of him. They rained down among the advancing creatures, and he raised a cheer as half the creatures fell to the onslaught.

"*Nock,*" *he called. The men nocked another arrow.* "*DRAW!*"

"*FIRE!*"

Another storm of arrows flew through the sky, raining down on the advancing creatures. The horde was closer now, and he could see their warped forms. Small creatures holding twisted blades of steel made up most of their number. Throughout their ranks were animals that looked like dogs, but two to three times the size. Their bodies were twisted, however, and they seemed to be fed by the bloodshed around them. Sparsely, throughout the advancing horde, he saw normal sized men, but they were covered in black cloaks, their hoods drawn tight over their heads. Vampires, he thought.

"Nock," he yelled, quickly followed by, "DRAW! FIRE!"

Another swarm of arrows erupted from the battlements, falling towards the back of the quickly advancing horde. He saw that they were closing quickly.

"Squad one, draw your swords and prepare to defend the breach! Squad two, continue to fire on the enemy and prepare to defend the wall!" He drew a massive sword, a foot wide and five feet long. "Squad one, TO VICTORY OR DEATH!" he screamed. The men cheered as he vaulted over the wall, falling twenty feet before hitting the ground. He grabbed his sword in both hands and charged the oncoming horde. Arrows poured from the wall behind him, hitting the front line of goblins rushing towards him.

The scene swirled into smoke again, but refocused quickly, this time from a view above the field of combat. Joshua watched as Alaric hit the front line of goblins, squad one only paces behind him. Alaric's massive sword struck out, cutting two goblins in half as he met them. His weapon was a blur as he lashed out at the enemy, and Joshua watched as blood and limbs flew out from Alaric's position. In a moment the horde was so thick that Joshua was only able to follow Alaric's positions because of the light reflecting off the large man's polished armor.

The battle seemed to last seconds and hours at the same time. Men fell in heaps on the front line, and all the while Alaric was screaming rallying cries and carving through the enemy force. One of the large dog-like creatures charged Alaric, but his sword struck the center of the animal and lifted it off the ground, throwing it behind him in a spray of blood and gore. The distraction proved enough for a throng of goblins to swarm him, however, burying Alaric under a heap of the small, twisted creatures.

For what seemed an eternity Joshua watched the combat. The men of squad one all fell to the onslaught, stacked in a twisted heap of death along the front line. The goblins began to scale the walls of the keep as the cloaked vampires and dogs began to tear down the gate.

As the gate was beginning to fall Joshua noticed a glimmer of light, centered on where Alaric fell. Alaric erupted from the pile of goblins that had buried him. He stood and screamed towards the sky, and cheers erupted again from the wall. The arrows fell heavier upon the goblins scaling the wall, and a swarm of arrows so dense that it appeared to be a singular black cloud fell just outside the gate. The goblins and dogs there were consumed by the onslaught, but the vampires continued their attack on the gate, finally breaching its defense. Alaric turned and charged towards the gate, but the vampires were already through.

Half of squad two abandoned their bows and drew longswords, jumping from the wall to the inside of the keep. They rushed the gate and formed a line of defense thirty men deep. The dozen vampires that had breached the gate began to tear into the men.

Outside the wall Alaric began to fight his own way towards the gate. Goblins fell to every swing of his massive blade. The dogs began to shy away from him, with most falling back. Those that continued towards the wall were struck down by the continuous volley of arrows. Alaric met his first vampire, but in a flurry of movements the vampire fell in pieces around him.

It was only minutes before Alaric had reached the gate, and he destroyed three vampires as he entered. Four more turned to face him, and Joshua watched the exchange of blows with wonder. Two of the vampires fell to Alaric's first attack, and one leapt onto his back. Alaric skewered the fourth vampire before reaching behind him and throwing the last vampire off of him. As the vampire slid across the ground Alaric leapt into the air, thrusting his sword downward through the vampire's neck as he landed.

The battle raged on as the world swirled into smoke before Joshua's eyes. Joshua cried out in protest, but when the scene focused again he was looking at the gate through Alaric's eyes.

The ground beneath him was soaked red with blood, dismembered limbs lay scattered around the field. The world was quiet, and he turned to survey the area. All around him were the corpses of goblins and vampires. The last few minutes of his memory were nothing but a red blur, a forgotten fury state in the heat of battle. He walked through the shattered gate of the keep and out into the field beyond. The grass was stained red with the blood of his fallen comrades and the countless slain goblins. He turned back and found the same inside.

"Anyone!" he shouted. "Is anyone alive!? Can anyone hear me!?"

His cries echoed back to him off the abandoned houses of the outer quarter of the city. He began to walk towards the inner gate, but the only thing he saw along the way were the bodies of his fallen soldiers, intermingled with the corpses of the fallen vampires and goblins. The bodies of the vampires *were smoking, the sun beginning to disintegrate their flesh. He continued to search the outer quarter, what had been the military quarter, but failed to find anyone alive.*

The world swirled into smoke again. Joshua found himself face to face with Alaric by the fire.

"I searched the rest of that day," Alaric said, "and well into that night. I did not find a single survivor. I do not know how it came to be that I survived the onslaught, nor why the horde failed to take the inner city. The fury of battle overcame me, and my memories of the end of the fight are blurred at best."

The large man hung his head, and Joshua moved towards him, placing a hand on his shoulder.

"After that I instructed the people of Onryx to flee, to find a home elsewhere. I myself took a boat across the sea with a number of them to Erith. There I met with the Utherrian, who had been appointed Steward of the Realm while I had been deployed."

The smoke swirled again, and Joshua found himself standing in a great stone hall. The stone was polished to a shine, and a thick, richly colored gold carpet ran down the middle of the room. Pillars of ornately carved stone ran along the sides of the carpet, and Joshua could see stained glass windows set high up the walls. The windows cast a myriad of colors into the hall. The light seemed to center on an empty throne at the end of the carpet. Just below the throne was another seat, but this one was occupied by a man in a gray robe. Joshua recognized Utherrian immediately.

As he approached, Utherrian rose from his seat. He fell to his knee at the end of the carpet, bowing his head to the Steward.

"My liege," he said, "I bring ill tidings from the east. Onryx has fallen, and I am to blame."

Utherrian looked down at him for a moment, then touched his shoulder. "I have heard some news from Onryx," Utherrian said, his voice gentle. "I do not believe that the fall of Onryx was the fault of any one man. A force of goblins, vampires, and dire hounds that large seems too much for any one man to fight back."

Alaric remained silent.

"Please, knight, rise. Tell me your name."

"My name is Alaric Lado, my liege," he said. He looked up at Utherrian and stood. "I failed to hold the eastern front, I failed to hold the

military quarter, and in doing so I jeopardized the lives of the countless men, women, and children who lived in the city."

"By my count almost all of those people made it to safety, and that is because, at least from the stories that have reached my ears, you stood to your last bit of strength to defend them. I have heard stories of you single-handedly holding the inner gate, of fighting back the horde that threatened the city. If not for you, the city would have fallen completely." Utherrian explained. "I know that you have come to me now expecting punishment, but in fact I offer you my thanks and gratitude. Thousands of servants of the Light were saved by your hand. You have my thanks, Alaric, Captain of the Lightguard."

"But sir," he protested, "the Lightguard has all perished. There is none left but me, and the enemy now has free hold of the port that will lead them to Erith's door."

Utherrian patted Alaric's arm. "Through no fault of your own. If anything, the fault lies with me. I was foolish to think that we could hold the shore so close to Ska'ell. The rising darkness there is too strong at the moment. The only thing that could push such a darkness back would be the King of Galion reclaiming the throne." Utherrian paused and looked up at the empty throne, the stained glass casting a rainbow of light around it.

"But there is no king," he responded.

"Ah, but there is!" Utherrian exclaimed. "We need only to look harder in order to find him, and find him we shall! I have begun to assemble a Guard, Alaric, a new Guard to act as the King's personal protection once he arrives."

Utherrian grew quiet, looking him up and down. He stood tall, but his eyes remained downcast.

"Alaric," Utherrian continued, "I would like you to serve in this Guard. For now I would ask that you swear fealty to me, as my protector, but with the understanding that you shall soon swear to the true King of Galion and no other. What say you?"

He looked up and met Utherrian's gaze. The Steward's eyes were pure silver and shone with an intensity that he had never seen before. More than that, however, was the depth of belief that the man contained. There was nothing but absolute belief within him. He did his best to maintain the gaze, but when he felt it begin to falter he fell to one knee again.

"Steward, I swear my life to your protection," he said. "If... When the true King of Galion appears my allegiance will be to him. My armor and *sword will be yours until the day that I reach the door at the end of my path. Will you accept my oath and my service?"*

"With great pleasure," Utherrian responded, laying a hand on his shoulder.

The world swirled into white smoke again, and Joshua felt himself lifted from the great stone hall. The smoke cleared quickly, and he found himself back by the fire.

Martin withdrew his hand and stood, walking back towards Utherrian without a word. Joshua turned and looked towards Alaric and saw tears staining the man's stubbled cheeks.

"Alaric..." Joshua said, not knowing what else to say.

Alaric wiped his eyes and coughed to clear his throat. "Please, my King, do not pity me. I failed my men in Onryx. I do not know, to this day, how I made it out of there alive, but the simple fact is that I somehow survived. I can only hope that I did so in order to avenge my fallen comrades there, and serving you is the best way to get that chance. If you will accept it, I would like to offer my service to you directly, rather than relying on the transfer of an oath from Steward to King."

Alaric stood before lowering himself to one knee in front of Joshua. "My King, I swear my life to your protection. My armor and sword will be yours until the day that I reach the door at the end of my path. Will you accept my oath and my service?"

Joshua was still overcome with emotion from the memory that he had just witnessed. "Alaric, this doesn't really seem necessary-"

"My King, I am sorry to interrupt, but it is."

"Ok," Joshua said, "if you insist." Joshua stood up and placed his hand on Alaric's shoulder. "Alaric Lado, last of the Lightguard, I accept your oath. I can only hope that I can do my part to earn and deserve such a faithful protector. You have sacrificed so much for Galion already, and I promise that I will do my best to make sure those sacrifices weren't in vain."

Alaric looked up from his position and into Joshua's eyes. "My King, I know that they were not. I will avenge my men, and together you and I will stand by the funeral pyre of Ska'ell."

19
Into the Sea of Grass

The rest of the night went by quietly, and the Guard was on the move again with the rising of the sun.

"Dollet is a two day journey," Utherrian said as the Guard prepared to set out. "That is assuming that we do not run into any trouble. We will need to camp in the open tonight, and I need not tell you the troubles that invites. Everyone must remain vigilant. If everyone is ready," the Guard nodded in response. "Good. Ryland, lead the way."

Ryland lifted his hammer onto his shoulder and led the way out of the trees. The Guard fanned out once in the clear, assuming their usual positions: Ryland twenty paces ahead, Rainira and Corwin a dozen paces to the left and right, Alaric twenty paces behind, with Joshua, Utherrian, and Martin in the center. Ryland set a fast, maintainable pace, his head turning to scan the area ahead of him as he moved. Nitika had disappeared again as they set out, but Joshua caught sight of her occasionally on the horizon. The land was completely flat, a vast plain that stretched on for miles. The grass was thick and brushed their calves as they walked. Above them the sky was clear, appearing bigger than any sky that Joshua had ever seen. He felt small as he moved across the grass.

Joshua quickly lost track of time as they marched. With

nothing to break up the scenery he felt that they could have travelled miles or yards. An hour could have passed, or half the day, only the sun shifting through the sky gave away the passing of time. Ryland had slowly decreased the pace they were moving at, finally settling on a quick walk. Everyone was quiet as they moved, but Joshua didn't get any sense of unease, just one of overly protective vigilance.

"What's in Dollet?" Joshua finally asked Utherrian, just to break the silence.

Utherrian looked a bit surprised at the question, or possibly it was just the breaking of the silence that surprised him. He chuckled, his face losing the intense expression and forming a friendlier one. "Dollet is a small town just outside the walls of Erith. We should reach it by sunset tomorrow, and we will find friendly lodging there before heading into Erith the day after."

Joshua nodded. "What happens then?" he asked, a little timidly.

"Then we go to the castle. We will be spending a good deal of time in Erith, for there is much to do. We must determine our best course of action to defeat Lacrym. More importantly though, you must take the throne and give hope back to the people of Galion."

Joshua did not respond at first. He was still trying to accept that he could be King. "Utherrian, what if you were wrong? What if I'm not the king? What if you pulled the wrong person across?"

Utherrian smiled at Joshua. "I did not make a mistake, and I drew exactly who I meant to draw. I have something for you back in Erith that I think will help you understand. Until we reach the castle, however, I must ask simply that you trust me."

"Ok," Joshua replied, his mind already trying to think of what Utherrian could possibly have in Erith to erase his concerns. At least the thought was something to occupy him on the journey across the plain.

Martin called a halt at midday, or at least what Martin said was midday. Utherrian pulled bread from his bag and passed it around, along with water to refill everyone's skins. Once the food was handed out they continued on, walking slowly and eating their lunches. When the food was gone Ryland picked up the pace again and they continued the march.

Two hours after the meal was done Joshua saw something in the distance. He pointed it out to Martin, who scowled. "I saw it a couple miles back, but I do not know what it is. We will find out soon enough, but I do not believe that it could be anything good."

They reached the object after another hour, as the sun was beginning to hang low in the sky, stretching their shadows across the flowing grass. Ryland stood before the heaping mass and turned as the rest of the Guard walked up. "You may not want to look, my King. 'Tis not a pretty sight."

Joshua ignored the offer and walked to stand next to Ryland. He looked over the blackened heap and at first couldn't discern what he was seeing, but it only took a moment for the reality to become clear. The heap was the twisted remains of a dozen people, along with what appeared to have once been a horse. The bodies had been mutilated, cut up and burned. Joshua could see the remains of a cart, a couple crates, and a blackened sword among the corpses. He looked down at his feet and saw something in the grass. He leaned down to pick it up and found a rough, hand-made doll. Joshua looked from the doll to the pile and realized it had been a family. He dropped the doll, turned, and threw up into the grass. He continued to vomit, bent at the waist, until there was nothing left in his stomach, yet he continued to retch. Corwin took Joshua by the arm and led him away from the heap a few paces and sat down in the grass with him. Joshua chanced a glance towards the heap and saw Alaric and Rainira pulling up grass from around it, covering the mound in a green blanket.

Joshua took a deep breath and stood up. The world spun a bit, but another deep breath steadied him. He walked over and began to pull grass along with Rainira and Alaric. The others joined in, and before long the mound was completely covered. Alaric picked up the doll that Joshua had dropped and frowned at it. He was about to lay it on the mound when Joshua placed a hand on the large man's arm. Joshua took the doll and placed it in his pocket, then turned to nod to Martin. Martin looked at Utherrian, who gave a slight nod. Martin uttered his guttural words and the mound burst into flame. They watched as the mound became a funeral pyre, and waited until the remains were reduced to ash.

"May they rest easy," Corwin said softly, "and may they find peace on the other side of the door."

"We need to move on further before setting camp," Utherrian said. "The smoke will have alerted whatever killed this group to our presence, and I would prefer to not be here should they return. Ryland, lead the way."

Joshua took one last look at the ash and followed as Ryland led them onward.

20
Vengeance

The Guard travelled well past sunset. Nitika rejoined them as the dark set in around them, taking up Ryland's place at the head of the group, acting as their eyes in the night. The stars offered some light, but it was still difficult to see anything. When Utherrian finally called a halt Joshua fell to the ground, his head spinning. Corwin handed Joshua a water skin and Joshua took a long drink. Utherrian handed out more bread, along with bowls of the previous night's stew. They ate in silence, and when the meal was done Joshua felt steadier.

"Do you know what happened?" Joshua asked.

"My guess, my King, would be that the family was heading towards the mountains." Corwin explained. "There is a small village along the mountains, about twenty miles south of where we crossed. They may have intended to settle there, or follow further to the river. From the river they could have gone east to Artek, or west to Pirn, or even Aerillon beyond."

"I do not think the King needs a geography lesson at the moment," Rainira interrupted. "No offense Corwin."

"None taken, Rainira, you are right."

"My King, many families have begun to flee towards the mountains and beyond in recent years," Rainira said. "As the darkness has spread from Ska'ell they seek a life further from the conflict.

Aerillon, a town on the opposite end of this continent from Erith, has easily tripled in size. Whether the people are actually safer there is not what is important. They feel safer, which allows them to continue living their lives as normally as they can. The family we found likely moved on trying to find a peaceful place to raise their children away from the war. To their misfortune, the war found them before they made it. Now the Light will guide them through the door, where they will have peace."

Joshua reached into his pocket and pulled out the doll he had found. He turned it over in his hand, trying to imagine the child who had owned it. He closed his eyes and imagined: *a little girl, running around a yard playing on her own. Her mother walks out of the house and calls to her, holding out the doll that she had spent days making for her daughter. The little girl shrieks with glee, throwing her arms around her mother. She takes the doll back into the yard with her and dances in circles with it as her mother watches, a smile on her face.*

"My King, are you alright?" Rainira asked.

Joshua looked at her and realized he was crying. He wiped the tears from his eyes and met Rainira's gaze. "I think so," he said. He looked towards Utherrian. "I still don't know for sure if I'm truly the king, but I do know that I'll help regardless. I want to meet Lacrym, and I want to give him this doll. I want to bring justice for this family, and for all the others that his darkness has ripped apart."

Utherrian smiled softly at Joshua, "We shall, my King. We shall."

The Guard unfurled bedrolls close to one another and set a rotation of two guards for the night. Nitika disappeared on their back trail, and Joshua laid down to sleep, the doll tucked safely away in his pocket again.

As the sun began to rise he was shaken awake. He looked up to see Nitika kneeling next to him. "My King, I need to show you something," she said.

Joshua stood up, wiping sleep from his eyes. "What is it?" he asked.

"Follow me," Nitika said, and began walking the way they had come. In the distance Joshua could see the mountains they had crossed, though their peaks were hidden in clouds. He looked up to the sky and saw grey clouds moving in. "We are going to have rain today," Nitika said, following his eyes. "It will make the final leg of our journey to Dollet harder, but we may still make it today if we move fast enough."

They walked a quarter mile before Nitika stopped and pointed to something lying in the grass. Joshua walked to it and found five bodies, all of them with their throats slit. They were large, possibly bigger than Alaric. Their heads were different from a human's with jutting lower jaws and broad brows, all heavily tattooed. He looked back at Nitika. "Who are they?"

"Orcs, likely from Ula'ree, a town in northern Ska'ell made up of their kind," she said. "They are willing allies of Lacrym, unlike the servants that he has forced into his service. I found them last night searching near the remains of the pyre we set. I wanted to give you some peace, some justice for the family we found."

Joshua looked at the corpses for a moment, absently touching the doll in his pocket. He finally turned to Nitika and embraced her. She stiffened at first, but relaxed when Joshua stepped back. "Thank you, Nitika, you did well."

Joshua saw Nitika smile under her hood. "We should get back to the others, maybe we can be closer to Dollet before the rains hit."

The Guard was putting the last of their gear into Utherrian's bag when Joshua and Nitika rejoined them.

"Is everything alright?" Martin asked.

Joshua looked to Nitika and nodded. "I took out the group that I believe slaughtered the family last night. I took Joshua to see them."

"Very well," Martin said. "Were you able to learn anything from them?"

"Nothing," Nitika said. "They were five orcs, but beyond that I do not know, as I did not give them a chance to speak."

"Orcs, this far to the west?" Martin said, looking to Utherrian.

"Lacrym's forces are growing bolder. We will need to be extra careful as we travel today. Orcs generally travel in large raiding parties, so there may be more about. The rain may slow us down as well. If everyone is ready, I would suggest that we get moving."

Ryland led the way again, but Nitika stayed close this time, only fifty or so paces ahead of Ryland. They jogged through the morning, and by mid-day the sun had been covered by the clouds. They ate a quick meal of bread and water, then continued on. After lunch Joshua saw a town on the horizon.

"Dollet," Martin said. "We are nearly there."

21
Fighting to Dollet

The rain began to fall with Dollet still miles away. It was gentle at first, a calm shower. An hour later, however, a strong wind blew across the plain that seemed to split the sky open. Rain fell in torrents, soaking them all in an instant. Thunder boomed around them as a bolt of lightning arced across the sky.

"Everyone remain alert, we may have trouble!" Utherrian called. "Ryland, we must go faster."

Ryland picked up the pace as the Guard's formation tightened up. They ran in a close group, their feet sinking into the wet ground with each step. Another roll of thunder filled the plain as more lightning lit the sky. The wind continued to gather strength until the rain seemed to be falling sideways. The town of Dollet grew ahead of them, and as they neared Joshua heard Alaric call out from the back of the Guard.

"Enemies to the south!" Alaric yelled.

"More to the north!" Rainira called. Her hand was a blur as she pulled an arrow, nocked it, and sent it flying in that direction.

"Do we flee or stand and fight?" Alaric called.

"Keep moving!" Utherrian yelled over the wind. "We can stand with the guard in Dollet to fight. Martin, make them aware of the danger!"

Martin produced his horn and raised it high as he ran. It sounded as if blown by the wind, its tone cutting through the storm. Ryland picked the pace up even more until the Guard was running. Water flew into the air with each footfall as the ground became one unending pool. Joshua looked to his left and saw a group of large creatures closing in quickly. To his right another group of smaller creatures was gaining as well. Ahead of them Dollet continued to grow closer, but it seemed like they were going to be overtaken before they reached the town. He heard Martin curse beside him.

"We're going to need to fight on the run," Martin said, stowing his horn.

Martin threw his arm out to the right and a ball of fire flew from his fingers towards the group of small creatures to the south, exploding amongst their ranks. Rainira continued firing arrows into the group to their north, and Joshua saw one of the creatures fall to the ground.

A mile outside of Dollet the two groups of enemies caught up with them, the smaller creatures attacking from the front while the larger ones attacked from behind.

Ryland grasped his hammer in both hands and charged into the group of small creatures. Joshua recognized them now that they were close. They stood only a few feet tall and held twisted metal blades. Their sharp teeth were bared in snarls of hatred. Goblins. Ryland swung his hammer as he met the group, sending three of the small creatures flying through the air. Ryland used the momentum to turn and bring the hammer down on another goblin, crushing it into the ground.

Nitika was near him, guarding Ryland's back, her daggers striking out in a blur at the goblins. Joshua saw three fall to her blades in quick succession. It appeared that Nitika was smiling as she blocked a thrust that came towards her. She kicked the goblin backwards, and it disappeared under Ryland's hammer. Nitika laughed and plunged back into the fray.

Behind them Alaric stood fast as the large creatures approached. It was a group of ten orcs, and Joshua realized that he had been wrong about their size when Nitika had shown him the corpses that morning. They were a full head taller than Alaric, solid masses of muscle charging towards them with axes and clubs.

Alaric had drawn his great sword, holding it to his side in both hands. Rainira stood behind him and to his right, still firing arrows into the advancing group. Joshua watched as an arrow sunk into the shoulder of the leading orc. The creature didn't seem to notice. Alaric swung his sword in a horizontal slash as the orc got closer, and Joshua saw the creature's head fly through the air as its body fell to the ground. Alaric brought his sword back around and slashed across the chest of another orc, staggering it. Rainira fired two arrows at the staggered orc, sinking them into its eyes. The orc fell backwards, only to be trampled by its companions.

Utherrian had drawn a longsword and moved back to assist Alaric, while Martin drew his katana and moved to the front to join Ryland and Nitika.

"Joshua, with me!" Martin yelled. "We need to break through the front line and make it to Dollet for aid."

Joshua raised his hand and his rapier appeared in it, steadier than the night before. He followed Martin forward and struck out at the first goblin he saw. The sword passed right through the creature, cutting through it easily. He thrust the blade towards another one of the creatures, but the goblin turned and blocked. Joshua stepped back as the goblin swung at him, then slashed out as the goblin's blade hit the ground. The goblin's head fell to the ground.

"Well done my King!" Martin yelled. The wizard cut down two goblins before holding his hand towards a group of five. A bolt of energy erupted from his outstretched arm, engulfing the goblins. When it disappeared the goblins were gone, nothing remaining of them except for their shoes.

Joshua jumped towards another goblin but missed with his strike. The goblin struck out at Joshua and hit him in the leg, the twisted metal blade sinking into his calf muscle. Joshua screamed in pain, and as the goblin pulled the blade out for another strike an arrow appeared in its chest. Joshua's injured leg gave out beneath him and he began to fall to the ground. Large arms embraced him as Alaric scooped him up on the run.

The Guard had broken through the goblins, but seven of the orcs were right behind them. The Guard ran for Dollet, the orcs hot on their tail. Rainira jumped as she ran, spun, drew, fired an arrow, and landed again without losing step. Joshua watched over Alaric's shoulder as the arrow sunk into the leg of one of the orcs. The orc fell, but quickly regained its feet and continued after them. Martin raised his hands into the air and then threw them towards the ground at his feet. The ground rumbled as they ran over it until Martin pulled his arms up to his chin. Rock and water and mud flew from the ground in a wall behind them, taking out the lead orc and slowing the rest. The Guard continued to run, putting space between them and the orcs. Joshua looked around and saw the town, along with a line of men holding bows. As the Guard passed them the men all lifted their bows and fired flaming arrows towards the orcs.

Ryland, Nitika, and Rainira joined their line. The group fired another volley of arrows into the orcs, felling all but two. Ryland and Nitika stepped forward as the last two orcs closed on them. Nitika leapt onto the first orc, sliding around it and driving her daggers into its neck. The orc fell as Nitika rolled off of it, regaining her feet in a flash. Ryland swung out with his hammer at the last orc, connecting with the creature's skull. A sickening crunch filled the air as it fell to the ground.

The world was quiet for a moment except for the sound of the rain. The sounds of thunder were distant, but they had travelled past the worst of the storm. Alaric set Joshua down carefully, but when he tried to stand pain seared through his leg again. Joshua fell to the ground, the world going black.

22

Healing Light

Joshua opened his eyes and shut them again quickly against the intense light that flooded in. Taking a breath, he slowly opened them and blinked. His vision came into focus bit by bit, and when it did he found himself in a small room, lying in a bed. The walls were wood, with an open-rafter ceiling. He looked around and noticed a small bedside table with a candle burning on top of it to his right. When he turned to his left he saw Rainira looking back at him.

"My King," she said, letting out a sigh of relief. "Thank the Light that you are alright!"

Joshua sat up slowly, feeling aches throughout his body.

"Should I go fetch Corwin?" Rainira said, reaching out a hand to steady him.

Joshua took her hand and squeezed it, offering her a weak smile.

"I think I'm ok," he said. "What happened? Where am I?"

"You passed out after the battle," Rainira said, her voice soft. "It is not much of a surprise, what with it being your first fray. You did wonderfully though, my King, you handled yourself admirably."

Joshua let out a laugh that turned into a cough. "You don't have to be nice to me Rainira."

"I was not being nice, my King, merely telling you the truth.

A wound like the one you sustained would normally be much worse. Thankfully Corwin was able to tend to it quickly, and the power of the Light in the Sigil helped to keep the infection at bay..."

"Infection?"

"You were pierced with a blade forged in darkness. The goblins all carry them. Cheap weapons made of poor iron, but the magic within them is dangerous. Once pierced, the darkness begins to spread. If left untreated by the Light for too long, the darkness alone can turn a small injury into a mortal one."

"Then I'm glad Corwin was able to get to me in time," Joshua said, giving Rainira a slightly stronger smile. "How are the others?"

"Everyone else is fine. They are in the local inn, waiting for you to wake up."

"How long was I out?"

Rainira lowered her head before responding. "Two days."

Joshua was struck silent for a moment at the news, but quickly recovered himself. "If everyone else is at the inn, where am I?" he asked.

Rainira looked back up and met Joshua's eyes, her frown instantly blooming into a beautiful smile. "At my parent's house!" she exclaimed. "We wanted to be cautious, as we did not know if Lacrym's men knew of your return. So while the Guard has stayed at the inn, acting as if they are still searching for the true King, I suggested bringing you to my parent's home. This is actually my old room." Rainira blushed at that.

Joshua turned and swung his feet from the bed and stood up. Pain flared through his calf again and he fell back into the bed.

"I thought Corwin's magic could heal anything," he said.

Rainira smiled at him, the way a mother or loved one smiles at an injured child. "Corwin has great power to heal, but when fighting the darkness even the strongest Light can struggle. Your waking tells us that the darkness has been purged. If you will give me leave, I can fetch Corwin and he should be able to finish healing you."

Joshua nodded and Rainira stood and left the room.

Joshua laid back in the bed, trying to ignore the intense pain still flaring from his calf. He looked around the room again to distract himself, and saw a small bookshelf tucked into the corner. Next to it was a writing desk, with a quill and rolls of parchment. Joshua smiled at the idea of a world in which computers and even ink pens were a foreign concept. Everything was so foreign, yet oddly comforting to him, like the worlds of old fairy tales.

The door opened as he was lost in thought and Corwin came through, followed by Utherrian, Martin, and Rainira.

"It is good to see you awake, my King!" Corwin called with a wide smile. "Feeling better, I hope?"

"Yes, Corwin. My leg still hurts though, and I can't seem to walk," Joshua responded.

"We shall have that rectified in a moment, my King." Corwin knelt by the edge of the bed and pulled the blanket back to expose Joshua's injured leg. Joshua looked down and saw the puncture wound, surrounded by a dark red inflammation. *Infected*, he thought.

Corwin clapped his hands together and bowed his head. He began to move his palms back and forth, rubbing them together. Joshua noticed a light slowly blooming between his hands, and when Corwin placed them against his leg he expected to feel the flare of pain again but instead felt an intense concentration of warmth. Joshua watched as the bright red infection in his veins began to slowly flow back towards the wound. Corwin's hands grew brighter as the infection receded, and finally the cleric rubbed his hands over the hole in Joshua's leg. When he removed them Joshua was amazed to see that the hole had closed up, leaving no trace whatsoever.

"Try to stand, my King," Corwin said, offering a hand.

Joshua swung his legs out of the bed again, took Corwin's offered hand, and attempted to stand. He slowly put pressure on his leg and found that there was no pain at all. He let go of Corwin's hand and laughed. "That is amazing, Corwin. Thank you."

Corwin smiled and said "It is my pleasure, my King. I am happy to be of service."

Martin stepped forward. "I am glad to see that you are healed, my King. Now, if I may get on with business -"

Rainira stepped forward and cut Martin off. "The King needs to rest. He has not had an actual night's rest since we arrived. Whatever you need to say can wait until morning, Captain."

Martin looked shocked at Rainira's outburst, or possibly at the idea of being addressed as Captain. He took a step back from Joshua and shook his head. "Of course, you are correct," he said to Rainira. He turned to Joshua. "My King, please take the night to rest, we can have our discussion in the morning. The town is safe for now, but I want to get you to Erith as soon as possible. If you are up to it in the morning, we will continue our journey then."

Martin turned and walked from the room, followed by Utherrian. Rainira moved forward. "You really should rest, my King. You have not slept well the past two nights."

"Have you stayed with me the whole time?" Joshua asked.

Rainira smiled. "Yes, my King. Someone needed to watch over you. I slept during the days while Corwin sat with you, but the rest of the time I was here." She looked towards the door. "Is there anything I can get for you? Food? Drink?"

"I could definitely go for a bite to eat," Joshua said, feeling his stomach rumble at the mere mention of food.

"Then let us head downstairs. I think my mother is making dinner as we speak."

Rainira turned and walked towards the door. When Joshua hesitated she asked, "My King, is something wrong?"

"Nothing's wrong, Rainira, but can I ask a favor?"

"Anything, my King."

"Could you please call me Joshua?"

Rainira balked, but before she could say no Joshua continued, "If not forever, then at least while I'm a guest in your home?"

Rainira relaxed and responded "I suppose that is fair my Ki-... Joshua." She opened the door and held it for him. "Shall we eat?"

Joshua smiled and touched his rumbling stomach. "Lead the way," he said.

23
Manda Hospitality

The first floor of the house was small, with a cozy country charm. The walls were the exposed interior of a log cabin, and on the floor was a rug that had been well worn by years of footsteps. Paintings adorned the walls around the room, and Joshua noticed one above the fireplace that was a portrait of Rainira. He walked over and looked up at it, smiling and a bit taken aback. In the painting Rainira was wearing a flowing green gown. In one hand she held a single red rose, and in the other she held her bow. He looked to Rainira and back to the painting.

"This had to have been done recently," Joshua said. "You don't look much younger in it."

"My mother asked for it just before we set out to find you, actually," Rainira said. "I stood for it two weeks ago and gave it to her as we passed through Dollet on our way to the forest."

"It's beautiful," Joshua said.

Rainira smiled. "Thank you Joshua." She touched his arm to pull his attention from the painting and gestured across the room to a small table.

The table was set with four bowls, and as Rainira led Joshua across the room to it a man and woman walked in from the kitchen. The man was carrying a large black pot, steam rising out of its open top. The smell of beef and vegetables filled the room. The woman had a copper pitcher containing something cold enough to cause condensation to drip onto the floor. They set the pot and pitcher on the table and turned to Rainira.

"Joshua, I would like to introduce my parents," Rainira said. "This is my father, Onder Manda, and my mother, Amelia."

"It's a pleasure to meet both of you," Joshua said, offering his hand.

Onder was the first to take it, giving Joshua a firm handshake. "The pleasure is ours, my King," he said.

"It really is nice to meet you, and I am glad that you are healing well," Amelia added, taking Joshua's hand and squeezing it.

Joshua nodded to them both and said to Onder "Please, call me Joshua."

"My King, I could not, it would not be proper!" Onder replied.

"I insist. You've been kind enough to let me stay here." When Onder didn't seem convinced Joshua continued, "I am a guest in your house, I really do insist that you call me Joshua, please."

Onder took a deep breath and let it out in a sigh. "I suppose that would be alright while you are here in our home," he said. "But no longer than that!" he added quickly.

"Thank you."

Rainira laughed. "Perhaps we should sit and eat before the food gets cold?" she asked.

Onder nodded and pulled a chair out for his wife. Joshua took his cue and pulled out the opposite chair for Rainira. She smirked at him and took the offered seat. Joshua sat as Onder dipped a ladle into the pot. He served heaping portions of stew into each of their bowls as Amelia poured a sparkling liquid into their cups. Once everyone was served Joshua took a scoop of the stew. It was hot enough to scald his tongue, but after the past couple of days eating straight meat and mushrooms the flavor was amazing. His eyes widened as he looked towards Amelia, who laughed.

"Rainira makes that exact face whenever she stops by after time out in the world," Amelia said. "There is nothing to lift the spirits like a good home cooked meal, I say."

"It's wonderful!" Joshua replied. He dug into the bowl with

intensity, finishing it quickly. Before he could even ask for a second helping Onder had already ladled one into his bowl. Joshua finished four helpings in total before being too full to continue, while Rainira ate three and her parents ate two each.

"You are going to sleep like the dead tonight," Onder said with a laugh. He clapped his stomach and let out a hearty belch.

Joshua lifted his forgotten glass and was about to take a sip when Onder stood up. He lifted his own glass and looked at Joshua. "I would like to raise a glass to you Joshua." Joshua smiled at him, but didn't respond. "I would like to raise a glass to the coming of the King, and offer Amelia's and my own blessing that the road to victory will be swift and safe. May the Light shine again!"

"May the Light shine again," Rainira repeated, raising her own glass. Amelia lifted hers in the air, her smile broad but her eyes revealing her true concern.

Joshua raised his glass into the air and met theirs. "Well said, sir, thank you."

They all drank, and Joshua discovered the liquid was a sparkling wine with a flavor of crisp apples and grapes, similar to the Prosecco he had had back home. He drank the entire glass, as did the rest of the table. Amelia poured another glass of wine as Onder invited them to the seats around the fireplace. Onder lit the fire as Joshua took a seat, and between the warmth of the fireplace and the comfort of the cushioned seat, not to mention the large meal he had just eaten, Joshua began to feel drowsy at once. As he began to lose himself in the fire he heard someone say something.

"I'm sorry?" Joshua said.

Onder chuckled. "I asked what your world was like," he said. "Utherrian was telling me that you came from another world. It seemed unbelievable to me at first, and he added a whole lot of details that I did not understand about 'parallel worlds,' but upon seeing your strange clothes and hearing your way of speech there is no longer a doubt in my mind that he was right."

"Oh," Joshua replied. "I really don't know where to start, to be honest."

"How about you tell us about yourself," Amelia suggested.

"Ok. Well, before Utherrian brought me here I was a college

student. I don't know if you have colleges here," he looked to Rainira who shook her head. "College is basically advanced schooling, more specific to a chosen career. I was studying computers-"

"What is a computer?" Onder asked.

"It's a machine that can do all sorts of tasks, like act as a journal or access the internet, which is basically the collected knowledge of my world with a lot of other things mixed in."

"That sounds amazing!" Onder exclaimed.

"It is. I didn't really have a lot going on, other than my school work and my cat, Cleo. My studies kept me busy. It was snowing the day I left, and I had just gotten into a car accident on the highway...I thought I was going to die, but instead I wound up here."

"Car?" Onder asked.

"Dear, stop pestering him. If you ask about every word we will never get to know him, and this may be our only chance to have him to ourselves," Amelia said.

Joshua laughed. "It's really fine. A car is another machine, much larger than a computer, which is our main transportation. You use horses and carts, correct?" Onder nodded. "Well, a car is like a cart, only it doesn't have horses pulling it. Instead an engine moves it. I can't really explain the details of that, but basically they are just large metal machines that carry multiple people around without horses."

Onder was visibly impressed, but didn't follow up after his wife's admonition. Instead it was Amelia who asked "And do you have someone back there?"

"I'm not sure what you mean," Joshua said.

"A girl!" Amelia said. "Do you have a special lady waiting for your return?"

"Mother!" Rainira exclaimed.

"There is no harm in asking," Amelia responded, dropping a wink to Rainira and quickly looking back to Joshua, who chuckled as he saw Rainira blush.

"No, ma'am, I don't have a lady waiting for me. I don't even know if I'd be able to go back once the war is done. I don't even know if I'll survive long enough to face the choice."

"Our Rainira will make sure that you do," Onder said. "Best shot with a bow in the entire world, our Rainira."

"I've seen her in battle already, and I have no doubt that you're right"

Rainira's blush darkened as she stood up. "It is getting late, my King. You should get some sleep, tomorrow we will be on the move again with the rising of the sun."

"What happened to calling me Joshua?" he asked. When Rainira looked away Joshua stood and stretched before finishing the last of his wine. He turned to Onder and Amelia. "Can I help you clean up?"

"Absolutely not," Amelia said. "Onder and I can take care of that."

"Thank you for the meal and the wine, both were delicious. And thank you again for allowing me a room in your home."

"Any time, Joshua, our door is always open to the King," Onder said. He shook Joshua's hand and said "I hope you sleep well. If there is anything that you need, do not hesitate to ask."

Amelia stepped forward and grasped Joshua's hands again. "I know that it is Rainira's job to look after you, but if you can, please look after her as well. I worry so much when she is away."

"I will do everything I can to make sure she gets home safely," Joshua said.

Amelia surprised him then by throwing her arms around him and planting a motherly kiss on his cheek. He smiled as she stepped back. "Good night Joshua, and good luck."

Rainira led Joshua up the stairs and back to the room he had awoken in. She opened the door and set to work stripping the sheets from the bed that were stained with blood. She laid out new ones, working quickly, and when she was done she turned to Joshua. "Is there anything else you will need?"

"I think I'll be fine. I'm just glad to be sleeping on an actual bed for a change. You know, while not unconscious."

Rainira laughed. "I hope that they were not too forthright tonight."

"Your parents? No, they were wonderful. Your mother is an amazing cook. They both seem like great people."

"They are," Rainira said.

Joshua looked at her as she shifted from one leg to the other, obviously feeling awkward. He noticed that she had let her hair down for the first time that he had seen. It fell in waves down her back, a dark brown that complimented her tanned skin. When he looked back at her face and met her eyes he saw that they were a bright green.

"Are you ok Rainira? You seem uncomfortable. If me being here in your home is causing that I'm sure that Utherrian can find me another place to stay."

"I am fine, my King. There is just a lot on my mind. Of course I do not mind you staying here." She met Joshua's eyes again and smiled. "If there is nothing else that you need, I should be getting to bed myself."

"I'm all set," Joshua said, deciding that trying to convince her to call him Joshua was a futile fight.

"Then good night, my King. I will wake you in the morning when it's time to meet the rest of the Guard."

"Good night Rainira."

Rainira left the room quickly, brushing past Joshua and closing the door behind her. Joshua shook his head, unsure of what he had done to make her so uneasy. He pushed the thought from his mind and stripped down to his pants before sliding into bed beneath the blankets. Sleep took him moments after his head hit the pillow, and for a change they were blessedly without dreams.

24

An Archer's Eye

Joshua woke to a knock on the door. He sat up and looked towards the window to see the sun rising in the distance. He stood and dressed quickly before opening the door to find Rainira waiting, holding a bundle of cloth.

"Good morning Joshua," she said with a smile.

"Back to Joshua, huh?" Joshua said with a laugh. Rainira just glared at him, so Joshua pointed to the cloth and asked "What's that?"

"Clothing. It is my father's, so it will likely be a bit large on you, but we will be able to get you better clothing in town. Utherrian mentioned it to me yesterday, better that you not stick out as we move about, and your current garb is very out of place here."

"So I've noticed," Joshua replied. "I thought Dollet was safe?"

"It is, but you never know if Lacrym's spies are about. Better to be cautious when out in public, at least for now." Rainira handed him the clothing. "Get changed and then come downstairs. Mother has breakfast prepared, and once we have eaten we are to meet Utherrian outside the inn. If there is time after we will get you more appropriate clothing."

Rainira left, shutting the door behind her. Joshua laid the clothing on the bed, and stripped to his underwear. He looked down and noticed a scar on his leg where he had been stabbed that hadn't been there before. The scar was a twisted knot, darker than the area around it. He made a mental note to ask Corwin about it when he saw the cleric.

Joshua sifted through the clothing and found pants and a rough leather belt. He slipped them on, using the last notch of the belt in order to cinch them closed. He put on the socks and large leather boots next, followed by the shirt. When he was done he looked down at the fabric hanging from his body and laughed.

Joshua rolled his own clothing into a ball and tucked them under his arm as he left the room. As soon as he hit the steps he could smell toast and onions. Rainira and Onder sat at the table, sipping something from mugs. Onder waved Joshua over with a smile.

"Good morning Joshua!" he said jovially. "Sit, m' boy, sit! Have you ever had coffee? It is a wonderful drink that picks you right up in the morning."

"Good morning Onder. Yes, I've had coffee, it's basically a staple in my world." Joshua sat as Onder poured a cup of thick black liquid into a mug. Joshua lifted the mug and took a sip, spitting it out almost instantly.

"Is something wrong?" Onder asked, still with a hint of laughter in his eyes.

"No, it's just much thicker than our coffee and I wasn't expecting it. It tastes like there's something else in it as well."

"Probably the whiskey," Onder said with a wink. When Joshua stared at him, mouth open, Onder laughed. "What? You do not put whiskey in your coffee?"

"Only on the weekends," Joshua responded. He took another sip of the coffee, this time expecting the flavor, and found that it tasted quite sweet, once you got past the bitter beans and the oaky whiskey flavors of course. He took another sip and laid his mug on the table. Amelia came into the room carrying a tray of plates loaded with eggs, fried onions, and toast. Joshua's mouth began to water at once. After Amelia had passed out the plates and sat down Onder picked up his fork and dug into the food. Joshua followed his lead.

Once the meal was done Rainira quickly excused herself and Joshua, explaining that they had to meet the Guard. She kissed her father and hugged her mother. "Just in case there is no time to stop by later. I love you both," she said.

"And we love you dear," Amelia responded. Onder put his arm around his wife and nodded.

"Thank you both for the amazing meals, and for offering your home to me," Joshua said.

"It was our pleasure, sir. You can repay us by bringing our Rainira home safe," Amelia replied, taking Joshua's hand.

Onder reached out and shook Joshua's hand and said, "And you could bring peace back to these lands, that would be nice repayment as well."

Joshua laughed. "I will do my best, on both counts."

With that Rainira led Joshua out of the house. The street they exited into was full of people moving about. To his left Joshua could see a faint outline of the mountains they had crossed, and he was struck silent again at how far they had come in just a few days. When he turned to his right his mouth fell open, however, at the sight of a towering wall less than a mile away.

"The walls of Erith," Rainira said. "If you think they're impressive just wait until you see the gate, and the castle."

When Joshua didn't move she reached out and took his hand and pulled him away down the street, weaving in and out of the people. When they reached the square she let go of his hand and continued across. Joshua followed, looking around. There were so many things he had never actually seen before, like the blacksmith working a forge and hammering metal into something useful on an anvil, or the butcher hanging fresh deer carcasses from hooks outside his shop. The sounds that filled the air gave hints of other things beyond the square, but Joshua couldn't place them. As they neared the other side of the square Joshua looked forward and caught sight of Utherrian and Martin outside of a taller building that he assumed was the inn.

When Joshua and Rainira reached them Martin greeted Joshua with a laugh. "I am sorry, my King, it is just that you look absolutely ridiculous! Utherrian, if I am to have any length of conversation with him today, we really must get him some suitable clothing."

Joshua blushed, feeling self-conscious. Joshua could see that Utherrian was consciously attempting to hide a smile of his own as he reached into his bag and pulled out a small leather pouch. He tossed the pouch to Rainira, who snatched it out of the air. "Go and take Joshua to find some clothing that fits. Give your father our thanks as well."

"Yes, Steward," Rainira said. She tapped Joshua on the shoulder and gestured towards a small road leading out from the central square. She led him down the road only a couple of paces before turning into a short building. Inside there were racks overflowing with clothing along the walls, and crude shelves piled high with socks and other smaller garments. Rainira led Joshua around the room, holding different pieces of clothing up to him and putting the ones that seemed too big back on the shelves. When she had gathered a full outfit she led him to a small curtain in the back of the shop, pushed him inside, and handed over the clothing before drawing the curtain shut.

Joshua changed quickly, noticing that everything Rainira had picked out fit perfectly. When he exited the curtain she looked him up and down, turned him around for a moment, then handed him a pair of shoes. They were only ankle high, unlike the knee-high boots he was currently wearing, and made of a dark brown leather. Joshua took off Onder's large boots and slipped on the new shoes. They fit snugly, but without pinching. He moved around a bit and noticed the clothing didn't restrict any of his motion.

"It is archer's garb, the kind we wear when training. You should be able to move freely in it, without any hindrance," she explained. "Does it all fit?"

"Yeah, it all fits," Joshua replied. "How'd you do that? It takes me longer to find clothes that fit, and I know my measurements!"

"An archer's eye," Rainira said with a smile. She walked to an older woman sitting nearby, putting stitches into what seemed to be a pair of partially finished pants.

The woman looked over at Joshua, and turned to Rainira. "All told we are looking at 30, but for you my dear I'll make it 20, the Kingdom does not have money to burn ya know!" she said with a dry laugh.

Rainira pulled the money out of the pouch and handed it to the woman. "Thanks Marla."

Rainira gathered up her father's clothing and led Joshua out of the store. As they reached the door the old woman, Marla, called out "Rainira! You gave me twice what I asked for!"

Rainira turned and offered Marla a wide smile before slipping through the door. She led Joshua back to the town square and pointed towards the inn. "Utherrian and Martin are likely waiting inside. If not, just find a seat and wait for them. I am going to return these clothes to my father and I will join you in a while."

"Thank you Rainira," Joshua said.

She smiled at him and walked away across the town square. Joshua watched her until she was out of sight, wondering what it was about her that made his stomach lurch as though he had missed a step.

"A beautiful girl, my King," a voice said softly from behind him. Joshua turned to find Martin watching him. The wizard laughed. "It is perfectly alright sir, since you were not interested in my dashing looks it would be odd if you did not appreciate hers. If you are ready though, may I suggest we head inside? There is much that we need to discuss, and now that I can look at your clothes without laughing I think we should get on with it."

"Yes Martin," Joshua said, blushing in front of the captain for the second time in only an hour. "Lead the way."

Martin walked towards a nearby building and opened the door, ushering Joshua inside. Joshua had to duck to avoid hitting his head on the door frame, and once inside he found himself not in the entrance of an inn, but rather in a dark barroom that reeked of stale beer and vomit. Martin followed behind him and pointed to a table in the back corner where Utherrian sat. Joshua made his way through the dark room and took a seat across from Utherrian. Martin slid into a chair between them.

"I hope that you slept well, my King," Utherrian said, keeping his voice low. "It is time to get back to work, and I am afraid there are some complications."

"What's wrong?" Joshua asked.

Utherrian looked to Martin, who nodded and turned to Joshua. "I split the Guard up last night and sent them scouting for any sign of Lacrym's forces nearby. After the attack when we arrived I wanted to be sure that the threat was indeed taken care of. They were all given horses and told to ride out two miles in pairs before circling back, with strict orders to return before sunrise."

"So what's the problem?" Joshua asked.

"Alaric and Nitika arrived back four hours ago, an hour before sunrise." Martin said. "Corwin and Ryland, however, have yet to return."

Utherrian leaned forward. "No member of the Guard has ever missed an ordered rendezvous. Something must have delayed them. We sent Alaric and Nitika out again to follow their back trail, but we have not heard back yet. If we do not hear soon we will have to follow and try to find them."

"Why don't we just leave now? If Alaric and Nitika found the others, we'll meet them as they come back. If not they may need our help," Joshua said.

"We cannot all go," Martin said. "We need to ensure your safety above all. Perhaps Utherrian could take you into the city to the castle while I take Rainira and go out-"

"No!" Joshua interrupted. "I'm not going to sit by while they may be in trouble. I'm going with you."

"My King, I cannot allow such a dangerous request," Martin said.

"I'm your King, correct?"

"Yes, sir."

"Then don't consider it a request. Let's go."

Utherrian smiled as Joshua stood and walked towards the door. Martin turned to protest to the Steward, but Utherrian only raised his hand, his smile widening. Martin begrudgingly stood and followed his Steward and his King out of the barroom and back into the square.

25

The Red Dragon

Rainira was waiting for them outside the bar. She smiled at Joshua, but when she saw his expression her face fell.

"What is it?" she asked.

"Corwin and Ryland are missing," Joshua said quietly.

Rainira turned to Martin when Joshua didn't continue. "They have not returned from last night's scouting. Nitika and Alaric have gone out again in search of them," Martin explained. "Our King has ordered that we all follow."

Rainira looked to Joshua, who nodded. "Then let us find horses and be off," she said.

She led their small group through town, taking a couple turns as she went. When they finally emerged from the small streets and clustered buildings Joshua saw a stable. He walked past Rainira, intent on moving as quickly as possible, but she caught his hand. "We can take care of readying the horses. Wait here."

"Wouldn't a king's word move things along faster?" Joshua asked. He shifted from foot to foot, impatient at the delay.

"We cannot let it be known yet that the King has returned," Rainira explained. "No one but the Guard and my parents know, and we must keep it that way. We do not know who may be under the influence of the Darkness, and we must be cautious until we are ready to move. Utherrian will get the horses, the word of the Steward is the word of the King until you officially take the throne."

Joshua looked at her for a moment, took a breath, and said, "Ok. We have to hurry though, they could be in trouble."

Utherrian nodded and moved off to speak with the stable hands. Martin laid a hand on Joshua's shoulder, and Joshua felt calm spread through him like a wave.

"My King," Martin said softly, "we will find them, and I am sure they will be safe. Lacrym's forces rarely move about during the day, as they are weakened by the daylight. Unless our intelligence is wrong, there has been no large-scale movement of forces while the sun is shining, and the day is clear in all directions."

"Thank you, Martin, I'm just concerned," Joshua said with a sigh.

"Martin's right, my King," Rainira chimed in with a reassuring smile. "They all know how to take care of themselves."

"I'm just worried about them, Rainira. I know I only just met you all, but you've already done so much for me and I don't want to lose you, any of you."

Utherrian appeared and clapped Joshua on the shoulder. "I hope you can ride, sir. The horses await us."

Utherrian led them to the edge of town where they found four horses waiting, their reins held by a young stable boy.

"Here you are, sirs!" the young boy yelled. Seeing Rainira he quickly added, "and lady!"

Rainira laughed and took one of the reins from the boy, tousling his hair as she walked by. She checked the saddle and then mounted the horse in one fluid motion, sliding into the saddle and sitting with the ease of experience. She laid her bow across the pommel of the saddle as Joshua watched, her grace captivating his attention. It wasn't until Utherrian coughed that Joshua realized he had frozen. He blushed as he took the next horse and went through his own check, being extra sure the strap across the horse's stomach was tight. He placed one foot in the saddle and threw the other over the top of the horse.

"I believe you have ridden before," Rainira said with a smirk.

"I used to volunteer at a stable in my hometown," Joshua

explained.

Rainira nodded her head and looked behind them. Utherrian had mounted his horse, but Martin seemed to be having some trouble getting his mount to stand still. Every time he placed a foot in the saddle the horse whinnied and stepped to the side, out of reach. Finally Utherrian maneuvered his horse beside Martin's, blocking the mount's path. When Martin finally made it into the saddle, Joshua and Rainira both laughed, receiving a dark glare from Martin.

"Let us be off," Martin said, kicking his horse and riding off ahead of them.

"Someone is a bit touchy this morning," Rainira said to Joshua.

They both laughed as they urged their horses forward with Utherrian just behind them.

They rode at a steady trot, with Martin leading the way, Rainira riding next to Joshua, and Utherrian bringing up the rear. Martin seemed intent on a straight course, and Joshua asked Rainira, "Does he see something that I'm missing? How does he know where he's going?"

"Martin has plenty of magic at his disposal," Rainira said. "I am sure he used some form of it to find the rest of the Guard. I do not fully understand the magic he employs, I only know that he has more control of it than anyone I have ever known or heard about."

"What do you mean?"

"There are only a few alive today who possess magic: Martin and Logan Lacrym are the two most powerful. The only known ways to gain that power is to slay a dragon, or befriend one. Since almost all of the dragons were killed in the Dragon Wars a thousand years ago, there is no way to access the power anymore. Martin is a remnant of that war, and we are lucky to have his power on our side."

Joshua glanced behind him at Utherrian, wondering why the Steward had never revealed his secret self to the Guard. "Almost all of the dragons?" Joshua asked.

"We know of one that survives for sure. Droven, an obsidian dragon allied with Lacrym. Droven is how Lacrym has the power he does, how he has been able to twist the souls of those under him to form his vampire and goblin armies." Rainira paused for a moment as her horse stepped over a small ditch in the plain. "There are rumors of another that are all but confirmed. Lillith, a red dragon rumored to wander the world as a beautiful woman, manipulating the people into doing her bidding. Beyond that there are only whispers. There are some who speak of a great silver dragon seen in these parts, but the silver dragons had gone extinct even before the Dragon Wars, killed off by the other dragons because they allied themselves with humans."

Joshua struggled to keep a straight face, thankful that Rainira was too distracted to see his reactions. "So why is Martin the only one that survived?" Joshua asked, even though he knew about Martin's sealing himself within a tree to silence the voices in his head.

"Martin sealed himself away soon after the Dragon Wars, and Utherrian only undid the seal recently, using knowledge that he gained from a book from the Artek archives. You see, every time a person uses magic they sacrifice a part of themselves. The stronger the magic, the more you sacrifice. Different magics take away different parts of you, according to the stories. Dark magic chips away at one's soul, elemental and psychic magic chips away at one's body, and Light magic slowly erodes one's mind. Used responsibly, as Martin does now, the effects can be managed and quelled. Used recklessly, as many people did after the Wars in an attempt to seize power, the magic ravages one's being until there is nothing left."

They rode on in silence as Joshua digested the information. It wasn't long before Martin pulled his horse to a halt. Joshua and Rainira slowed and stopped beside him and were joined shortly after by Utherrian.

"What have you sensed, captain?" Utherrian asked.

"Trouble," Martin replied. Joshua saw that Martin's eyes were closed and wondered to himself if the wizard had ridden this whole way without opening them. Martin took a deep breath, seeming to struggle to concentrate. After a moment his eyes flew wide.

"A dragon," he whispered.

Utherrian looked at him, his eyes alarmed. "A dragon? In these parts? Where is it? Can you sense anything else?"

Martin closed his eyes again, screwing them shut. He sat that way for more than a minute before responding. "Not far ahead, nearer the shore. I cannot tell if the dragon is still there, but..."

Martin opened his eyes and kicked his horse into a full gallop.

He sped off across the plain, with the rest of them following behind. Their horses moved swiftly, and before long Joshua noticed the smell of salt in the air, a scent that brought back memories of summer trips to the shore. They kept moving, and soon Joshua was able to see an expanse of blue in the distance. As they drew nearer, Martin pushed his horse faster, drawing further ahead of them.

"Martin!" Utherrian yelled after him, but the wizard didn't slow down.

Joshua pushed his own horse to move faster, with Rainira and Utherrian following suit. Martin was still drawing further away, no doubt assisted by some magic. A strip of sand appeared in the distance ahead of them. Just after he noticed it Joshua saw something leap into the air in the distance. At first he couldn't be sure what it was, but then massive wings unfurled from the center and a slender dragon flew into the air. It went straight up before swooping downwards and flying in a bolt directly towards him. Joshua saw Martin's horse rear ahead of them. The wizard raised his staff and pointed it towards the dragon. A massive bolt of solid white light erupted from the end of the staff. The bolt flew towards the dragon, but the dragon lifted itself further into the air with ease, the bolt of light passing harmlessly beneath it.

Joshua watched the dragon as it looped in the air. It seemed smaller than Utherrian had seemed, but still larger than any creature Joshua had ever experienced. Its scales were a bright crimson red in the evening light. Martin screamed something in the distance, and another bolt of light erupted from his staff. The crimson dragon flew to the side this time, but the bolt caught its tail. The dragon let out a deafening cry before soaring higher into the sky. Martin let another bolt of energy fly after it, but the dragon dodged easily in the distance. The dragon continued to soar higher and further away, its wings flapping furiously to give it speed; before long it disappeared into the horizon.

"Was that..." Joshua's question trailed off as he watched the dragon disappear into the distance.

"Lillith," Rainira whispered. "So she is real."

Utherrian rode ahead of them to Martin, and when Joshua looked he saw the wizard slumped in his saddle. He rode forward to meet them, Rainira close behind.

"Go to the shore, see if the others are there," Utherrian called as they neared. "I will take care of Martin."

This time Rainira rode ahead with Joshua following. They reached the shore and quickly spotted the Guard. Joshua slid from his saddle and ran towards them. Ryland turned to him as he approached, his warhammer held in both hands. He swung over-hand at Joshua. Joshua dove to the side, barely avoiding the massive weapon. He looked up just as Rainira passed him, her momentum throwing her towards Ryland. She struck the larger man in the jaw with her bare hand, sending Ryland to the ground.

Joshua stood and walked to Ryland. He bent and picked the warhammer up from the ground, surprised by the weight of the weapon. With some effort he threw the hammer behind him. Ryland was on his hands and knees, shaking his head. When he stood up Joshua's armor appeared around him, ready for the large man to strike out. Instead Ryland turned and looked around. His eyes focused on Joshua and he fell to his knees.

"My King!" Ryland exclaimed happily before his face fell. "What happened? Why are you in armor?"

Joshua looked down and noticed his armor, then closed his eyes and concentrated on it vanishing. When he opened them again he held out a hand to Ryland. "It's alright Ryland."

Ryland stood slowly, still shaking his head a bit. He reached up and touched his chin. "That is going to swell you know," he said to Rainira.

"Serves you right," she snapped back. "You tried to crush the King!"

Joshua looked around for Rainira and saw her with the rest of the guard huddled on the ground nearby. He rushed over to them and placed a hand on Nitika's shoulder. She looked up at him, careful to keep her hood over her face, and offered a weak smile. Joshua looked to Corwin and Alaric and found them both sitting up, dazed but safe.

"What happened?" Rainira asked.

"The dragon..." Alaric responded, his voice distant. "The red one...Lillith...she ambushed us and knocked us out cold."

"We came looking for them and were also taken by surprise," Corwin continued. "As we approached a slender woman in red appeared. She touched Ryland and said something to him, and before I knew it he hit me in the chest with his hammer. I must have fallen here, because that is the last I remember."

Utherrian approached, followed closely by Martin, and looked over the group. "Corwin, can you do something to heal your wounds? We can get more help back in town, but for now we need you to be able to ride with us back to town."

Corwin nodded and brought himself up to his knees. The cleric bowed his head and whispered an incantation. A soft glow emanated from his chest, then swirled out around the rest of the Guard. As the light faded the Guard all began to get to their feet..

"Rainira and Nitika, take one of the horses and get the King back to town, as quickly as you can," Utherrian instructed. "We will follow behind, but you three can move more quickly with two to a horse and Nitika running beside."

Rainira and Nitika both nodded before moving towards the horses. Joshua began to protest, but Utherrian insisted, "Night is nigh, you need to be back in the safety of town before darkness falls. Now go."

Joshua gave one last look to the remaining Guard before following after Rainira and Nitika. As he mounted the horse behind Rainira he noticed for the first time how late it had gotten. He held on to Rainira's sides as she pushed the horse into a gallop. Nitika disappeared in front of them, moving in and out of sight as she ran loops ahead of them in search of threats. Rainira pushed the horse harder as the sun began to set, intent on reaching town before night fell completely. In the distance Joshua could faintly hear the beating hooves of the rest of the Guard following behind.

26
New Plans

Joshua and Rainira sat in front of her parents' fireplace. Nitika was outside, intent on acting as lookout until the Guard had all returned. Onder and Amelia had gone back to the kitchen to sit after bringing Joshua and Rainira steaming mugs of tea. Joshua had sipped his at first, but now the mug sat on the small table beside him, forgotten.

"They should be back by now, shouldn't they?" Joshua asked for the third time, standing up to pace in front of the fire. "Do you think something happened to them?"

"They were not that far behind us," Rainira said. "If they had been attacked we would have heard the town guard sound the alarm. Since no alarm has been heard, my best guess is that they are attending to some other business before coming to join us."

Joshua looked at Rainira, who sat cradling her mug of tea. "You're right," he said, slumping back into his chair. He lifted his own mug and took a sip before laying it aside again. "I just don't like not knowing, I don't like waiting. I feel so useless..."

"Well, stop that!" Rainira said with a sharp tone.

"What?" Joshua replied, a bit taken aback.

"I am sorry to be blunt my King, but it does not really matter if you feel useless. It does not matter if you have to sit and wait. Your safety is the most important thing to me right now. I need you to stay alive. The country needs you to lead them. So I do not care if you are restless, we are going to stay right here until the Guard returns!"

Joshua looked at Rainira in shock. She was fuming, her face bright red. As she began to calm down Joshua burst into laughter, holding his sides and rocking from the force. Every time he tried to speak up the laughter redoubled, causing him to lose control all over again. It wasn't long before Rainira was smiling at him, and a few more moments later she had joined her laughter to the chorus.

When Joshua was finally able to calm himself down enough to take another sip of tea the mood had lifted considerably. He smiled at Rainira and reached across the table to take her hand. "Thank you for caring about me, for keeping me safe," he said.

"It is my honor and my pleasure, my King...Joshua. Just please understand that we have been searching for you for a very long time, and we are now too close to risk anything. Tomorrow we will be within the walls of Erith, and we will all be sleeping within the white halls of Eringhal. The city itself may not be perfectly safe, but you will find no haven safer than Eringhal throughout all of Camledor. For now, just try to relax. I am sure that Utherrian or Martin will be here shortly with orders."

The front door opened and Nitika stepped in. She stopped for a moment at the sight of Rainira and Joshua's entwined hands, but recovered and moved into the room quickly. Joshua let go of Rainira's hand, trailing his fingers absently across hers as he did, relishing the warmth and already missing the shared moment as it dissipated. "Are they back?" he asked Nitika.

"They just made it to the center of town. Alaric, Corwin, and Ryland are heading for the inn, while Utherrian and Martin are heading this direction and should be arriving any moment."

"Thank you Nitika," Rainira said. "Would you like to have some tea with me while Joshua talks with the Captain and the Steward?"

"I would rather resume my watch, Rainira," Nitika said. She turned and was gone from the room in a flash.

Utherrian caught the door before it even shut and walked into the house, Martin close at his heels. "I would not mind a mug of tea," he said. "Something warm would be most welcome right about now."

Rainira stood to get a mug for the Steward. "Martin, can I get anything for you?"

"A small cup of your father's ale would be most welcome, if at all possible," he replied.

Rainira nodded and walked into the kitchen. Joshua could hear her talking with her parents as Utherrian and Martin sank into the two chairs nearby.

"Is everyone alright?" Joshua asked.

"Yes," Utherrian replied. "Ryland is a little shaken up, but he seems to have broken whatever control Lillith had over him. For now I believe that we are safe, but I will feel much more content once we are safely within the city walls."

"How did Lillith take control of Ryland?" Joshua asked.

"That would be her magic," Martin explained. "The red dragons were masters of the mind. Their magic is able to sink into the persona of an individual. The stronger a person's will, the more capable they are of resisting a red dragon's control."

Rainira came back in, carrying two mugs. She handed the one billowing steam to Utherrian and the other to Martin. As she turned to walk back to the kitchen to rejoin her parents Utherrian said, "Rainira, stay. There is no reason you should not be here right now."

"As you wish Utherrian," she said, taking a seat next to Joshua on the sofa.

"So what happens now?" Joshua asked.

"We need to get you inside Eringhal, but there is a problem," Utherrian said.

"No need to be cryptic with them Utherrian," Martin snapped. "We have received word that a small group of Lacrym's men are working within the city walls. We do not have all the details, but the information that we do have points to a very small number, likely no more than ten men. We do not yet know what their aim is, but we believe that rumors may have spread of your return. There would be no proof of your identity, but the fact that the entire Steward's Guard marched across the continent of Galion, only to return with one more person, a person dressed in strange clothes, could very well be common knowledge. If Lacrym even suspects that you may be the true King of Galion, he will stop at nothing to remove you before you have an opportunity to rally the nation behind you."

Joshua was silent, his face ashen. Rainira laid a hand on his shoulder and said, "You have your Guard, we will protect you."

"I know," Joshua replied. "I just don't want any of you getting hurt for me. I want to believe that I'm the King you all think I am, and there's a part of me that does, but there's still a large part of me that questions it, that thinks this is all some huge misunderstanding, or even a really vivid dream I'm having..."

"I can assure you that this is no dream," Utherrian said.

"How can you be certain?"

"How did you arrive here?" Utherrian asked.

"I was in a car accident, then in a weird dark place, then I heard your voice and came out of the dark place into the clearing in the forest."

"Do you remember the time before the accident?"

"Yeah, I was in classes all day. And I remember waking up and thinking about a dream filled with vampires and a knight...Ok, what does remembering all this have to do with me thinking I might be in a dream right now?"

Martin leaned across the table and slapped Joshua across the face, then calmly took his seat. "I am sorry for that, my King," he said. "It needed to be done, however, to clear your head of this ridiculous notion. Regardless of the past, you are here now, and you are the only hope that we have. You need to stop behaving like a scared child and accept your place-"

"Martin!" Utherrian yelled. "That is enough."

"Sir, he needs to-"

"He 'needs to' nothing. He is doing the best that can be expected of anyone in such a situation as this. If nothing else, have some respect for your King."

Martin fell silent. He turned to Joshua and said "I am sorry, my King, I acted poorly. I beg your forgiveness."

"Of course I forgive you," Joshua said. "You're not wrong, I'm freaked out and failing in a lot of ways. I don't know what I'm doing, and I need all of you to help me figure it out. That's why I hate when any of you risk yourselves for me...if you all die and I'm the only one left, well...I'm screwed..."

Rainira reached out and turned Joshua's head to her. "Joshua, you are doing fine, and you are going to be amazing. If at any point you forget that, just remember the mountaintop. You saved my life...I would have fallen off the side and plummeted to my death if you had not risked your life to save me. And then you saved all of us with the power of the Sigil. Any time that you doubt yourself, remember those two things: my gratitude and the Sigil of the King's power within your hand."

Joshua nodded and took Rainira's hand from his face. He felt a connection through that touch, one that grounded him and gave him some clarity. He held on tight, and Rainira seemed happy enough to offer the comfort.

"So," Joshua started, taking a breath. "What happens now?"

"First, we are sleeping in Dollet tonight," Utherrian began. "Rainira, if your parents do not mind, it would likely be best for Joshua to sleep here."

"I am sure that will not be a problem," Rainira said.

"Good. Second, we are heading out at first light. We will meet at the northern edge of town before daybreak. My hope is that we are well within the city gates by the time the sun rises. If all goes well we will be through the city's outskirts by midday, and to the castle proper by nightfall. If something should go wrong, we will rendezvous at Chapel Lux."

Utherrian looked at Martin. "We will move in pairs. Utherrian and Nitika will go first," Martin said, "as the two are often seen together within the city, and are also more than capable of protecting themselves should the need arise. They will be followed by Alaric and Corwin. Ryland and I will be next, as I want to be with him in case Lillith's spell retakes his mind. Finally, Joshua, you will come with Rainira. Each pair will stay within sight of the pair in front of them in case aid is needed."

"Understood," Rainira said, squeezing Joshua's hand. "I will protect the King."

"Very good," Martin responded. "Joshua, I want you to wear this as you move through the city tomorrow." Martin pulled a long gray cloak from behind him. "We do not want any additional attention drawn to you. I think that is all, so for now let us all get some much needed rest and put this wasted day behind us."

Martin rose from his seat, drained the remaining ale from his mug, and followed Utherrian out of the house. Joshua stood, releasing Rainira's hand, and nodded to the two men. They returned the nod and left the house.

"Are you alright?" Rianira asked Joshua after they had gone.

"Yeah, I guess. It's just all been a lot, you know?" he responded, rubbing his neck.

"You have handled everything admirably thus far," she said, standing to face him. "Just hold on another day and we should be safe within the castle. Utherrian has hinted at something there that may help you, though I do not know what it is. Let us just hope that it helps you as much as he thinks it will."

Joshua nodded, then threw his arms around Rainira. She embraced him in return. They held each other for a moment before Joshua stepped back. "Thank you for all of your help, and your kind words. It really has helped."

"You are welcome, Joshua," Rainira responded with a smile. "We really should be getting to bed, we only have a few hours before we need to be moving again. I will wake you when the time comes."

Joshua nodded. He walked to the kitchen to thank Onder and Amelia one last time, and to bid them farewell. After that he followed Rainira up the stairs, where they went their separate ways to sleep. As Joshua laid in the borrowed bed he looked toward the window, barely making out the walls of the city in the distance. He sighed as he closed his eyes, and moments later sleep took him.

27

The Great Gates of Erith

Rainira woke Joshua quietly. He dressed quickly, throwing the long gray cloak Martin had given him over his shoulders. They left the house silently, moving swiftly once outside. It was still dark out. Joshua couldn't see the moon or the sun, only a vast expanse of stars.

"Dawn is still a couple hours out," Rainira said, seeing Joshua looking up.

Joshua merely nodded as they moved through the barren streets, doing his best to stifle yawns. Rainira had her bow in her hands, but did not have an arrow at the ready. She looked down every side street as she led Joshua through the town, taking a circuitous route and avoiding the town center. They moved quickly, and half an hour later they had reached the northern edge of Dollet. Joshua looked around, trying to find the rest of the Guard, but saw no sign of life. Rainira led him to a bench and they sat down in the shadow of one of the buildings.

The time passed quietly, neither one of them willing to break the silence of the night. Eventually Joshua saw movement to his left. Rainira grabbed his hand to keep him from standing and the group kept moving out into the field.

"It is them," Rainira said, letting go of Joshua's hand. "Sorry, I needed to be sure. We are getting too close to be careless now."

The two of them stood and moved towards the rest of the Guard. Ryland was the first to step forward. He fell to his knees in front of Joshua. "My King," he said. "I beg your forgiveness. I was not myself, but I nearly killed you."

"Silence you damned fool!" Martin snapped, pulling Ryland to his feet. "You can beg his forgiveness later, prostrate yourself before him for all I care, but for right now we need to blend in. There will be no more references to Joshua as King, at least not within earshot of others, until we are safely within Eringhal."

Ryland bowed his head and stepped back into the group. "Now, you all remember the plan, correct?" Martin asked.

There was a muffled response of "Yes, Captain."

"Good, let us get on with it then, no sense dallying about."

Martin started off, leading the group. They walked along the edge of town, staying in the shadows as best they could. Half an hour passed in the silent dark before Joshua noticed the sun beginning to break the horizon. As light began to flood the world Joshua noticed it illuminating the walls of the city less than a mile away. Martin led them out into the open field and onto a broad, cobblestone road before long. Joshua looked ahead of them and gasped.

Nitika appeared beside him and whispered "Behold, the great Gates of Erith."

Joshua could barely believe the size of them. Two solid doors, made of some shimmering metal, rose into the sky ahead of him. Their facades were beautifully etched with two knights facing outward, holding spears across the entryway. As they moved closer Joshua had to crane his neck to see the tops of them. Martin moved off ahead of the group towards one of two small stone buildings that flanked the gates. Joshua watched as he disappeared within and Utherrian called a halt.

When Martin finally returned he looked angry. "May as well pass some food around Utherrian, we will be stuck here a while," he said.

Utherrian looked at him quizzically. "Did you inform them that the Steward had returned?"

"Yes, sir, but apparently two of the mules that open the gates were killed in the night. Our suspicions were correct, it appears that there are spies within the city."

Utherrian sighed, then reached into his bag and began to pass out small loaves of bread. "This is the last of our rations. Let us hope that the delay is not too long."

They ate in silence, mingling on the side of the road together. As the sun rose higher other people began to appear on the road, approaching the guard houses only to be told to wait. Some returned the way they had come, while others sat on the short walls bordering the road.

"People are beginning to arrive," Martin said. "Damn the luck. Everyone, spread out, mingle about the people, stay in your pairs. We will need to trust the Light to get us through this safely, but for now we need to separate before we are noticed together. Be safe, and remember: should something go wrong, delaying us from the castle tonight, meet at Chapel Lux by nightfall."

Utherrian and Nitika left, joining a group by the gates who immediately started asking the Steward questions. Alaric and Corwin followed, and Joshua heard the cleric call out a greeting to another group. Martin and Ryland moved a dozen paces forward before falling in behind the last larger group. Rainira moved to the side of the road and sat on the stone wall there, patting a space beside her for Joshua.

"Hopefully they get the gates moving soon," Rainira said.

Joshua had a flash of his vision from the Shaded Wood, a vision of giant gates swinging open against a bright blue sky. He looked towards the west and saw the sun just coming up over the mountains in the distance. The day was definitely clear if he could even make out the mountains. "They'll open soon," Joshua said softly.

"How could you possibly know that?" Rainira asked with a laugh.

"I don't know, I just...do," Joshua said, shrugging his shoulders and touching the Sigil within his pocket.

A moment later they heard a loud crash from the gates. Rainira turned to him with a look of amazement, but Joshua missed it. He was watching the gates as a line of light appeared in the center of them. Slowly, the gates began to move. They opened into the city, the knights engraved on them seeming to invite the waiting people in. As soon as the gates were wide enough people started to move through.

Joshua saw Utherrian and Nitika enter the city with the first group. The gates swung open faster as they began to move, but the pace was still sluggish. They were only halfway open when Alaric led Corwin through. There was another large crash as the gates stopped moving, and Joshua found himself wondering what kind of mechanism was inside the walls to move such massive slabs of metal.

Martin and Ryland entered the city, and Rainira stood from the wall. She held her hand out to Joshua, who took it. As they walked forward she let go of his hand and placed hers on his forearm instead. "If people think that we are together they will be less likely to question us," she explained.

Rainira led Joshua along the road, and as they passed through the gates Joshua couldn't help but look up at the clear blue sky beyond. Rainira pulled him away from the sight and into the city of Erith.

28
Erith

Rainira led Joshua from the gates into Erith's outer quarter, where the streets were barely an arm's width across and the air smelled of rotten food and urine. Everywhere Joshua looked he saw either people wearing clothing that was well made or people in rags. Those in finery were just passing through the outer quarter like Joshua and the Guard, and they seemed out of place amongst the beggars. There were hundreds of men and women sitting along the streets, and twice that number of children. All of them had their hands out.

Joshua looked to Rainira. "Do you have anything we could give them?"

"Utherrian has all of our supplies," Rainira replied. She hung her head. "I hate to say it, but be sure to protect the Sigil. Many of the children are experienced pickpockets. I am not worried about them making off with the Sigil, but if any of them tries to take it they will surely burst into flames. So for your sake and theirs, be sure to protect it."

Joshua fished the Sigil out of his right pocket and moved it to his left, where he could hold onto it with his free hand. They continued through the street while Joshua did his best to ignore the children that gathered around them at every step. It broke his heart, and when he looked to his right he could tell that the effort was taking more of a toll on Rainira. She seemed to be in physical pain, and Joshua increased their pace in order to get out of the area quicker.

As they moved on through the city the throngs of children and beggars began to thin. Soon they found themselves in a stretch of city that seemed abandoned.

"This is the most obvious break between districts within the walls," Rainira said. "The outer quarter is only the area nearest the gate. Soon we'll enter the lower quarter, followed by the inner quarter. Beyond that is the castle."

In the distance Joshua could see Ryland over the crowd moving towards the lower quarter. As he made a turn he caught a brief glimpse of Martin. Rainira and Joshua followed the throng of people further into the city, caught in the swell pushing forward. Rainira slowly moved them to the center of the crowd as they moved.

"We are less likely to be noticed in the middle," she whispered.

Joshua nodded and continued on. Soon he found himself in an area that reminded him of Dollet. Small wooden buildings lined the roadway that they followed. Signs dangled above the street, advertising tanneries, butchers, blacksmiths, and alchemists. The lower quarter took them half the day to walk through, mainly due to the large crowd of people stopping at random shops to sell and buy goods. By the time they reached the inner edge of the lower quarter the sun was directly above them. Rainira led him onward, weaving between the crowds stopped all around. As they entered the inner quarter Joshua caught his first glimpse of the castle, and he gasped at the sight.

The tallest peak loomed high above them, and he could just make out the walls that surrounded the castle itself. While the buildings of the inner quarter seemed to be made of stone rather than wood, the castle itself seemed to be built of the same shimmering metal that the gates were made from. The midday sun reflected from the facade, making the castle appear as though it were made of pure light.

"That is Eringhal," Rainira said. "That feeling of wonder never goes away. I have been around the castle for years, and it always takes my breath away. Just wait until we pass through the inner gates to Eringhal."

Joshua was speechless. He let Rainira lead him forward while he gazed upward at the tower above them in the distance. It wasn't until he ran into someone that he broke his gaze and watched where he was going. He heard an angry comment from behind him, but by the time he looked around the offended person had already disappeared into the crowd.

As they passed through the inner quarter Joshua noticed that the layout was similar to the outer quarter, the only difference was that the buildings were much more grand. Instead of the weathered wood, the shops here were made of worn stone. It was obvious that this area was older, but the buildings had stood the test of time better than the poorer districts. The further they advanced through the district, the nicer the buildings became. They walked onward as the sun became lower and lower in the sky above them. By the time the sun was setting the castle was still a distant sight.

"How big is Erith?" Joshua asked.

Rainira thought about it for a moment before answering. "Well, the city is not a circle, so it is difficult to estimate the distance. From the gates to Eringhal it is just about a half day's walk, a bit more when there is a crowd like today. From the castle to the port it is another half day's walk, but from the gate to the port it would take just under a day. The inner quarter surrounds the castle on all sides, maybe a quarter day's walk in all directions. If I had to guess, I would say it would take two full days of light to walk from one wall to the opposite side in any direction."

Looking around, Joshua wasn't surprised at Rainira's estimates. The city was larger than any he had ever seen. The closest he had come would likely be New York City, but even that seemed to pale in comparison.

"What's that?" Joshua asked, pointing to a tall spire in the distance that seemed to gleam a radiant gold in the setting sun.

"That would be Chapel Lux," Rainira said.

Joshua nodded as Rainira led him further along. He could still see Ryland in the distance, but couldn't see anyone else in the crowd, even though it had thinned considerably.

The light dimmed considerably as they moved onward, and as the day faded into night Joshua heard the sounds of commotion ahead of them. He looked to Rainira, but her face showed no signs of concern as she continued to lead him forward. The noise continued as they moved, however, and Joshua noticed Rainira's face begin to fall.

"What is it?" Joshua asked.

"I do not know," Rainira responded, her voice flat. She let go of Joshua's arm and drew her bow, holding it in her left hand, keeping her right hand free to draw arrows as needed. "Stay vigilant, just in case."

The crowd had almost all disappeared, no doubt making their way to homes or accommodations at inns around the city. Joshua followed by Rainira's side, watching the road ahead without seeing anything. Rainira stepped up their pace until they were jogging forward. Joshua looked ahead but couldn't see Ryland in the crowd. Either the large man and Martin had made a turn or something had gone wrong.

Joshua noticed that a silence seemed to have fallen around the crowd. Ahead of them he heard the sounds of a fight. Metal on metal. His first thought was of the Guard. He began to run forward, but before he had made it even two steps Rainira had grabbed his arm to stop him and screamed. Joshua raised an arm in front of him, a shield of shimmering light appearing just before an arrow struck it. Joshua pushed the arrow aside and stepped in front of Rainira, searching for the source of the shot.

In the distance Joshua finally caught sight of Ryland. The large man was locked in melee combat with two figures dressed in black robes which billowed out around them. They moved fast, almost too fast to track. Ryland was defending himself well, however. One struck out at him, but Ryland spun to the left of the strike. His hammer came down in a wide arc, crushing the figure beneath the blow.

"Move aside!" Rainira yelled in Joshua's ear. He reacted right away, moving behind Rainira. She raised her bow, an arrow nocked. She drew and fired in an instant. Joshua watched the arrow sail through the air and bury itself into the second attacker's back. The figure arced in pain, a howl echoing through the dusk. Ryland spun at the sound, bringing his hammer over his head and smashing it through the figure's form. Even from a distance Joshua heard the sound of crunching bone and winced.

Joshua saw a burst of blue light off to Ryland's left as Rainira grabbed him and pulled him down an alley. She set off at a run, leading Joshua by one hand while she held one of her long swords in the other. She took a turn to the right, then another, followed by one to the left. She continued to weave through the city streets until Joshua had lost any track of where they were. The sounds of the skirmish faded behind them as they moved. Joshua tried to stop, to go back. He wanted to help the Guard, but Rainira held his hand tight and pulled him forward. Finally he gave in and let her lead him onwards.

Joshua stopped trying to keep track of their path, letting Rainira guide him. He looked over his shoulder whenever he could, ready to raise the Sigil at any moment. Rainira kept pressing forward, seeming to take any turn she could. It seemed to Joshua that they ran for hours, but when Rainira finally stopped Joshua looked around, the building ahead of him catching his attention in an instant.

Even in the dim moonlight, the Chapel Lux shone like the midday sun.

29

Ambush

Rainira threw herself against the gate outside Chapel Lux, but it didn't budge. They could still hear the sounds of fighting far behind them. Joshua hoped that Ryland was unharmed, along with the rest of the Guard, and he desperately wanted to go back for them. Rainira continued to throw herself against the closed gate, the crashing sound snapping Joshua out of his worry. He turned and laid a hand on Rainira's shoulder. She stopped her assault on the gate and looked at Joshua. He offered her a weak smile and stepped to the gate himself.

"Is anyone there?" he called. He waited a moment, then tried again. "Is there anyone inside?"

When there was still no answer, Rainira moved to continue trying to break down the gate with her shoulder. Joshua held out his hand to stop her. Rainira looked at him questioningly, but Joshua only smirked back. He closed his eyes and rotated his hand. Light emanated from his closed hand, stretching out above and below in a long line. The light solidified into a long bar.

Joshua looked at Rainira and gestured to the streets behind them. She drew her bow and turned to watch the streets around them. Joshua lifted the long bar of light and slammed it into the space between the two sides of the gate. The bar of light slid between the bars and Joshua began to push. He put all of his weight into it, and as he strained the light from the bar grew brighter and the bar seemed to feel more solid. He continued to push, but the gate showed no sign of shifting. With one last effort he put everything he had into the push, but still the gate stood strong.

Joshua stepped back, dropping his hands, the bar of light disappearing. Rainira turned and looked at him.

"What now?" she asked.

"I don't know," Joshua responded. He looked up at the chapel's spire. The stones themselves seemed to be sources of light, but no one answered their calls or came to check on the commotion in the streets. Rainira continued to look around, growing more nervous by the second.

Joshua tried to think. Obviously force wasn't the answer. He had tried pleading. He had even tried using the power of the Sigil to open the gate. A thought struck him then. He stepped forward and pulled the Sigil from his pocket, holding it in both hands and clutching it to his chest. He bowed his head, thinking of the Light and trying to think of himself as King. As he did the stone shone brighter and brighter, becoming a single spot of intense light. When there was still no movement from Chapel Lux he looked up and spoke in a loud voice.

"I am Joshua, King of Galion. By the power of the Light, please, help us. "

Silence filled the street, and when nothing happened Joshua turned to Rainira. Just as he was about to tell her that they should go back and help the others a crash echoed through the silence. He spun and looked at the gate as it slowly began to open before them, the hinges squealing in the night like a banshee's cry. The gates swung open slowly, rust breaking from the hinges as they moved. When they were wide enough Joshua grabbed Rainira's hand and led her through the gates and into the courtyard of Chapel Lux.

< < < > > >

Ryland blocked a strike from one of the masked assailants, then turned and kicked the other that moved towards him. When his hammer was free he swung it in a wide arc around him, connecting with the first masked man, sending him flying across the road. The second had regained his feet and was advancing fast. Ryland attempted to swing the hammer back, but the arc had too much momentum and sailed past the man. As Ryland braced for the strike he heard a cry of pain. He looked around to find Nitika, one of her daggers buried in the man's shoulder. She smiled at Ryland before pulling the blade back and striking with her other hand, slicing the man's throat. Blood sprayed through the night as the man fell to the ground, gasping for air.

Ryland turned his attention to the man he had sent flying. It took four steps to reach the prone man, and without a thought Ryland brought the hammer over his head and down upon the man, crushing his chest beneath the weight of the blow.

The immediate attackers taken care of, Ryland turned to look for Martin.

Nitika shouted as she turned to move, "Alaric and Corwin were ambushed by seven men. Martin already moved forward to help them. We must hurry."

Ryland rested his hammer on his shoulder and followed Nitika up the street. They ran forward, and it wasn't long before Ryland caught sight of Corwin laying on the ground ahead of them. Alaric was straddling the downed cleric's body, striking out with his massive blade in a fury. Three men were trying to find an opening to attack the paladin, but Alaric's blade was keeping them at bay. Nitika ran to the left as Ryland went right, both advancing on the nearest of the three attackers. When Ryland reached the man he spun, swinging his hammer in an arc from the ground to the sky. The hammer caught the man in the lower back, lifting him from the ground with a series of cracking sounds. The man fell to the ground a dozen paces away, limp, as Ryland looked to the other attackers. Nitika had already taken the head off of one of them, and as Ryland watched Alaric brought his blade across in a horizontal slash at the third man, cutting him cleanly in half. The man fell in two pieces, his mouth still moving as he lay, split from shoulder to hip, on the ground.

"Alaric, are you alright?" Ryland asked.

"Yes, but-"

"Then tend to Corwin, we will find the others!"

With that Ryland and Nitika were off, moving forward. It

wasn't long before they found Utherrian and Martin. The two men stood in the middle of a small square, a dozen masked bodies lying around them. Martin raised his staff as Ryland entered the square, but quickly lowered it when he recognized Ryland and Nitika.

"Is everything sound?" Ryland asked.

Martin took a breath. "Yes," he said, seeming to struggle to maintain his composure.

"What of the King," Utherrian asked. "What of Joshua?"

"I do not know," Ryland responded.

They stood in silence for a moment, all of them trying to catch their breath. The silence held for a moment before being shattered by a loud creak echoing through the night. They all looked at each other before moving backwards towards Alaric and Corwin. When they met them Alaric had Corwin in his arms. He fell in line with them and kept the fast pace they had set. They moved into the city, making their way towards the source of the sound. Without a word between them the entire Guard began to sprint.

Nitika called out a warning from the back, disappearing into the night. A muffled cry was heard to the left of the Guard, followed a couple seconds later by another from the right. Nitika appeared behind the Guard again, matching their pace. Ryland turned his head and smiled at her, a smile she returned with violent glee.

It took them only a couple of minutes to reach Chapel Lux and the source of the noise. The gates stood firm before them, the street deserted. Ryland moved forward and slammed his fist against the gate.

"Where are they?" he snarled into the night. He turned back to the Guard, his gaze falling on Utherrian. "Where is my King?"

"I am right here," came a voice from behind him.

Ryland spun to see Joshua moving towards them from the chapel's doors. Joshua was moving slowly, seeming to glide over the illuminated pathway. When he reached the gate he raised a hand. The gates swung open again, this time without the loud squeal they had produced the first time.

Ryland smiled at Joshua, taking a step forward and picking him up in a massive hug. Joshua's feet left the ground as Ryland lifted him into the air.

"Come inside, the place seems to be empty, but it also seems to be protected," Joshua said. He led the Guard into the Chapel, sparing a glance towards Corwin's limp form, but tried to keep any thought of the cleric's fate from his mind. He realized that his efforts were in vain, however, and a tear fell from his cheek as he led the Guard through the doors of Chapel Lux.

30

The Chapel Lux

The Guard entered through the chapel's large wooden doors and found themselves in a wide room. There were no lights or candles, but the illuminated stones that the chapel was made from lit the room in a brilliant radiance. At either end of the room were long wooden tables, atop which sat an assortment of books and quills. Across from them were three sets of doors, smaller than the main doors. As Joshua led the way into the room the large doors behind them swung shut, closing with a gentle click.

Ryland jumped in front of Joshua, holding his hammer in front of him. There was no sound beyond the breathing of the Guard, and Joshua laid a hand on Ryland's shoulder.

"It is ok, Ryland. We are safe here," Joshua said, his voice calm, almost melodic.

"My King, how would you know that?" Utherrian asked.

"You said this was the rendezvous," Rainira said, appearing amongst the Guard. "And this is a chapel of pure Light. What servant of the Light would be at risk here?"

Joshua nodded to her with a smile before walking around Ryland. He went to the middle of the three doors and took the handles. Someone protested from behind him, but Joshua ignored the sound and pushed the doors open. Rainira followed close behind him, and they each held one of the doors open for the Guard. They moved through the doors reluctantly and found themselves in the main hall of the chapel.

The room was even wider than the entry hall, and easily three times as long. The walls seemed to fade into light as they rose, and the ceiling was obscured by clouds that seemed to glow internally with a golden radiance. Two rows of benches ran from the back of the chapel to the front. At the front they saw a stained glass window, fifty feet tall. Depicted in the glass was a woman in white robes, her hands clasped in front of her chest. Platinum blonde hair fell down across her shoulders, billowing out around her. She floated in a glowing background of swirling light.

Below the window was an altar. A silver stand sat atop the altar, upon which was cradled a spherical crystal larger than a pumpkin. A dim light pulsed in the center of the crystal, growing and shrinking in a steady rhythm, almost as if alive.

Two chairs sat beside the altar, facing the crystal. The chairs were occupied.

"Hail!" called Alaric. "We are the Guard of the King, and we seek aid and protection within the Chapel Lux for the night! Are you able to offer such?"

The figures didn't shift.

Ryland began to lead the Guard down the center aisle of the chapel slowly, his hammer held in front of him. "Please! We have a member of the Guard who requires aid!"

"Lay him before the altar," Joshua said from behind Alaric. "There he shall receive the help you seek."

Alaric turned and gave Joshua a curious look. Ryland moved aside as Alaric moved ahead and down the aisle quickly. When he reached the altar he laid Corwin's body in front of it. He leaned his head close to the cleric's face, listening for breath. He was able to hear the faint sound of breathing, but it was weak.

The Guard joined Alaric at the front, moving in front of the chairs to address the figures as Joshua and Rainira each walked to the backs of the chairs. Nitika gasped when she saw the figures.

Joshua sat in the chair to the left of the altar, while Rainira sat in the chair to the right. Both sat upright with their eyes closed, their chests rising and falling as they breathed. Almost simultaneously, Nitika drew her daggers and held them at the standing Joshua's throat while Martin drew his katana and held it to the standing Rainira's neck.

"What is the meaning of this?" Utherrian demanded.

The standing figures were still, seemingly unconcerned about the weapons raised against them.

"What kind of sorcery is this?" Martin snarled. "A trap of Lacrym?"

False Joshua flinched at that. "How dare you speak the name of the King of Darkness within these halls?"

"I will speak whomever's name I wish until you explain this treachery!" Martin shouted. "Do you know who this is that you threaten?"

"There is no threat here," False Joshua responded calmly. As he spoke an aura of Light surrounded him. He reached up and pushed Nitika's blades aside before walking to the altar. False Rainira mirrored the action, a matching aura growing out from her as well, standing beside him before Corwin.

Both of the glowing figures clasped their hands in front of them. They bowed their heads and began to murmur something beneath their breath. The light in the crystal on the altar began to pulse brighter and brighter.

"Stop!" Martin exclaimed. "You imitate the King! Explain yourself or face the wrath of the King's Guard!"

The luminous Joshua and Rainira both began to laugh softly as the light in the crystal faded back to its original dim pulse. False Rainira turned to Martin. "Do you not wish for protection? Do you not wish for aid for your injured guardsman?"

"Of course we do," Alaric responded, stepping in front of Martin and pushing the wizard's blade down. "We just do not know what is going on and would like some answers."

"Of course," False Joshua said. "We are servants of the Light, manifestations of the Light's power. We needed you to follow us within the Chapel willingly, and most refuse to follow us in our true forms. So we borrowed the forms of your guardsman and your King-"

"He is your king as well!" Martin interrupted, still fuming.

Alaric grabbed Martin's shoulders and held him still.

"That is yet to be proved," False Joshua said. He looked towards the real Joshua in the chair. "The man still has much to prove, and there is much that is not yet known."

"In any case," False Rainira said, "let us offer aid to your friend as a token of goodwill, then we may speak at our leisure." She turned to Utherrian. "If it is alright with the Steward of the realm, of course."

"Of course," Utherrian responded.

"Thank you, Steward. We shall also take on our true forms so that your friends may join the conversation," False Rainira responded.

The two shimmering facsimiles turned back towards Corwin, lowering their heads and clasping their hands together again. They began to murmur again, and the light within the crystal grew. Martin watched as the light held within the crystal grew brighter and brighter. Within seconds it was too bright to look at directly. Martin looked away, and almost immediately the light exploded outward through the chapel. The entire Guard was blinded by the brilliant white light. They could still hear the figures murmuring, but could see nothing.

The light faded almost as quickly as it had exploded. The Guard blinked, trying to clear their vision. When they could see again the first thing that they noticed was Corwin, sitting up and looking about with a confused expression. The next thing they noticed was Rainira and Joshua stirring out of the chairs they sat in.

Joshua looked across at Rainira, then looked up at the Guard standing in front of the altar. "What happened?" he asked. "Where am I?"

"That is a good question, my King," Martin responded. He looked around, but the two false figures had vanished.

Joshua stood, wobbling a bit, and made his way to Rainira. He took her hands and helped her to her feet. "Are you alright?"

Rainira looked around, then met Joshua's eyes. "I think so," she said.

Joshua turned back to the Guard, still holding Rainira's hand. "What's going on?" he asked.

"We are inside Chapel Lux," Utherrian said. "Beyond that, I know little more than you do."

Joshua stared at the Steward for a moment, trying to discern whether he was telling the full truth or not. Before he could make up his mind, Joshua's eye was pulled towards the stained glass window. The light within the glass seemed to grow brighter, and the figure depicted there shifted. The woman's hands went from clasped together to being held out to her sides in a welcoming gesture. Her palms glowed brighter, and the two points of light exploded outwards. Joshua and the rest of the Guard shielded their eyes against the light. When they could see again they saw two tall, slender figures standing by the altar.

The figures had a human form, but were definitely not human. They both hovered slightly above the floor, and their skin glowed with an intensity that obscured their features beyond recognition. Their faces were blank, only the suggestion of features present. Their bodies were obscured with shining robes.

"We are servants of Light," the figure on the right said. "That is, we are the manifestation of the Light."

Utherrian stepped forward. "I am Utherrian, Steward of Galion, and I am also a servant of the Light." He bowed his head. "Thank you for aiding Corwin, we are in your debt."

"You are already serving the Light," the figure on the left responded. "There is nothing more that we would ask of you."

Joshua stepped forward, trying to find the words to match the questions circling in his mind. When none came, he asked "What do we call you?"

"You may call me Lumi," the figure on the left responded.

"And you may call me Luce," the figure on the right followed.

Alaric stepped forward. "You offered aid to our friend, and for that we thank you. But you have not answered my second question: will you offer us protection until the night is through?"

"Of course we will," Luce responded. "You are within Chapel Lux. Few mortals have stepped foot within these walls. You will be safe here until morning, at which point I am sure that you will be moving on."

"Yes," Utherrian said. "We need to reach Eringhal as soon as possible."

"You will be on your way with the dawn's first light," Lumi said. "For tonight, let us hold counsel, for there is much that you should hear."

The two figures floated down from the altar and stopped by the first row of benches. The Guard followed and took seats along the benches. Once they were all seated Luce and Lumi floated back to the altar and turned to them.

"Please, feel at home here," Luce said. "There is much to discuss, and there is no need to be uncomfortable as we do."

He raised a hand and snapped his fingers. Pillows appeared along the benches. Joshua was the first to reach for one, laying it on the bench and sitting on it. Sitting on the pillow was like sitting on a cloud, and Joshua felt instantly at ease. The rest of the Guard slowly followed suit, each relaxing into the pillows easily. A calm fell across them all, causing all of them to feel rested and refreshed.

"Now," Luce said. He and Lumi both sat, their legs crossed beneath them, still hovering a foot off the ground, and looked out at the Guard. "Ask your questions, and we will offer what knowledge we have."

31
A Gift of Light

"I suppose that we could start with the most obvious question," Utherrian said. "Will we succeed in our cause?"

"The Light is not omniscient," Luce responded. "But I can say that having a man carry the Sigil of the King into Ska'ell gives us hope."

"The King will carry the Sigil," Ryland snarled. "Not just a common man."

"That is yet to be seen," Luce said. "As of now he is just a man. There are things that he must overcome, and one of the greatest challenges will be rallying the people of Galion to his cause. Without the people around him, the Sigil's power will wane."

"I have something in Eringhal that will help with that," Utherrian said.

"Really?" Lumi asked. "What is it?"

"That is for the King to discover, but you will know in time," Utherrian responded. His expression made it clear that the subject was closed.

"What can you tell us about the Darkness," Martin asked. "Specifically, what can you tell us about the forces of Ska'ell throughout Camlidor?"

"As I said, the Light is not omniscient," Luce said. "But we do see much. Currently, the world is balanced on the edge of a knife. The Darkness can never be completely eradicated, but it can be tampered. Right now there is a great deal of activity at Karanlik, as well as Astrakhan and Ula'ree. Lacrym is gathering an army to him. If left to his own devices, he will have a force large enough to sweep across Galion without issue in three years, perhaps less."

"Karanlik is Lacrym's fortress in the south of Ska'ell," Utherrian explained, looking to Joshua. "Astrakhan is a tower in the southeast of Ska'ell, and Ula'ree is the Orc village to the north of the desert there."

Lumi picked up where Luce stopped. "So far Galion has remained fairly untested. There are a number of roving bands throughout the continent, but they have been scouting more than attacking. The seas are, as usual, treacherous, but they should remain traversable with the usual precautions."

"There is one oddity," Luce said. "The Tower of Esterash in the middle of the ocean between Galion and Ska'ell has broken from the island and risen into the air. We do not know what has caused this, though we do not think it was Darkness, and we know that it was not the Light. We do not believe that this occurrence will have any effect on your efforts, but it is an oddity."

"Esterash has been floating for more than a millenia, it is not a new occurrence," Martin said, his voice harsh.

"Is that so?" Luce replied. "As I said, the Tower is an oddity, not caused by the Light or Dark, so perhaps that is why our information regarding it is incorrect. My apologies."

"It is getting late," Utherrian said, moving the conversation back, "and the Guard needs rest. If there is anything else that we need to know, now would be the time."

"Joshua already knows what needs to be done, as the Sigil has offered him a vision of the future," Lumi explained. "Know this, Joshua: the vision was but a possible outcome, not a definitive accounting of events. There are two things that must happen, however. You must head east with whatever force you are able to gather in one year. Any longer and Lacrym's forces will have reached a critical mass and the threat of the war spilling onto the shores of Galion will grow exponentially. The second thing that you must do is pay a visit to the Cave of Shadows-"

"No," Martin interrupted. "I will not take the King within a league of that place."

"But you must," Lumi insisted. "Joshua must conquer the Darkness within himself before he has any chance of defeating the Darkness in Ska'ell."

Martin stood and walked up the center aisle without responding. Joshua stood to follow, but Utherrian held up a hand for him to stay.

"Lumi is right," Utherrian said. "The Cave of Shadows is dangerous, but it is something that must be done."

"Very good," Luce said. "I believe that is enough for tonight." He floated down from the altar and stopped in front of Joshua. "Joshua, if you seek any information, guidance, or counsel, please know that you are welcome in the Chapel Lux at any time."

"Thank you, Luce," Joshua said.

"Now, please feel free to rest wherever you would like within the chapel, you will be perfectly safe within these walls."

"Good luck to all of you in your efforts, and thank you for your service to the Light," Lumi said.

The Guard stood and began to walk out of the chapel and back to the entryway.

"Joshua, a moment, if you would," Luce said. Utherrian stopped and turned. "I only require Joshua, and rest assured that I mean him no harm."

Utherrian nodded and reluctantly made his way out of the chapel's entry hall to join the rest of the Guard. When the room was cleared, Luce led Joshua to the altar.

"Joshua, I did not mean to insult you, and hope that I have not," Luce said. "But the truth remains that you are not yet King. A king, a true king, must have the support of the people, and must be able to protect the people from all threats. The city of Erith is currently under threat from a group loyal to Lacrym, and they must be eliminated before you lead Erith's forces across the ocean."

"How do I find them?" Joshua asked.

"Once you have reached the castle you will have plenty of information at your disposal. I urge you to set your guard on this task as soon as possible. The sooner the city is safe, the sooner the people will begin to support and join you."

"I'll be sure that it gets done then."

Lumi floated down to Joshua and laid a hand on his shoulder. "We have a gift for you," she said. "If you are to ascend the throne, you will need the qualities to protect and hold it. Tell me, what do you value most: protecting your friends, eliminating your enemies, or serving the people?"

Joshua thought about it for a moment before responding. "Aren't they all the same?"

"Please, explain."

"Well, to protect my friends I need to eliminate those who would threaten them. And to serve the people, I'll need to protect them from the dangers that those enemies threaten them with. In the end, if I fail to do any one of those things I'll fail to do all three."

"Very good," Lumi said. Even with her obscured features Joshua was able to sense a smile on her face. "Another question then. Would you lay down your life to serve the Light?"

"I would like to believe that I would," Joshua said. "I'm here, and I will do whatever I can to help Galion."

"And do you believe that you are the true King that Galion needs?"

Joshua hesitated before answering. "No," he said. "I know that the Guard believes it, and Utherrian in particular seems to know something the rest of us don't, but I don't think that I'm it."

Luce joined Lumi in front of Joshua and laid a hand on Joshua's other shoulder. "That is a good answer," Luce said. "A man who doubts his power is a man who will wield it responsibly. You have the makings of a king, Joshua, you merely need the confidence of one. That will come in time, I am sure."

Joshua nodded.

"Now, our gift, then you may join the Guard and rest," Lumi said. She led Joshua to the altar. "Please, lay your hands upon the crystal."

Joshua looked from Lumi to Luce, who merely nodded. He lifted his hands and laid them on the crystal. Its surface was perfectly smooth, and it was surprisingly warm to the touch. The light inside the crystal grew in intensity.

"You have been told that magic comes from the dragons, and that is accurate, but that is because it was gifted to their kind by both the Light and the Dark ages ago, when the balance was pure," Luce explained. "In that time, the Light and Dark swirled together, creating the dragons to watch over Camledor. As time passed, mankind fell further and further from the Light and began to see the dragons as a threat rather than protectors. Eventually, one of the dragons was killed, and the man who slayed that dragon gained incredible power. When word spread, more men hunted the dragons out of greed. The dragons fought back, and eventually the Dragon Wars began."

"We wish to grant you access to the Light, Joshua," Lumi said. "As you lead the forces of Galion into Ska'ell you will face many perils, but the power of the Light will guide you."

Lumi and Luce both began to float higher into the air, stopping in front of the stained glass. The woman depicted there now had a hand extended downward towards the altar. "This is our gift to the potential King of Galion," Luce said. He and Lumi began to fade from view, their forms turning translucent before fading out completely.

A voice unlike Luce's or Lumi's whispered from the crystal as the light within grew brighter. It was sweet, motherly, a voice that calmed Joshua and made him feel safe. "Spread the Light into the darkest reaches of the world Joshua," the voice said. "Bring the people back to the Light. Bring them back to safety."

The light in the crystal seemed to explode. Light washed through the chapel, blinding Joshua. He tried to pull back, but his hands seemed to be fused to the crystal. The light subsided slowly, and Joshua looked into the crystal. Tendrils of light bloomed from it, wisping through the air. The tendrils twisted upwards before spiraling down into Joshua. As they did he felt a warmth within him, along with a growing power.

32

The Cleric's Blessing

When the tendrils disappeared Joshua found that he could lower his hands again. The crystal had resumed pulsing with its inner light, and when he looked up Joshua saw that the woman in the glass had returned to her original position, her hands clasped in front of her chest. Joshua turned and walked up the aisle and through the doors into the entryway.

"What did they tell you?" Utherrian asked.

Joshua told Utherrian about the group operating within the city.

"We can dispatch people around the city to try and find them," Utherrian said. "I will be sure that they start as soon as we reach the castle in the morning. Was there anything else?"

"We talked about a lot of things, they even told me more about the dragons. I didn't realize they were originally protectors of mankind."

"Yes, they were," Utherrian said with a frown. "That all ended with the first dragon slayer, however, and the Dragon Wars ended them for good."

"They gave me something as well," Joshua added.

"What did they give you?"

The rest of the Guard gathered around Joshua, curious, as

Joshua lifted his right hand and took a breath. Tendrils of light rose from the tips of his fingers, swirling in the air above his hand. There was a cumulative gasp from the Guard as they watched the display of magic. Joshua closed his hand and the tendrils of light disappeared.

"They have given you power over Light magic," Corwin said in a whisper with an excited smile. "I can help to teach you to wield it."

"I would appreciate that, Corwin. I don't even know what it does."

"Light magic heals and protects. With practice you will be able to mend wounds, grant yourself protection from Dark magic, and perhaps even extend that protection to others. It is an amazing gift."

"Training will have to wait for another time," Utherrian said. "We all need rest. At first light we will make our way to Eringhal, where we can begin the preparations for our push east. We have one year, and there is much to do."

The Guard spread out around the entryway and laid out their bedrolls, almost everyone going to sleep. Corwin sat against the wall near one of the tables, lost in thought. Joshua walked to him.

"May I?" Joshua asked, pointing to the ground next to Corwin.

Corwin looked up, distracted. "Of course, my King."

Joshua lowered himself and the two men sat silently beside one another for a while, the only sound in the room that of Ryland's snores. Joshua looked at Corwin, worried about the cleric.

"What's wrong, Corwin? I can see that something's on your mind," Joshua asked.

"It is nothing, my King," Corwin said. "At least nothing that you need to concern yourself with."

"Please," Joshua pushed. "I'm curious."

Corwin remained sullenly silent for a moment before letting out a long sigh. "I was thinking of the door, the one we all walk through in the end. I saw it, and almost opened it."

"I'm glad that you didn't."

"Thank you, my King, but that possibility is not what concerns me now. The door has always been described to me as a gateway leading to the peaceful embrace of the Light. But something has gone wrong in that realm, I fear. The door seemed darker than I imagined. I don't know if it was just my imagination, or if the Darkness growing in the east is rippling through the doorway, but my mind is shaken by the implications."

Joshua thought about it, trying to understand what was troubling Corwin, but couldn't wrap his mind around the concept. Instead he clapped a hand on Corwin's back and offered the cleric a smile. "Cheer up," Joshua said. "You saw the door and lived to tell the tale. Whatever is wrong with it, we'll fix it."

Corwin offered a weak smile.

"Anyway, I've had something I've wanted to ask you since back in Dollet, but I haven't had the chance yet. Something Luce said before granting me magic made me think of it again."

"What is it, my King?"

"Martin had told me that magic was either a gift from a dragon or taken by force from a dragon, but Luce explained that it originally came from the Light and the Dark."

"I do not understand the question," Corwin said.

"How did you get your magic?" Joshua asked bluntly.

Corwin laughed. "It was about twelve years ago, right after Ryland joined the Guard. I had known Utherrian for a couple of years already, though I had yet to join his Guard. I had travelled with him to the Galatian Mountains, investigating reports of an attack on a town in the area."

Corwin trailed off, lost in his own thoughts. He reached over and wrapped his hand around Joshua's wrist. Joshua closed his eyes—

—and found himself standing in a field at dusk, mountains rising up into the sky less than a mile away. He turned to his left and saw a small town, made of only a dozen or so small buildings, all of which were on fire.

"We are too late," a voice said from behind him. Joshua turned to see Utherrian and Martin, with Ryland scanning the area behind them for threats. "Let us see if there is anyone left alive," Utherrian said.

Martin led the way towards the town. When they reached the edge the wizard raised his staff into the air. Blue light launched into the sky and rain began to fall over the town. The small Guard and Corwin stood and watched the rain fall, quenching the fire beneath it. After twenty minutes the fire had died down, after another ten it was out completely.

Utherrian took the lead then, walking into the center of the town. The buildings were all burned beyond repair, and they saw no one as they walked. It wasn't until they reached the center that Joshua saw the bodies: dozens of men, women, and children lay dead throughout the small square, the dirt and grass stained red beneath them.

"What happened here?" Corwin asked.

Martin knelt by one of the bodies, looking it over for any clues as to what had happened. When he finally stood the wizard looked grim.

"Arrows," he said, "and the wounds are fresh. Whoever slaughtered these people did so from a distance, fetched their arrows, lit the town on fire, and are likely waiting to spring a trap. Stay vigilant!"

Joshua drew his longsword with his right arm and raised a buckler with his left. The Guard and Corwin spread out in pairs, Martin and Ryland going one direction while Joshua went with Utherrian in the other. They reached the edge of the town before the attack came. A flaming arrow flew through the air, sticking into the building next to them. The wet wood didn't catch, but three more arrows followed. Joshua stood against the building on the left side of the street while Utherrian pushed himself against the building opposite. The arrows fell where they had stood, sticking up from the ground.

"What do we do?" Joshua called.

Utherrian waited until a second volley fell to the ground before stepping into the middle of the street. He raised his hand toward the sky and thrust it forward, sending a split bolt of light across the plain towards the archers. Corwin heard screams of pain, followed by one of rage. Another arrow came flying towards Utherrian, and Corwin saw the Steward was moving too slow to get out of the way. Corwin pushed off the building, leaping through the air, his buckler extended. The arrow missed the buckler, sinking into his upper arm instead. Corwin screamed in pain as Utherrian sent another bolt of light flying.

Utherrian grabbed an arrow from the ground and inspected it. He sniffed the tip before whispering "Poison."

As Utherrian reached out to help Joshua a man flew into the Steward, knocking him to the ground. Joshua thrust his sword through the man's neck, killing him instantly. Ryland and Martin appeared then.

"I think that's all of them," Martin said. He looked down and saw Utherrian on the ground. Martin knelt and checked for a pulse, giving a sigh of relief when he found one. "He'll be fine, just out cold for a bit."

Ryland looked at Joshua and noticed the arrow. "A bit is too long," Joshua said, his voice strained. "The arrow is poisoned, I need his aid before *it spreads."*

Ryland tried to rouse Utherrian, but with no success. Joshua screamed into the night and held out his arm. "Take it!" he yelled at Martin. "Take the arm before the poison takes me!"

Martin hesitated only a moment before drawing his katana and slicing downward. The blow was clean, cleaving directly through Joshua's arm. Martin stepped forward with a hand full of conjured fire, shoving the flames against the wound, cauterizing it and stopping the bleeding. Joshua howled in pain before the blackness took him.

Joshua's eyes snapped open in Chapel Lux and he looked at Corwin.

"I woke up two weeks later," Corwin said quietly. "They carried me back to Eringhal. Utherrian was able to stabilize me on the journey back, and kept me sedated while he worked to clear the poison from my system. When I finally woke the wound was healed over my shoulder and the poison was gone. I was grateful to be alive. It was not until two days later that I realized I had gained the power to wield the Light. I asked Utherrian, and he told me that the Light must have blessed me. It is the only answer I have ever gotten."

Joshua thought about that. It was possible that the Light had granted Corwin the magic, but more likely that Utherrian had gifted it to the cleric in thanks for saving his life.

"Thank you, Corwin," Joshua said, standing up. Corwin nodded to him. "I'm going to turn in, it's been another long day. You should get some sleep yourself."

"I think that I will stay up for a little while yet," Corwin said. "My mind is still far from easy. Thank you for the distraction, my King, it has helped to lessen my troubles."

"Any time Corwin," Joshua said with a smile. He left Corwin to his thoughts and laid down on one of the bedrolls. Joshua drifted to sleep quickly, thinking of the Light.

33
Eringhal

Joshua was woken by Utherrian. The Guard was already up, their gear packed. Joshua packed his bedroll, stowing it in Utherrian's bag, and accepted a piece of bread from him. When he finished eating the Guard opened the chapel's large main doors and stepped outside.

The sun was still low in the sky, but the streets were already teeming with activity. "We will move together today. Just be sure to stay close, do not let anyone get separated," Martin said. He pushed the gates open and led the way towards the castle.

Joshua was in the center of the Guard and kept pace easily. His senses were bombarded by new smells and strange sounds. The road they followed had a few scattered shops, but seemed to be more homes than anything else. When they reached the main road it seemed that every building was selling something. The smell of baking bread and meat filled the air, and Joshua could hear music coming from somewhere distant. They passed two men having a heated argument in a language that Joshua had never heard.

They moved through the city undisturbed, and they entered a large square just as the sun was reaching its peak. People mingled throughout the square, but the largest group stood before two large iron gates at the opposite edge. Joshua looked past the gates and saw the castle.

"Erignhal," Rainira said from beside Joshua. "We are finally home."

The castle was the largest building that Joshua had ever seen. It was square and made of white stone, its roof reaching up to a single point. Thin towers rose up at the corners of the castle, but ended well below the tip of the castle proper.

Utherrian led the Guard to the crowd at the gate. Martin called out, "Make way! Make way for the Steward of Galion!"

The crowd shifted and turned at the call. Utherrian held himself tall as he walked through the opening that the crowd made. The people were shouting things, all asking for something, but Joshua could not make out any of the individual requests. The tumult was quieted as two men in heavy gilded armor approached the gate. They held long halberds at their sides, and as Utherrian reached the gate they pulled it open. Utherrian led the Guard through the gate and onto the castle grounds. Joshua expected the people to attempt to surge through the gate, but they held their ground, still calling out their requests as the guards closed the gate.

The open area of the castle grounds felt odd after the density of the city, but Joshua welcomed the sight of grass and trees. The wall surrounding the castle stood twenty feet tall, and beyond it he could just make out the towers of the city's main gates. He saw a number of small buildings around the grounds, though he did not have time to look at them closely as Utherrian led them up to the steps of Eringhal.

At the top of the steps were two more guardsmen, dressed in the same armor as those at the gate, also holding halberds. They opened the tall wooden doors to the castle as the Guard approached. Utherrian nodded to them as he led the group inside.

They entered into a large room with vaulted ceilings. Banners made of silver cloth hung from the walls, each emblazoned with a golden bird, its wings spread wide.

"The seal of Galion," Alaric said, following Joshua's gaze.

Joshua nodded as he continued to look around the room. Along the walls were dozens of large golden planters filled with brightly colored flowers. He counted three doors, one ahead of them, one to the left, and another to the right.

Utherrian stood in the middle of the hall and turned to the

Guard. "We have made it home safely," he said. "Corwin, how are you doing?"

"Just fine, sir," he responded with a smile.

"Very good. Now, there is much to be done, but let us take the remainder of the day to tend to ourselves. I will need a volunteer to show Joshua around the castle while I deal with some business."

Rainira stepped forward, and Joshua's stomach fluttered at the thought of more time with her.

"Thank you Rainira. You can start with the kitchens, as I am sure the King is hungry. As for the rest of you, the day is yours. Do not leave the castle grounds, but beyond that you are dismissed."

Alaric and Corwin nodded and went back through the castle's main door. Nitika and Ryland left through the door to the left, and Martin followed Utherrian through the door ahead of them.

Rainira turned to Joshua, "Are you hungry?"

"Very," Joshua answered.

Rainira led him through the door to the right and down a short flight of stairs to a long hallway. Five doors lined the inner wall, while the outer wall had a row of windows. Joshua looked out across the grounds as they walked. He saw more of the small buildings, and as they walked he spotted Alaric and Corwin walking towards one of them near the wall, behind which was a large dirt circle. "Those are the training grounds," Rainira explained. "I do not know why, but Alaric and Corwin are likely going to practice. They should rest, but they never do."

Rainira led Joshua through the last door and into a long room filled with tables. They walked up the side of the room past more windows. At the end of the room was a raised table with a large, ornate chair in the middle. Beside it sat two chairs with raised backs, and to either side of them were three normal chairs. Joshua looked back across the other tables and saw at least a dozen chairs at each. "This is the Dining Hall, obviously," Rainira said. "It can seat around 300 people, but it has been rarely used in recent years. The kitchens are just through here." She pushed through another door that seemed almost hidden in the corner of the hall.

The kitchen was filled with noise. Joshua counted at least a dozen people moving about, some carrying food while others worked over stoves. Two stood in the back of the room washing dishes. One of the people working a stove noticed them and waved them over.

"Rainira!" the cook exclaimed. "How nice to see you! When did you return?"

"It is good to see you too, Megno," Rainira responded. "We only just returned, this is our first stop."

Megno noticed Joshua then. "I am sorry, I do not believe we have met before. I am Megno, head cook of the kitchen here at Erignhal." Megno extended his hand.

Joshua shook the cook's hand. "I'm Joshua," he said.

"Are you a new member of the Guard?"

"I guess you could say that," Joshua responded.

"Megno," Rainira said, cutting off the line of questioning. "Do you have anything prepared that we could eat?"

"Of course, of course, how foolish of me! Go on out and find yourselves a seat and I will have plates prepared for you in a moment."

With that, Megno hurried Joshua and Rainira from the kitchen and back into the dining hall. Rainira led Joshua to the first table outside the kitchen and took a seat.

34

An Archer's Tale

Joshua sat quietly while Rainira talked about past events that had been held in the hall. "I was not here for most of them, obviously, but the stories always reached Dollet. They were extravagantly grand events. The only one that I ever attended here was after the annual Steward's Tourney."

"What's that?" Joshua asked.

"Every year Utherrian held a Steward's Tourney," Rainira explained. "It is a competition open to anyone. It has events ranging from cooking to swordplay. Utherrian has hired a number of people that won their events. Megno started as head cook seven years ago after winning the cooking event, and Johan became our head cartographer after winning the map making competition last year. I came to join the Guard three years ago when I won the archery competition and drew in the swords competition."

"I didn't know that. Granted, I don't know much about most of the Guard yet. I've only heard Martin, Corwin, and Alaric's stories in detail – and Utherrian has told me some of his past – but that's it."

They were interrupted briefly by Megno. He carried two large silver bowls to the table, steam rising from them. As he laid them in front of Joshua and Rainira he smiled and said "May I present to you my pork and greens soup."

Joshua looked into the bowl and saw large chunks of pork surrounded by different vegetables. There was very little broth, for a soup, but the smell was intoxicating.

"Thank you Megno," Rainira said.

"Yes, thank you," Joshua added. "It smells amazing!"

Megno bowed his head and left for the kitchens. Joshua picked up his fork and took a bite before the door had even closed. The flavor was even better than the smell. Rainira ate slowly, but Joshua dug in with enthusiasm.

"Tell me more," Joshua said between bites.

"About what?" Rainira asked.

"About you."

"Oh," Rainira took another bite as she tried to figure out where to start. "Well, I got my first bow when I was five, a gift from my father. He used to be one of Dollet's hunters, and he taught me to shoot. I followed him everywhere. He would even take me on his hunting trips, all the way across the plains to the mountains. By the time I was ten I was a better shot with a bow than he was, and almost as good with a sword. For my sixteenth birthday my parents gave me one hundred gold pieces, nearly their entire savings, so that I could enter the Steward's Tourney in two events. I left that summer, and have not lived at home since."

Rainira grew quiet for a moment, taking a few more bites of her food before continuing. "The city was beautiful and huge and overwhelming to me, but the entire main road was decorated with banners and lights, so it lifted my spirits. I stayed with my uncle that week, a drunkard and an idiot, but overall a sweet man. I was rarely at his house anyway. The Tourney was held on the castle grounds, and I spent my days here. The first two days were the artisan competitions. The air was filled with the smell of food and the sound of music. Carpenters displayed their best creations, cartographers stood before their maps. There were painters and poets, and that year there was even a living statue who entered the sculpting competition. He came in second, I think mostly due to his hubris."

Rainira laughed at the memory. Joshua closed his eyes and could see the grounds filled with people, the gift from the Light allowing him to see the offered memory with ease.

Children ran around with candied apples while their parents kept a watchful eye. Men and women everywhere were doing their best to be cheerful despite the competitiveness of the Tourney.

A large stage had been erected in front of the castle, festooned with banners and ribbons. Utherrian stood atop the stage, announcing the winners of the cooking competition. An old woman walked up when she was announced the winner, her face lit with a smile. Utherrian shook the old woman's hand and pinned a ribbon to her apron before handing her a bag of coins.

The day went on and on, with the winners of other competitions being announced. It wasn't until well after sunset that the people began to leave the fairgrounds.

"The first two days were the busiest, as all of the events were packed tightly together. The third day was the livestock competitions, so the grounds were filled with the smell of animals. It rained that year, so the smell was even worse than usual. The fourth day began the martial competitions, and it started off with archery..."

Joshua watched from the crowd as Rainira, a few years younger, walked up to a rope line with her bow. There were four targets ahead of her, one set at ten paces, the next at twenty five paces, and the third at fifty paces. The fourth was set far in the distance, barely visible to the crowd that had gathered.

Rainira walked to the firing line to a stand with five arrows. She lifted the first one, seemingly oblivious of the crowd cheering around her. She nocked the arrow and lifted her bow. She fired without taking any time to aim, and the arrow appeared dead center in the first target. She repeated the exact same movement for the next two targets, scoring bullseyes with both.

She nocked the fourth arrow and raised her bow, taking her time to aim with the furthest target. She took a breath, held it, and released the arrow. It sailed through the air and stuck in the wooden log holding the final target aloft. The crowd erupted in cheers, as Rainira was the first to even come close to the final target. She nocked the final arrow and took aim, releasing it towards the final target again. The arrow sailed through the air and came down fast, landing in the target. Judges rushed to the final target and waved red flags in the air.

Bullseye.

The rest of the morning was spent finishing the qualifying round.

Rainira was already the crowd favorite by the time the ten contestants were chosen. For the second event the three targets were set up in a row at fifteen paces. Each contestant was given three arrows and fifteen seconds to fire them. The first four competitors made one bullseye each, the other two arrows drifting from the center. The next two made two bullseyes, and the last three before Rainira made three. When Rainira stepped up, she nocked all three arrows at once and fired. The arrows flew out and buried themselves in the bullseye of each target, sending the crowd into another roar of cheers.

The events continued, with Rainira leading them all easily. The final event was between her and a tall elven man. One target was placed at one hundred paces. Rainira and the man both took the line and were given ten arrows each. They took turns firing at the target, each landing bullseye after bullseye. The red dot in the center of the target was black with arrows as they each reached their final arrow. The elven man took the first shot, plunging his arrow into the center. Rainira closed her eyes as she nocked her final arrow. When she opened them she looked towards the sky and took a deep breath. She fired her arrow, sending it into the mass in the center. A tie.

Utherrian walked up to the two contestants. "Generally, in the event of a tie, the prize money is split between the two contestants. However, since we still have daylight left, I propose one final challenge, the results of which will determine our winner. Do you accept?"

Rainira accepted immediately, determined to prove herself the best. The elven man looked reluctant, but agreed at the urging of the crowd. Utherrian nodded and signaled to the event staff off to the side. The target was removed, and another was placed by the far castle wall, five hundred paces away.

"The rules for this event will be simple. You will each be given one practice arrow in order to judge the range. After that, the first to strike a bullseye will be declared the winner. In the event that you both strike true, the first to miss after that will be the loser. Understood?"

Rainira and the man nodded. They each took their practice shots. Rainira struck the wall just above the target while the man sunk his arrow into the bottom of the target itself. Staff ran out to clear the arrows and waved a green flag in the air to signal an all clear.

The elven man drew first. His arrow soared through the air, striking the bottom of the second ring of the target. Rainira took her shot, striking the second ring on the top. Their second shots both missed completely. The man's third shot hit near the center, and Rainira frowned. A staffer ran to the target and waved a black flag. The arrow had landed in the first ring outside the bullseye. Rainira nocked her arrow and fired, hitting the same area.

The elven man took a breath and sent his next arrow flying. A red flag this time.

Bullseye.

Rainira took a deep breath as she drew her next arrow. She aimed, closed her eyes, and fired. The arrow soared through the air and struck the target with a splintering sound. Another red flag. A man ran forward with the arrows to show the crowd that Rainira's arrow had split the man's in half. The crowd cheered.

The elven man sneered at Rainira before firing his next shot. In his haste he pulled the shot and it shattered against the wall of the castle. Rainira took her time, firing another arrow directly into the target. Another red flag. The crowd erupted with cheers and chants of "Rainira!" The elven man threw his bow on the ground and hung his head. Rainira approached him and offered him her hand.

"You shot amazingly," she said.

The man shook Rainira's hand, his face still sour. "As did you," he said, his voice melodic with his elven accent.

Utherrian led Rainira to the stage where he tied the winner's ribbon around her bow. He handed her the coin purse and said "Congratulations, Rainira. I have not seen shooting like that in many years."

"Thank you, Steward," she responded. She left the grounds that day elated.

35

A Tour of Eringhal

They finished their food and Joshua took the bowls into the kitchen. Megno was nowhere to be found, so Joshua left the bowls with the dishwashers in the back. When he came back out Rainira was standing by the door.

"Are you ready to continue the tour?" she asked.

"You haven't told me about the rest of the Tourney, about the swords competition," Joshua said.

"There is not that much to tell. The next day was unarmed combat, and the swords competition was the next. The week ended with jousting, an event that always drew the largest crowds."

"You said you fought to a draw in the swords competition, right?"

"Yes. It was a long day, and the championship match lasted over an hour. I faced Alaric, who was already a member of the Guard. Between my speed and his reach neither of us was able to land a hit. By the end we could barely lift our swords, and we shook hands on a tie. At the awards ceremony I was given the winnings anyway, since members of the Guard were not eligible to win the funds, having sworn themselves to the crown. Utherrian asked me inside after, and in the throne room he asked me to join the Guard. I was shocked at first, but honored to accept. I took my winnings home to my parents, nearly two thousand gold pieces, enough to last them the rest of their lives. I said goodbye to them and came to live in the castle."

Joshua smiled and said "I'm glad that you did."

Rainira returned the smile and gestured toward the door at the far end of the hall. "How about we finish the tour?"

"Lead the way," Joshua said, and followed her out the door. She led him through the next two rooms quickly. The first was a smaller room, and the walls were lined with maps. A tall, slender man stood at a table in the back, drawing on a large piece of canvas.

"This is Johan, the cartographer I told you about. He became Eringhal's only map-maker after the Tourney three years ago, so we came to the castle at the same time."

"It's a pleasure to meet you. I'm Joshua." He looked around the room and said "Your work is beautiful!"

"Thank you Joshua," Johan said, offering a small bow.

Joshua walked to a large map that dominated one of the walls. On it were two continents. The one to the west was drawn in golden and silver ink, while the one to the east was drawn in black and red. "The known world," Johan explained. "Galion to the west, Ska'ell to the east."

Rainira pointed to a large castle, surrounded by mountains, drawn in the south western part of Ska'ell. "That's Karanlik," she said. "Lacrym's castle. And over here," she pointed to a city in the north east of Galion, surrounded by walls. "Over here is Erith, where we are now."

Joshua looked over the rest of the map, amazed at how far they had come from the forest in the west. There was still a long way to travel.

Rainira led Joshua from the map room to the next door in the hall. "The last two doors here both lead into the armory. It used to be two smaller rooms, but Utherrian had the center wall taken out to make more room."

The armory was completely filled with weapons. Racks of swords lined one wall, while axes and hammers lined another. The back wall was covered in shelves all the way up to the ceiling, overflowing with armor.

"The city's smiths and armorers have been busy the past few

years. Utherrian has had them making blades and armor as fast as they could, in preparation of the day that we march on Ska'ell, or they march on us."

Rainira led Joshua back to the entry hall. She gestured to the door straight across from the main doors. "That is the throne room, and from there you can get to the counsel room and the larger conference hall. I am sure Utherrian will show you that later."

Rainira took Joshua through the doors to the left of the main entrance. He found himself in a long hallway, with three doors to the left. Another hall branched off from the middle, forming a large "T." Rainira led him down this hallway. "This entire wing is the sleeping quarters. The three rooms we passed at the beginning are guest rooms, though they are rarely used anymore. Along this wall," Rainira gestured to her left, "are the Guards' rooms. The first room there on the right is Utherrian's, and this final room will be yours."

She opened the door and led him into a large room. The floor was covered in a thick golden carpet. A fireplace was set into the far wall, with large wooden chairs with silver cushions placed in front of it. To the left, at the end of the room, was a bed larger than any Joshua had ever seen. Posts rose from the four corners of the bed, each thicker than Joshua's chest and intricately carved with beautiful designs. A blue blanket was draped across the bed, and at least a dozen pillows laid against the headboard. A large window was set into the wall high above the bed, the transparent section made of large glass blocks that looked surprisingly solid.

"You will get a tour of the grounds some other time. For now you should get some rest. Utherrian will likely be by in a short while to get you."

"Thanks Rainira," Joshua said, his attention held by the sight of such a luxurious bed. He broke his stare and looked at Rainira, offering her a big smile.

Rainira laughed and left the room, leaving Joshua alone. He walked around the room, looking at the paintings on the walls. One in particular, hung above the fireplace, caught his eye. It was a portrait of a man and his family. The man wore a crown, and his arm was around the waist of a beautiful woman. His right hand rested on the shoulder of a small girl, and the woman's left arm held a baby wrapped in a silver blanket. Joshua walked to the painting and noticed a small plate at the bottom. It said "King Resavit and the Royal Family. 1072 AD."

Bookshelves stood on either side of the fireplace, filled with large, leather bound books. Joshua looked over them, their titles mostly names of places and things he had never heard of. Some caught his eye, like "The Dragon Wars: A History" and "On Light and Dark." There were catalogues and encyclopedias, and at the bottom he saw a couple without titles.

Joshua continued to move around the room, finally making his way to the bed. He took off his boots and fell into the center of the bed. Its mattress was even softer than it looked, and within minutes Joshua drifted off to sleep.

36

The Throne Room

The sun was beginning to set when Utherrian shook Joshua awake. Joshua sat up groggily, wiping the sleep from his eyes. He yawned and stretched.

"How long was I out?" he asked.

Utherrian laughed. "Long enough, my King. It is still the same day that you went to sleep, if that is what you are asking."

"It was." Joshua yawned again before standing up. He found his shoes and pulled them on, tying the laces tight as he looked at Utherrian. The Steward had moved to the fireplace and was looking up at the painting.

"The royal family," Joshua said. "At least that's what the plaque says."

Utherrian nodded, his face somber.

"Did you know them?" Joshua asked, walking to look at the painting with Utherrian.

Utherrian looked to Joshua. "Yes, I knew them." He stared back up at the painting, seeming to lose himself a bit in it. "I knew them very well."

"Were you with them when...when they were...when they died?"

"I was with the Queen, but could not save her," Utherrian said, hanging his head. He turned away from the painting and started for the door.

"Why not?" Joshua asked, standing his ground.

"I was following orders."

"From whom?"

"From King Resavit."

"What orders could the King have given you that could be more important than protecting him?" Joshua demanded.

Utherrian turned and looked at Joshua, his eyes heavy. "He ordered me to protect his children."

Joshua glanced at the picture, specifically at the young boy and girl. "What happened to them? Were you able to protect them?"

A tear rolled down Utherrian's cheek, though no emotion showed beyond his eyes. "Not exactly," he said. With that he turned and left the room. Joshua paused a moment before following the Steward into the hall.

Utherrian was silent as he led Joshua through the halls. The Steward led Joshua through the entryway and into the throne room. Joshua stopped in his tracks upon entering the room, stunned.

The room had a vaulted ceiling taller than any he had seen in the castle. Directly above him the ceiling reached a point, and the slant in the ceiling, combined with the shrinking carpet below him, forced the eye directly to the far end of the room to a raised platform. Three steps above the rest of the room sat a large throne, gilded in silver and gold. Even in the fading daylight the throne seemed to shine, and Joshua saw that the same type of stones that Chapel Lux was made of were strewn throughout the throne, giving it a similar ephemeral glow. Two feet to the left of the throne sat a smaller chair, also gilded in silver and gold, but without the luminescent stones. At the base of the steps, to the right of the throne, sat another seat, this one made of simple polished stone.

Utherrian walked to the simple seat and sat down, beckoning Joshua to join him. Joshua walked through the hall, eying the windows set high above. There was no glass in these windows, only a small outcropping in the room above would keep the elements out in the case of a storm. Joshua recalled Nitika's story of her assassination attempt and kept checking the vaulted windows as he advanced up the aisle.

The rest of the room was simple. Pillars lined the aisle, though they stayed the same width apart as the carpet narrowed toward the throne, giving the appearance that the room was growing wider despite its rectangular shape. The walls were adorned with a dozen banners on either side, each bearing the seal of Galion. Above the throne Joshua saw three banners. To the left and right were larger banners bearing the seal, but in the center was a different banner. It was the same silver, but with golden edging. Rather than the bird in the center, this banner had a circle stitched in gold. Within the circle was a four pointed star, its points extending beyond the circle. The star was stitched with a thread that shone out from the banner, making it the focal point of the room, rivaled only by the throne itself.

Utherrian watched quietly as Joshua took in the room. When he saw the young king's eyes fixed on the banner directly above the throne he said, "That is the Crest of Light. The star has not shone in seventeen years. Not since King Resavit was killed, right in this very hall"

Joshua looked down to his feet, half expecting to see a dark stain in the golden carpet beneath him.

"What happened that day?" Joshua asked.

Utherrian sighed heavily. "It was night, actually, although you may have already surmised as much," he said. "I still do not know how, but a band of vampires got into the castle that night. Ten in total. Three of them came in through the windows above. Four came through the front door, killing the guards posted there in the chaos of their surprise attack. The final three came through the basement, following an entrance that we have since closed. King Resavit and I were here in the throne room, and as the vampires flooded in he ordered me to leave him and find his children. I disobeyed at first, but the King commanded me again and I left his side. Four guards had come into the throne room and so I left to find his children and the Queen."

Utherrian fell silent. He stood from his seat and paced in front of the throne, struggling with the memories of that fateful night. "The Queen and the Prince were in the King's quarters. Two of the vampires had arrived ahead of me, and the Queen was holding them back with a sword she had found somewhere. The sword gleamed with Light, and if not for that the vampires would have made short work of her. Even with the sword the vampires overtook her as she stood in front of the Prince. He was young, only four at the time, and he stood against the wall, terrified. As the vampires attacked she lowered her blade and cast a spell before they were upon her.

"I remember the scene as if it had only just happened," he whispered. "The two vampires tore into the Queen as light surrounded the young Prince. By the time they had finished with her the Prince had vanished. I dispatched the two vampires and rushed back to the throne room. The vampires had disappeared, leaving the King's body in pieces around the throne. One of the Guards was wounded but thankfully alive. He informed me that the Princess had come running into the throne room, and when the vampires saw her they grabbed her and made off into the night."

Utherrian stopped in front of the throne, looking up at the Crest of Light, his back to Joshua.

"So they killed the King and Queen and took the Princess?" Joshua asked. He turned the story over in his mind. "What happened to the Prince?"

Utherrian turned and looked at Joshua for a long while before answering. "That I do not know," he said, his voice distant. "I assume that Lacrym's forces found him and either killed him or converted him, as there has been no word of him since."

Joshua was silent, trying to imagine the fear and chaos that must have filled the castle that night, and beyond that to the terror that must have gripped the entire kingdom at the news of their royal family's demise. His mind couldn't even fathom the scale of it, and he shook his head in an attempt to clear it.

"In the end," Utherrian continued, "all I could do was continue as Galion's Steward and attempt to hold the kingdom together. I succeeded, for a time, but with no heir even I could not hold it together forever. Soon the people moved on, going back to their own lives and forgetting about the throne altogether, leaving their fates in the hands of the Light. Ten years after that night I began my search for the true King of Galion. That search took me seven years, and ended only when I found you."

Joshua hung his head, uncomfortable with the weight of the role Utherrian had thrust upon him. He looked at the Steward, at the dragon Utherrian, and saw the light from the throne and the banner shining around him. Joshua had sworn to do what he could to help Utherrian, to help all of the Guard, and he stood by his word. King or not, he would give his life for Erith and for Galion. He looked at Utherrian and said, "So what happens now?"

Utherrian smiled, a beaming smile that rivalled the light behind him. "Now we prepare. We start to plan. According to the manifestations of the Light, we have one year to gather our forces and take the fight to Ska'ell."

"Don't forget the band here in Erith," Joshua interjected. "We have to take care of them before we can even think of taking Erith's forces across the ocean."

"Very true, my King, very true," Utherrian began pacing again. "I have already dispatched a dozen spies into the city. We shall, hopefully, have information on this band of Darkness that lurks among us within the week. At that point we can move against them and begin our preparations for the true fight."

"I would like to lead the strike against them," Joshua said. "I think it would help to rally the people of the city."

"That is a noble idea, my King, but one that I cannot allow. Your safety is more important now than ever. Without you to lead, there is no hope of Erith's strength rallying against the Darkness."

Joshua looked down at the floor, upset that the Steward had refused the idea so quickly. He took a while to compose himself before looking back to Utherrian. "So what am I supposed to do in the meantime?"

"Take the throne," Utherrian said bluntly.

Utherrian sounded as if the idea was simple, as if the mere act of Joshua sitting on the throne would make some massive difference. "I can't, Utherrian, not yet. I can't sit on that throne until I've proved to the people that I'm worthy of leading them. I can't sit on it until I've proven that to myself."

Utherrian sighed, but walked to Joshua and laid a hand on his shoulder. "At some point you must, Joshua. If you do not take your place as King, if you do not take the throne and the crown, there is no chance that the people will accept you as King."

"I'm sorry, Utherrian, but I can't do it. Not yet."

"Then we must find a way for you to gain your confidence without putting you in harm's way."

"I can't think of another way. Can you?"

Utherrian thought about that for a long while, silent. He paced as he muttered to himself, his brow furrowed as he wracked his brain for options. When nothing came to mind he finally turned back to Joshua. "I do not know, my King. Hopefully, by the time the matter of the Dark forces within the city is resolved, we will have thought of something. Until then, let us move forward. There is plenty to do before you address the people."

Joshua looked to Utherrian, concerned that the Steward would try to force him to take the throne before he was ready. He pushed the worry aside, knowing that Utherrian would only insist as a last resort. "Then let's get to work," he said, offering a hand to Utherrian.

Utherrian looked at the young king and smiled. He still had many concerns, but for now he would accept that Joshua was willing to at least act the part. Utherrian grasped Joshua's hand. "Let us get to work."

37
War Plans

Utherrian led Joshua to the door in the back corner of the throne room. It was a plain door, designed to blend into the surrounding wall. Utherrian pulled it open and ushered Joshua inside.

The room was small compared to all the others in the castle. In the middle sat a long table made of some type of wood that had been polished to a reflective shine. The center of the table had been carved into a topographical map of Camledor. Placed on the table were carved wooden tokens, some painted white and others painted black. The table was surrounded by eleven chairs, ten of which had low backs and were made of the same wood as the table. The eleventh sat at the far end of the table from the door, its back substantially higher than the others and its spokes carved into elegant, flowing patterns.

On the wall across from the door Joshua saw the same three banners that hung behind the throne, though these were substantially smaller to fit in the room. A row of bookshelves lined the wall to the left, filled with large volumes bound in leather. The right wall was dominated by another large map. Instead of the artistic colors used in the map Joshua had seen in Johan's map room, this one was very utilitarian, drawn in black with faint grid lines, separating the map into districts.

Martin turned from one of the bookcases as Joshua finished

looking around the room. "Hello, my King," Martin said. He looked exhausted. "How are you settling in?"

"I'm doing fine, definitely glad to have had a chance to sleep in a nice bed," Joshua replied.

"That is good, very good," Martin said distractedly. "Come on in and have a seat."

Martin took a chair at the middle of the table. Utherrian took the chair at the end closest to the door while Joshua walked around and sat in the small chair opposite Martin.

"I am going to make this brief," Martin said. "I thought it would be best to give you an overview of what we are facing. The white pillars on the map here are representations of our forces throughout the world, while the black pieces are Lacrym's forces."

Joshua looked around the map. In Galion there were more than a dozen white pieces: one in Erith; another in a city to the south that was dominated by a large tower labelled Artek; another piece was in Dollet; and three pieces sat in separate towns around a lake in the southwest called Pirn, Aerilon, and Hwen. Two more white pieces, along with one black piece, sat in open areas on either side of the Galatian Mountains.

In Ska'ell there was one more white piece in the city of Onryx. The rest of the pieces on the continent were black. Karanlik in the southwest, Lacrym's castle, had one. A tower called Astrakhan in the southeast and Ula'ree to the north of it each held a piece. A volcano to the north of Karanlik had a piece. Four more pieces were scattered through the desert in the south, and three more were scattered around the north.

No pieces, black or white, were on any of the islands around the map.

"As you can see," Martin said, "we are currently outnumbered. The good news is that the pieces only represent current, official military units. Our hope is that once you have taken the throne and your presence is known throughout Galion, the people will come forward and volunteer for service. We will not force anyone to serve, but we must impress on them that we will need more men."

Utherrian leaned forward. "We have been working on a plan for months, one that was not based on your return, but it still seems to be the best course of action to me," Utherrian said. "Martin and I just altered the plan to include the information that we received at Chapel Lux."

Utherrian slid a drawer out of the table and pulled a small white wooden boat out and placed it at Erith's docks. He began to slide the boat to the east across the ocean. "We will depart in approximately one year. Two ships will leave at that time, the Guard on one and a small contingent of warriors on the other, and we will head to the Cave of Shadows-"

"Against all common sense," Martin interrupted.

Utherrian glanced at Martin but ignored the comment. He moved the boat to a large island to the north. There was a cave in the northwest of the island.

"What is the Cave of Shadows?" Joshua asked.

"It is a place of magic," Martin said. "Ancient magic. The veil between worlds is thin there, and any who enter confront the deepest, darkest parts of themselves. Many have gone mad within the cave, many more have died."

Martin pushed himself back from the table with force and stood up. He looked at Utherrian and yelled, "This is a needless risk! No good can come from such a distraction!"

Utherrian remained calm, staring at Martin. "The Light itself told the King to go there. I choose to place my faith in the power of the Light. There is plenty of time to discuss this at a later date. For now, let us move on."

Martin sat down, sulking in his chair as Utherrian continued. Utherrian placed another ship on the map by Erith and began to move it southeast across the ocean. At the same time he moved the first ship south. The two met at Onryx. "The remainder of our fleet will carry the rest of our forces across the ocean. We will leave ample forces within Erith to protect the city in the event that Lacrym launches an offensive while we are in Ska'ell." Utherrian placed a white piece on the map. "From Onryx we will travel north along the bay before turning south." He moved the piece as he spoke. "We will cross the desert near its center so that we can avoid the volcano and the forces placed there. We are hoping that the forces garrisoned there will come out to meet us. The more that we can draw into the open and away from their defences the better our odds in the final fight. If we are unable to draw them out, the force at the back of our advance will split off to keep them busy as the rest of us advance on Karanlik and attack Lacrym head on."

Utherrian moved the white piece against the black piece at Karanlik. He and Martin were silent for a while as Joshua looked at the map. When Joshua sat back Utherrian began to move the pieces back to their original locations.

"How will the battle go?" Joshua asked, his voice quiet.

"It will be bloody," Utherrian said somberly. "We will lose many of our own in the fight. There is no other choice, however, as any delay will only give Lacrym more time to consolidate his power."

Joshua stood from the table and walked to the tall chair at the end of the table. He laid a hand on the back of the chair and looked across at Utherrian. "There's not really anything I can add to this, you two know what you're doing more than I ever will, or at least more than I will in the next year. If you say this is the only way, it's the only way."

Utherrian nodded. "That is all that we have for you for tonight. Get some rest. We will be taking this week to start preparations here in Eringhal. We will hold your official coronation as soon as possible, followed by a feast in the dining hall. Until then, the castle is yours and you may do whatever you like. I would suggest that you speak with Nitika soon, hear her story. She can give you valuable information about Lacrym's forces. Over the coming months I want the entire Guard training with her as well, as we will be up against many vampires in this fight. Knowing their potential will be crucial to victory. There are books in your room, many of which you would do well to read, as they contain information about the creatures we will be facing."

Utherrian stood and walked to the door.

"Thank you Utherrian," Joshua said. "And thank you Martin."

Both men nodded to Joshua and left the room. Joshua glanced back at the map, especially at the black pieces. He looked up at the center banner on the wall, the one depicting the Crest of Light. He sighed, then turned and left the room, closing the door behind him.

38

The Grounds at Night

Joshua wandered the halls of the castle, thinking of the coming war. It all seemed too large, too real. He couldn't fathom how he was supposed to lead an entire nation to war, especially one that he didn't even know existed less than a month ago. He walked to his room, but after looking over the bookshelf he turned and left, too restless to go to bed. The thoughts spinning through his head were starting to overwhelm him, causing him to panic. He finally broke and ran from the room and back to the entry hall. He pushed his way through the doors and out into the night.

Joshua ran across the quad without thinking of the direction. It didn't take him long before he was met with the castle walls. He put his hands out and leaned against the smooth stone before turning and sliding to the ground. He began to sob, tears rolling from his eyes as he pulled his legs up. He threw his head back and screamed into the night, then pulled his legs to his chest and buried his face in his arms.

He did not know how long he sat that way, but after a while his sobbing subsided and he sat quietly, looking up at the strange arrangement of stars in the night's sky. He looked up and did his best to block thought from his mind. Eventually Joshua stood and wiped his eyes, taking a few deep breaths to compose himself before walking back towards the castle. He took the long way around, passing numerous small buildings and the large dirt circle that made up the training grounds. As he passed he heard noise coming from the training grounds. Still feeling a bit restless, Joshua turned towards the sound and walked into the dirt.

The dirt of the training grounds was dry, and as Joshua walked dust kicked up around him. He made it to the middle before a curved blade appeared in the night in front of him, its blade reflecting the light from the moon. A thought later and Joshua was encased in shining armor, his rapier held before him in the night. The light from the armor illuminated the space in front of him, and he saw a figure dressed in black, a hood obscuring their features. Teeth appeared beneath the hood, fangs gleaming in the moonlight as the figure smiled.

The figure struck out at Joshua, the small curved blade moving almost too fast to see. Joshua moved his rapier to his left quickly, pushing the strike to the side. In his left hand a small shield appeared. The figure spun and slashed, and Joshua moved the shield into the path of the attack, the sound of metal loud in the quiet of the night.

The figure backed off, then disappeared completely. Joshua looked around, unable to see where the attacker had disappeared to. Before he could spot the figure, a force threw him forward from behind. Joshua was sent sprawling into the dirt. As he rolled over he looked up to see the figure. The hood lowered and Joshua found himself looking into the smiling face of Nitika.

"My King," Nitika said, offering a hand. Joshua took it and accepted the help. Nitika sheathed her blade and bowed before Joshua. "I am sorry for the surprise, my King. I am happy that you were able to react quickly, but I apologize if I frightened you."

Joshua's armor, blade, and shield disappeared. He sat in the dirt, his heart racing. He looked up at Nitika and tried to laugh. "It's actually a relief," Joshua said. "It helped to distract me from my own thoughts."

"Is everything alright my King?"

"Far from it," Joshua said. "I'm freaking out, to be honest."

"About what?" Nitika asked, sitting in the dirt across from Joshua.

"Everything," Joshua admitted. "About being King, about

the war, about the battles that we're going to face...Hell, the Cave of Shadows is terrifying enough to face, let alone the idea that I'm supposed to ask hundreds...thousands of people to die for me. It's a lot to take in."

Nitika looked at Joshua for a while as he continued to attempt coming to grips with everything that had been thrust upon him. Finally Joshua looked up and offered Nitika a weak smile.

"We have a year to prepare," Nitika offered. "It is not much, but it is time enough for you to learn that this is not a weight that you must carry alone."

"I know that," Joshua said. "All of you have been amazing so far, and I know that you'll help me, I'm just overwhelmed."

"I would be surprised, possibly even concerned, if you were perfectly fine with everything."

Joshua laughed, finally beginning to calm down again. He looked across at Nitika. "Why do you seem so familiar to me?" he asked.

"I do not know, my King. All that I can say is that I feel the same way. I feel some draw to you, some feeling beyond duty that makes me want to protect and help you."

"It's strange, isn't it?"

"No stranger for you than a world filled with vampires and goblins, I am sure."

Joshua laughed at that. "I guess you're right there."

Nitika fell silent, her entire body perfectly still in the night. She looked over Joshua carefully. "My King, why are you out in the dark alone?"

"I just told you," Joshua said. "I was overwhelmed. Martin and Utherrian just gave me a summary of the state of the world. I can tell you, it was not a very reassuring presentation."

"I do not think that it was meant to be, my King. I think that they respected you enough to tell you the truth, not a pile of lies that would ease your mind."

Joshua nodded. "I understand that. It's just that...hell...I didn't even know this place existed not too long ago. I didn't know that any of you existed. I didn't know there was a possibility of magic, and had no idea that deities could actually be real."

"Give it time," Nitika said. She reached across and took Joshua's hand. "In time everything will make more sense. You have a year to settle in, to accept your place among us. No one expects you to do it all in one night."

Joshua pushed his hands against his eyes, trying to clear his head and calm his emotions. "I know that you're right. I'm sure that I'll get there eventually."

"You will, and we will all help you along the way."

Joshua smiled as he lowered his hands. "In any case, Utherrian told me that I should talk to you, that you had a story that would help me understand what we're up against."

Nitika looked away, gazing out across the castle grounds.

"You don't have to tell me if you don't want to-"

"No," Nitika interrupted. "It is fine. You should know more about the Darkness, and who better to tell you than a vampire."

"Nitika, I didn't mean to imply-"

"You implied nothing," Nitika interrupted again. "Martin did though. And Utherrian. They let me in, acted as if I was one of them, but they both constantly make it clear that I am different, I am the one on the outside."

"If it makes a difference, you're one of my favorites," Joshua said. Nitika snapped her gaze back to Joshua. "In all of this you've been the most understanding. I feel like you're the only one who understands what I'm going through right now. You're the only one that knows what it's like to be an outsider trying to be a part of this."

Nitika smiled, but her eyes betrayed the emotion within her. "You are not wrong," she said softly. "It has taken me a long time to convince the Guard that I could be trusted. I do not blame them, I was an agent of Darkness sent to assassinate their Steward, the highest office in Galion at the time. If I had succeeded you and I would not be sitting here right now. The Steward is the only one who believed that the King was still out there to be found."

"So what happened to you?" Joshua asked. "What brought you here? What made you serve the Light and protect Utherrian instead of killing him?"

Nitika sighed, but she looked at Joshua and forced a smile. "It all began a long time ago. I have no memory of my childhood, a side effect of being corrupted by Dark magic, but I remember every bit of my conversion...and the events that followed."

Nitika fell silent for a moment, and Joshua gave her a nudge. "Tell me, please."

Nitika took Joshua's hand in hers, inviting his magic to bring the memory to life, took a breath, and began to tell Joshua her story.

39

Darkness and Blood

"I was sixteen when Logan Lacrym corrupted my soul with Darkness," Nitika said, staring off into the night. "It was the most violated I had ever felt, like he reached deep inside me and ripped something pure out. I remember screaming in pain...

Nitika screamed in the darkness. Her arms and legs were bound by thick chains that stretched her out in all directions. The dark stone she was held to was cold against her naked body. Lacrym stood in front of her, leering at her young body as he cast his dark magic. He let her rest a moment, and she noticed that he appeared average in almost every way. Average height, a slightly hefty weight, and with short brown hair. The only thing that set him apart from other men that she had seen was the twisted coil of scars around his face that formed an upside down triangle connecting his eyes and mouth.

Lacrym lifted his hands into the air and twisted them towards her. She felt as though his hands reached directly inside her and took hold of something vital. He moved his hands downward slowly, the pain increasing within her chest and stomach.

"I have no desire to kill you," Lacrym said, his voice a soft melody. "I merely want you to serve me, and serve me you shall."

Lacrym ripped his hands backwards, pulling a scream from Nitika's throat. The pain was beyond anything that she had imagined possible. It wasn't long before she blacked out, the pain too much for her to bear.

When she awoke, Lacrym was still in front of her. She looked down to see that her body was dripping with water. Her throat was dry and burned.

"Drink..." she choked, her voice weak.

"I am sorry, dear, but I did not catch that," Lacrym said, a sadistic smile across his face.

"Thirsty," Nitika said, the word taking all of her energy.

"That is understandable," Lacrym said. "You are transitioning, the Darkness is working its way inside you. Soon you shall drink deeply and be more satisfied than you have ever been."

Lacrym turned and walked from the room, leaving Nitika alone in the darkness.

It was days before Lacrym returned, and in all that time Nitika never once became hungry. It was the thirst that dominated her world, a desperate thirst that blurred out every other feeling. There was no joy, no love, no thought beyond the thirst.

When Lacrym finally returned he was followed by a young girl, twelve at the most. The young girl stood in the middle of the room, silent, her head hung low before her. Lacrym went to Nitika and lifted her head. "It is time to complete the transition," he whispered, kissing her cheek. Nitika recoiled at the intimate touch and Lacrym laughed. "It is no matter," he said. "Either you will feed, or you will shrivel where you stand and die a hundred deaths."

Nitika glared at Lacrym, pushing against the chains as hard as she could, trying to get to the man's throat. Lacrym laughed, the sound making Nitika's blood boil. He walked back to the young girl in the center of the room and pulled a knife, drawing the flat of the blade sensually across the girl's shoulder. He looked back at Nitika and smiled before cutting the side of the girl's neck. The wound wasn't enough to threaten the girl's life, but the smell of blood flooded Nitika's senses. Her vision turned red and her entire body was racked with longing. Lacrym walked through the door and closed it behind him. Nitika barely registered a snapping sound before the chains around her fell away, casting her to the floor. Nitika landed on her feet, and in her red haze she rushed to the little girl and plunged her face into the girl's neck.

Nitika bit and blood gushed into her mouth, giving her a sense of relief stronger than any she had ever felt. She sucked at the girl's neck, the blood rushing down her throat. The girl's body went limp and Nitika's arms wrapped around her and held her close. She cradled the girl's body close as she *drained the blood from it, every drop a revelation to her body.*

Finally the girl's body was completely drained and Nitika let her fall to the ground. She stood slowly, noticing for the first time in days that she was naked. She crossed her arms over her breasts, then looked towards the door and saw Lacrym watching. He threw back his head and laughed with pleasure as Nitika rushed forward, slamming into the door.

Lacrym laughed even harder. "Do not fret, my dear, you shall soon serve me with joy. It will not be long now."

Lacrym was still laughing as he walked away down the corridor that led from Nitika's cell. She heard a snap echo down the hall and in an instant the chains jumped out and ensnared her again, pulling her back against the wall. A day later the thirst began again, wiping out all thought...

"I went on that way for a month," Nitika told Joshua. "He would starve me for a week, then bring me children to feed on. Every time after the first he would ask me if I would like to swear allegiance to him. It only took a month, four feedings, for me to give in to the darkness and swear to him."

Nitika was on her knees in the center of the dark stone chamber. Blood dripped from her chin as she stared at the body in front of her. It was another young girl, this time only six or seven. Nitika wanted to scream, to cry, to curl into a ball in the corner. When she looked up at Lacrym her sorrow vanished and rage washed over her. She leapt forward in a flash, but Lacrym knocked her back quickly, a black force throwing her to the ground. She sneered up at him from the cold stone. Lacrym twisted his hand and pain ripped through Nitika's head. She screamed, and when the pain stopped Nitika was left quivering in the pool of the young girl's blood.

"This all can end," Lacrym said. "All you need do is swear your allegiance to me and to serve the Darkness."

Nitika stayed quiet, her mind racing with a million emotions. She shook on the ground, trying to calm herself. The fire was back in her throat already, the blood from the child barely sating her thirst. It took all of her will, but she remained silent until she could finally pull herself back to her knees.

"If you continue to refuse, your meals will get smaller and smaller," Lacrym said, a sweet smile spread across his face. "Eventually they will stop altogether, and I will leave you to starve here, slowly. It will take years. There is nothing left for you to go back to, so you have two, simple options: you

may refuse my offer and wither and die here, slowly, in great pain; or, you may accept my offer and the pain will end. The choice is yours."

The truth sank into Nitika and she began to sob, though no tears came from her eyes. "Yes," she whispered, her voice cracking.

Lacrym leaned forward. "I'm sorry dear, I did not catch that. You will need to speak up."

Nitika closed her eyes and stood up slowly. She opened her eyes and looked at Lacrym. "Yes," she croaked, a bit louder this time. "I accept your offer."

"Very good!" Lacrym said. "This is wonderful news!"

Nitika hung her head, shame washing over her.

Lacrym walked forward and took Nitika's hands in his. He turned and spoke to one of the guards behind him. "Give me your cloak."

The guard unhooked his cloak and handed it to Lacrym. He turned and draped the cloak over Nitika's shoulders. She wrapped the fabric around her tightly, acutely aware of her nakedness for the first time in weeks. She looked up at Lacrym.

"Come with me my dear, we will get you properly clothed and fed. I have a very special place for you within my castle, one that I think you will be very happy with."

Lacrym led Nitika through the halls of the dungeon. She passed countless doors, sounds of pain or torture coming from behind many of them. She did her best to block out the sounds as she followed Lacrym up a flight of stairs and into the first floor of the castle. The rooms were still dark, but they were much more open than the rooms below. There were no windows, so the only light was cast by torches hung on the walls. She was nearly blinded, even in the soft light, but her eyes began to adjust quickly. Lacrym led her down a series of twisting hallways and past dozens of doors before finally leading her through one. Inside was a very small bedroom, completely windowless, with only a large standing cabinet in one corner and a small desk and chair in the other. She went to the cabinet and opened it, finding a number of outfits hanging within. She went through them quickly as Lacrym left the room, closing the door behind him. She selected one and slipped into it, the leather hugging her form like a second skin. Dressed for the first time in a month, she went back to the door and opened it.

Lacrym looked her up and down and smiled. "The outfit fits you stunningly. And it suits the role that I have for you to play in my kingdom."

"What is it that you would have me do?" Nitika asked.

"Now, now, my dear, that can wait. We have some business to attend to first. Follow me."

Lacrym led Nitika down another series of halls and opened a small, indistinct door. He gestured inside and Nitika entered. "Before we move further, please, drink."

Lacrym closed the door behind her and Nitika found herself alone in a room that was perfectly dark and filled with the smell of blood. It overwhelmed her, consumed her, and she tore through the room. The blood consumed all thought, her mind and vision going red as she was guided through the room by scent alone. The blood flowed down her throat in a torrent, silencing the screaming in her mind and squelching the fire in her throat. In moments she was satisfied and stood in the middle of the room. She still smelled the blood, but her need for it had disappeared. She walked back to the door and knocked on it. It opened and she stepped back into the hallway.

"How do you feel?" Lacrym asked.

"Better," Nitika responded. She could feel her strength returning, even more than before, and her eyes no longer hurt from the light. She looked behind her through the door and saw the bodies of the children she had just fed on. Dozens of them, ranging from very young to mere teens. As she looked on she saw movement at the back of the room: more children, huddled together, shaking in terror as they looked at her. Nitika felt something in her mind begin to bend under the strain of emotion, and as she repressed her feelings she felt it snap. In an instant her emotional turmoil faded to a dull throb, easily ignorable.

Nitika reached out and closed the door, leaving the children in darkness.

"Wonderful," Lacrym said, offering a sweet smile. "If you would, my dear, please follow me."

Nitika followed Lacrym as he led her through the halls. She was able to take in her surroundings again, and she noticed that there was very little to see. The halls were all bare, black stone, and the floors were a polished, shiny black, but beyond that there was nothing. No decorations, no banners, nothing but the occasional torch. Lacrym led Nitika through another door, this one larger and decorated with some form of gleaming black stone.

On the other side of the door was a massive room with vaulted ceilings. At the end of the room was a throne on a raised platform. Lacrym walked to the throne and sat, throwing a leg over one of the arms and leaning back.

"Nitika," Lacrym said, his voice contemplative. "Nitika, Nitika... what do you remember?"

Nitika tried to think. "I remember nothing beyond the dungeon."

"That is very good news. Very good indeed." Lacrym leaned back, arching his back across the arm of his throne, stretching. "Well, my dear, there is one order of business that we must take care of before we move on."

"And what would that be?" Nitika asked.

Lacrym smiled and stood from his throne. He walked towards Nitika. "You must kneel and take the oath," he said.

Nitika hesitated only a moment before kneeling.

"My steward, Fulhar Heark, will give you the words."

A large man walked forward in jet black armor. He had been standing in the shadows near the throne, blending in with them completely. He walked to Nitika and whispered in her ear. When he was finished he stepped back and moved into the shadows again. Nitika lowered her eyes and took a breath that she realized she no longer needed. She looked back to Lacrym and spoke the words.

"I pledge my soul to the Darkness. I will serve the Dark with all my soul.

"I pledge my life to the throne. I will serve the throne through the rest of my life.

"I pledge everything that I am, I pledge all that I have, I pledge all that I will ever gain, to King Logan Lacrym, King of Ska'ell, Lord of the Darkness."

Lacrym sat straighter in his throne, his leg still over the armrest. "Very good my dear," he said. "Welcome to the family."

40
One with the Darkness

Nitika fell silent and closed her eyes and lowered her head, doing her best to not look at Joshua. Joshua reached across the dirt of the field and took her hand in his.

"It's ok," Joshua said. He rubbed Nitika's hand. "You don't have to go on if you don't want to."

Nitika took a deep breath and opened her eyes again. "No, I need to get through this. You need to hear it, and I think that I need to tell it."

"Then take your time, I'm not going anywhere."

Nitika forced a smile and stood up. She walked around the training yard as Joshua sat and watched her. She moved easily through the field, seeming to almost float. She made three full laps around the training pitch before returning to Joshua.

"May we walk, my King?" Nitika asked.

Joshua stood up, dusting himself off. "Of course," Joshua replied. "Lead the way."

Nitika led Joshua around the castle grounds. As they walked she seemed to relax, and by the second lap she fell back into her story.

"After my vows I was thrown into training. I spent months training with the other vampires in Karanlik, Logan's castle. They taught me to harness the powers that the Darkness had given me. The speed and agility, the strength. It was not long before I was reaching the top of the group, besting even the most seasoned vampires. To this day I do not know if it was something that Lacrym did to me, or if it was something innate. In any case, I became the best, and Lacrym took notice."

Nitika sat at the small desk in her room, reading over one of the many tactical works she had been provided. The text was dry, but she devoured it, loving the feeling of knowledge that seemed to pour into her mind. She was broken from her studies by a knock at her door.

"Come in," Nitika called.

The door opened and Lacrym walked through. He was dressed in his usual black and silver, looking both regal and comfortable at the same time. He strode into the room with ease.

"Nitika, my dear!" Lacrym said. "How has everything been going for you? I hope that you are settling in nicely."

"Yes sir, I believe that I have," Nitika said, standing as Lacrym walked into the room.

"That is wonderful news, wonderful!" Lacrym said as he walked to the desk and picked up the book Nitika had been studying. "'Influences of Darkness and the Effect on the Common Man'," he read. "An interesting read, but quite useless for our purposes here. The effect of the Darkness on the common man is liberation, freedom from question, freedom from the burden of thought. Complete and utter freedom."

Lacrym walked around the small room, looking over the few things that Nitika had gathered as her own. The inspection did not take long, and when Lacrym finished he stood before Nitika, looking her up and down.

"The new outfit suits you," he said. He gave another moment to inspect Nitika's skin tight black leather that covered her from jaw to feet, leaving no skin exposed. "Come, my dear, I have your first assignment."

Nitika followed Lacrym through Karanlik's halls and into the castle's throne room. Lacrym walked to the throne and sat, slinging a leg over the arm of the chair as usual. Nitika stopped at the base of the steps leading to the throne and gave a short bow.

"There is no need to stand on ceremony, my dear. You are at the top

of my people, and to reward you I am sending you on a special assignment."

Nitika looked up at Lacrym. "What assignment, sir?"

Lacrym stood and walked down to Nitika. He stood before her and took her hands in his. He rubbed the backs of her hands as he said "I am sending you to bring me something, something very valuable."

"And what would that be, sir?"

"The head of the Lightguard's captain. He is stationed in Onryx. Once you've taken his head, my forces will move in and take advantage of the confusion to take the city back for us once and for all." Lacrym dropped Nitika's hands and paced in front of her. "Galion has been encroaching on our continent, taking bits and pieces as they can. Their new Steward, Utherrian, has given them hope. He talks of a new king to fill Resavit's seat. I would be worried if the idea was not so thoroughly laughable."

Lacrym paused, tilting his head to the side as if trying to hear a distant sound. He stood still for a moment before bursting into laughter. "Listen to me," he chuckled, "going on and on. None of this is any concern of yours. For now, you need only to know your task. Bring me the head of the captain of the Lightguard. If you succeed, the tasks that follow will be just as grand, possibly even grander."

Nitika bowed to Lacrym. "It will be done, sir." Lacrym smiled and waved her away. Nitika left the hall without looking back, and made her way out of the castle. Once outside, she moved faster, disappearing into the night.

< < < > > >

"I moved through that entire night," Nitika told Joshua. "I slept during the days and moved at night. It only took me two nights to make it to the outskirts of Onryx. Once there, I did recon for two nights, determining the captain's movements. On the third night I was confident and made my move. There is not much to tell of the attack. I scaled the wall and made my way into his home. I bypassed his children and his wife before running a knife through the captain's chest. Once dead, I ripped his head from his shoulders and made my way back over the wall, and not once was I seen. Lacrym's forces attacked that same night, and without a captain to direct them, the Lightguard fell easily. Only one made it out, Alaric Lado, who led most of the citizens away on ships, but the city was Lacrym's again..."

< < < > > >

Lacrym greeted Nitika in the throne room upon her return. Nitika pulled the captain's head from a bag and tossed it on the floor in front of Lacrym before kneeling. Lacrym looked down at the severed head before kicking it across the hall, laughing.

"Nitika, my dear! Well done! Because of your actions, Onryx is ours again. Well done indeed!"

Lacrym walked down and took Nitika's hands. "My dear, you are going to do great things, and together we will do many more wondrous things throughout Camledor!"

< < < > > >

"Over the next six months Lacrym sent me out on assignments to assassinate other captains and high ranking officials of Galion's army, as well as outspoken dissidents within his own forces. I'm ashamed to say that I completed every task perfectly, not once being detected. I became one with the Darkness, melding into the shadows. By the end of the year I had helped whittle Galion's forces down to almost nothing. It was then that Lacrym gave me what would become my final assignment."

41
A Final Assignment

"It has been an interesting half year," Lacrym said to Nitika as she knelt before his throne. "You have performed admirably. Not one failure, not one slip up. Every name that I have given you has fallen soon after."

"Thank you, my King," Nitika said. "I am happy to be of service."

"As a reward, I am moving up my schedule and sending you on a special assignment. If this next assignment goes as well as your previous ones, I am confident that we will be able to take Erith by the spring, and we will have Eringhal by the beginning of summer."

"Whose life shall I be taking, my King?"

"You will be going after the Steward of Galion himself. Utherrian."

"The Steward never leaves Eringhal, my King. How will I reach him?"

"Walk with me my dear," Lacrym said, descending from the throne and offering Nitika a hand up. She stood and hooked her arm through his and walked with him through the halls of Karanlik. Lacrym led Nitika through multiple halls and down countless stairwells. Nitika was not sure where they were until Lacrym opened a door into a long dark hallway. She would never forget the dungeons. The smell of blood and decay hung thick throughout this hall, the sound of weeping and desperation filled the air. Lacrym led her to the end of the hall and opened a door. Nitika let go of his arm and walked into what had once been her cell. She walked around the

small room, running the chains through her hands, touching the cold, blood stained stones. For the first time in six months she felt a twinge of emotion deep in the reaches of her mind.

Nitika walked back to Lacrym and lowered her head. Lacrym reached out and pulled her face up to his. "Nitika, my dear, I did not mean this to be a negative reminder. I merely wanted to remind you of how far you have come in such a short time. You have been truly magnificent, and I am sure that you will do just as well on this assignment."

"Thank you, my King." Nitika said.

Lacrym offered Nitika a hand and led her back through the hallways and out of the castle. They walked down the castle steps and out into the desert. The full moon hung low in the sky, illuminating the sands that stretched out in every direction.

"I will be honest with you my dear," Lacrym said. "This assignment will be more difficult than any you have faced before. First, you will need to infiltrate Erith without alerting the guardsman. If you alert the guards, you will need to abandon the mission. Second, you will need to make your way through the city without arousing suspicion. If you do bring any attention to yourself, you will need to abandon the mission. Finally, you will need to get into Eringhal. If it has not been made clear by now, you must do so without alerting the castle guards. The Steward is generally in the throne room, tending to the needs of Galion. There are windows, set very high in that room. These windows will be your point of entry. Get inside, and bring me the head of Utherrian, the last bastion of Light in Galion."

Nitika nodded. "Your will be done."

"Very good my dear. Once you have completed your task, return here and we shall have a feast to celebrate the beginning of the end. You have the opportunity to raise our kingdom to the final level. You have the chance to spread the Darkness into the far reaches of the world, finally snuffing out the Light."

"I serve with pleasure, my King."

"May you be one with the Darkness, my dear."

< < < > > >

"I left that same night," Nitika said. "I made my way to Onryx. From there I took a ship across the ocean, dropping me south of Dollet so as not to alert the guards of Erith. From the coast I sped north to Dollet, where I found an abandoned building to spend the day in. That night, I made my way into the city..."

Nitika sped through the night, fast enough to disappear among the shadows. She approached the walls quickly, and she used her momentum to launch herself into the air. She met the wall fifteen feet off the ground, using her speed to propel herself upwards. She met the top of the wall and stood fast, taking a moment to take in her surroundings. A guardsman was in the distance, but far enough away that she knew she hadn't been spotted. She leapt off the other side of the wall and landed within the city of Erith. The rundown outer limits of the city surrounded her. She moved again, picking up speed and slipping between the buildings. Chapel Lux shone in the distance, but Nitika knew to keep her distance from the Light.

She passed into the inner city, and as the sun began to rise she made her way under a bridge where she spent the day. The city came alive with the daylight, but as night fell again Nitika began to move. There were still people in the streets, but Nitika moved smoothly between them. She made her way east in the city, finding an area where the buildings were dense against the inner walls of the castle. She climbed to the top of one of the buildings, using the vines and window ledges to make her way upwards. When she reached the roof she merged herself with the shadows and waited. She watched the guards moving along the inner wall for more than an hour. When she was finally able to nail down their movement she made her move. She timed the space between two guardsmen and launched herself over the wall at a run. Her black-clad body flew through the air like an arrow. She hit the ground in a roll, coming to a full stop in a large dirt pitch. She looked around quickly, realizing that she was in a training arena of sorts. She moved quickly, hiding in the shadows of a small building nearby.

Nitika watched the guardsmen moving around the field for another hour, waiting for her chance. As she waited, she inspected the other buildings, plotting her path to the roof of the castle. When Nitika saw a gap in the guards she moved again. She sprinted across the inner path, launching herself off the ground and into the air. She made the top of the first building easily. From the roof she leapt across a gap onto another building, one that sat at the bottom of the walls of the castle. She knelt in the shadows of the building's roof while she readied her next move. She pulled rope from a pouch at her back and attached a metal hook to the end.

Nitika crawled to the edge of the roof and watched the guards below. When another gap appeared she stepped to the middle of the roof and threw the grapple into the sky. Her enhanced hearing registered the hook sliding across the roof before it finally caught on something. She pulled the line tight and made her way up the side of the castle.

Once on the roof Nitika coiled the rope together before stowing it back in her pouch. She looked around before finding the single raised area in the roof, windows running the length of it. She moved silently to the windows and looked down into the throne room of Eringhal. Her face fell as she saw that the room was empty. She stayed still against one of the vertical pillars between the windows, waiting for her target to enter the throne room.

Nitika stayed still for three days in that position. The overhang for the windows was deep enough to keep the sunlight away from her, the castle roof was high enough that the guards on the inner wall could not see her, and the outer wall was too far away for anyone to see her statuesque form. She watched as Utherrian went in and out of the throne room, always accompanied by at least one other person. At numerous points she was about to leap into the room, planning on dispatching both individuals, but her desire for stealth stilled her.

Finally, on the fourth night, Utherrian walked into the throne room alone. He went to the Stewards chair and sat. Nitika watched for two hours, waiting for some sign of movement through the rest of the room. Utherrian finally stood and walked to the center of the hall's aisle and looked up at the Crest of Light. Nitika moved to the center of the window, ready to make her move, when Utherrian turned slightly and looked up, directly into Nitika's eyes. The Steward did not call for aid as Nitika expected, but merely stood, waiting, challenging her.

Nitika made the decision in an instant and dropped into the hall, her curved blades in her hands as she landed silently on the ground fifty feet below. She stood and approached Utherrian, moving slowly. Utherrian stood his ground, seemingly unworried about the oncoming assassin. Nitika stopped five steps from him, hesitating, confused by his lack of concern.

"Do you have any last words, Steward of Galion?" Nitika asked, her voice barely more than a whisper.

Utherrian looked Nitika up and down. "You've changed a great deal in the last year," he said casually.

"How would you know?"

"I know a great deal about you, Nitika. I know that you were forced into servitude by Lacrym, that he took your life from you and replaced it with Darkness."

Nitika was shocked but did her best to mask the emotion.

"I know that you began your official service approximately half a year ago, and that in that time you have taken the lives of a great many good men. Those attacks paved the way for Lacrym to take the lives of countless more."

Nitika's composure broke and her shock became obvious on her face. "There is no way that you could know that I had anything at all to do with those attacks. I was never once spotted, there would have been no one to carry the message back to you."

"Your face remained hidden, but you cannot hide who you are inside, and you have a very unique soul."

"My soul is the Darkness that I serve. I am the best of Lacrym's assassins. Beyond that there is nothing unique about who I am."

"Try, Nitika, try to remember. What is the last thing that you can recall of your history?"

Nitika thought about it for a moment before responding. "I was in a dungeon, desperate for a drink, consumed by thirst. Before that there was nothing. Before that I was nothing."

Utherrian sighed. He turned away from Nitika and walked towards the Steward's chair at the base of the throne dais. He turned back to Nitika and said "There is much more before that. Push, you must remember!"

Nitika tried to push, but every time that she tried to remember anything before her time as a vampire she was blocked by that wall of red, that unending time of thirst. She pushed harder against that wall, and for a moment she found a glimmer of something more, some memory that was white instead of red. She took hold of that thought and used it to try and pull herself through, but the memory was nothing but white. That whiteness washed through her, and she could feel a part of her mind healing, bringing with it a wave of emotions. She staggered slightly as the wave crashed over her, six months of repressed feelings hitting her all at once.

She cleared her mind and realized that the Darkness still encompassed *her, shrouding those white memories from her conscious mind.*

"There is nothing before the Darkness," Nitika hissed, trying to mask the uncertainty that had crept into her voice. "In the beginning there was nothing but Darkness, and Lacrym will ensure that there will be nothing but Darkness again soon. As for your baseless notion that I was ever anything more than I am now, you are mistaken."

"It would seem that my desires have been thwarted by my own actions," Utherrian said. "Those actions may well cost me my life, but they will ensure that Galion will survive, that the Light will continue to shine against the Darkness."

"What actions?" Nitika asked.

"I locked something away one year ago today, something very precious, but something that must remain hidden."

"Take me to it," Nitika ordered. "Lacrym would be pleased with such a prize to commemorate the fall of Galion."

"I cannot, Nitika, it is locked away somewhere that even I cannot reach it."

"Then I believe you have outlived your usefulness, Utherrian."

Utherrian laughed, "That is probably true. I have lived a long time, and I have done much with my life, but I fall asleep each night worried that it will all have been for nothing."

"Are you prepared to die?"

Utherrian looked into Nitika's eyes. "Yes, Nitika, I am prepared. But before you do, there is something you should know."

"What is that?"

"You need not serve the Darkness. I can see that there is still Light within you."

It was Nitika's turn to laugh. "I swore an oath to the Darkness, to Logan Lacrym, and forsook all binds to the Light. I am an agent of the Darkness, and there is no way back from where I am."

"But there is, Nitika, there is!" Utherrian said, his voice hopeful. "You can still turn from the Darkness and choose to serve the Light. Nothing, save for death, is absolute in this world. Every choice is followed by another. Every mistake can be corrected. Every vow can be broken. Every oath can be undone."

Nitika held Utherrian's gaze for a while before looking down at her feet. She shuffled in place a bit before saying, "Lacrym would destroy me if

I broke my vow to him."

"I can promise that you will be safe, or at least as safe as anyone in Camledor is anymore. I will make you a part of the Steward's Guard, the King's Guard to be. You will be my shadow, my personal protector. You will protect the rest of the Guard and myself, and in return we will protect you. For Lacrym to destroy you, he would first have to kill all of us."

Nitika looked back up at Utherrian. "Why would you offer this to me?"

"Because we all make mistakes, and all of us deserve a second chance."

Nitika dropped her knives to the ground as tears welled up in her eyes. The knives clattered, the sound echoing through the hall. "Tell me what to do," she asked, her voice shaking as she clung to the wave of emotion that had swelled up within her.

Utherrian smiled and walked to her. He held out his arms and Nitika threw herself into them without a moment's hesitation. Utherrian embraced her, and when Nitika stepped back he saw tears on her cheeks.

"Nitika," Utherrian said, his voice gentle yet firm. "Kneel before the Crest of Light and forsake your ties to the Darkness. Swear that you will protect the Steward of Galion, that you will serve the throne once it has been filled. Promise that you will be fair and true and faithful to those around you."

Nitika walked past Utherrian to the base of the stairs that led to Eringhal's throne. She looked up at the Crest of Light and her legs buckled beneath her. She fell to her knees and bowed her head, her entire body shaking with her sobs. Tears fell in torrents down her face.

Nitika looked up at the Crest and spoke, her voice choked. "I renounce the Darkness that made me. I renounce my oath to Logan Lacrym, and hereby break my vow to his cause. In its place, I swear that I will protect Utherrian, Steward of Galion, and that I will serve the King of Galion, should such ever arrive. I will do all that I can to be fair and true and faithful in my duty."

Light burst forth from the Crest high above the throne. Tendrils of Light filled the hall and encircled Nitika. The tendrils came closer and closer before rushing inside her. Nitika threw her head back and screamed, an ear-splitting sound that was heard throughout Erith that night. The pain escalated inside her. She wanted to curl up, to protect herself from it, but it held her tight in its grasp. The pain continued to build until she thought that *she would burst into flame or simply explode. Just when she thought that she couldn't handle another moment, the tendrils of Light receded from her. She gasped for breath, and when she was finally able to sit up she noticed a figure standing before her.*

The figure was made of Light, with the tendrils spiraling out from its back, connecting it to the Crest. "Your oath has been accepted," the voice said, whispering and booming at the same time. "The Light has looked into you and found you worthy of a second chance. It has severed the Darkness's control over you, though it cannot return you fully to what you once were. Protect Galion, Nitika, as a servant of the Light."

Nitika looked at the figure, her body still. When she finally spoke it came out in a sob. "Thank you," she said through her tears.

The figure bowed its head to her before disappearing, dissolving back into tendrils of Light before disappearing within the Crest again.

Utherrian appeared at Nitika's side and offered her a hand. She took it and rose to her feet. Utherrian took Nitika into his arms again as she shivered. "It will be alright, Nitika. You are free of the Darkness, free of Lacrym's control. You are one of us now, and we protect our own."

41

A History Lesson

Joshua and Nitika had walked three laps around the castle as she told her story. When she finished they found themselves back near the training grounds. In the moonlight Joshua saw tears on Nitika's face. He reached over and took her hand, and as soon as he touched her she turned and threw her arms around him, burying her face in his shoulder. Joshua stroked her hair as he waited for her to calm down.

When Nitika finally stepped back she laughed. "It is odd to have so many emotions running through your head all at once," she said. "I am constantly ashamed of what I have done, but at the same time I am happy with where I wound up. I am grateful that the Light deigned to offer me a second chance. If not for that, I would be back with Lacrym. The war would have ended, Galion would have burned, and I never would have met you. I do not know what it is, but I feel drawn to you in a way I have never felt before."

Joshua smiled at Nitika. "I'm glad that you made the choices you did. You weren't yourself when you were under the Darkness's control." Joshua turned to start walking back to the castle. "And I feel the same connection," he said over his shoulder.

Nitika followed Joshua back into the castle. In the entry hall Nitika took her leave and went off to the right, heading towards the armory or dining hall or perhaps the map room. Joshua yawned as he turned left towards his room.

As Joshua opened the door to his room he found Utherrian within, sitting in one of the chairs by the fire. The Steward was gazing up at the painting of the Resavit family, lost in thought. Joshua swung the door shut behind him and Utherrian jumped when it clapped shut. He stood quickly, a book falling from his lap and onto the floor.

"My King, I apologize, I did not mean to intrude," Utherrian said.

"It's alright Utherrian," Joshua responded. "You're always welcome here. I feel like I'm the one intruding. I am the one who's new to the castle after all."

Utherrian bent and picked up the book that had been sitting in his lap. It was one of the large, unnamed works that lined the bottom of the bookcase. Joshua looked over and saw a space where the book had sat, the last in the series.

"What's that?" Joshua asked.

"This is the final journal of King Roland Resavit," Utherrian said, brushing off the cover of the book. "I doubt that anyone has read through these in the twenty years since he died."

"What's in it?"

"The last five years of the late King's life. There are details in here about the escalation in the war that brought us to our current point. King Resavit wrote nearly every night, detailing as much as he could. I think that it would do you good to read through it if you are sincere in helping us to win the war. It can bring you up to speed far better, and far more thoroughly, than countless meetings ever could," Utherrian said, holding the book out to Joshua.

Joshua stepped forward and took the journal. It was heavy, and easily a couple of hundred pages long. Joshua opened to the first page and looked at it. The text was written in a tight, looping script. At the top of the first page was a date: 1071 AD.

"Utherrian, what year is it?" Joshua asked.

"It is 1092 AD," Utherrian responded.

"AD?"

"It means 'After Dragons'," Utherrian explained. "The end of the Dragon Wars marked a new era for humans in Camledor. It was the end of the Dragons, and during the wars almost all of the recorded history of mankind was lost."

"So what happened after the wars were done?"

"Much has happened Joshua, more than I could possibly explain in a night."

"Then just give me an overview. If you want me to read about the last five years of King Resavit's life it might help to have some context."

"Very true," Utherrian said. He gestured to the chairs in front of the fire and they both sat. Utherrian closed his eyes for a moment, organizing his thoughts. "Just the big events, I do not think a detailed recounting will be necessary for you.

"As you know, the Dragon wars lasted five-hundred years. By the end the population of humans in Camledor was reduced by more than half, and all but three of the dragons had been killed. The new calendar marks the day that King Tamkiell took the throne. For many years the world was at peace. In 67 AD King Tamkiell died, naturally. His son, King Tamkiell II, ruled for the next 64 years before being killed in 131 AD by his court magician. His son, King Tamkiell III, took the throne next, and for the next 340 years his line held the throne and the world in peace. In 471 AD, King Tamkiell IX created the Assembly, a group of men chosen by all the people of Camledor. The Assembly ruled for another 342 years without conflict.

"In 813 AD, Ska'ell broke from the Assembly to form its own government across the sea. King Flagg took the throne in Ska'ell, and the peace held for another 130 years. Things began to turn dark when King Flagg III took the throne in 943. He refused to work with the Assembly on many things, demanding more than he offered. Then, in 999 AD, King Flagg III was killed on the throne by his only son, Logan. Logan took the throne and gave up the Flagg name. Instead, he took on the surname Lacrym. When the Assembly refused to acknowledge him as King, Logan Lacrym made a pact with the Darkness and the obsidian dragon, Droven, in exchange for power and declared war on Galion.

"Over the next 30 years the world became a much more dangerous place, and the 1000 years of near perfect peace was officially gone. In 1030 AD, with the war threatening the shores of Galion, the Assembly unanimously voted to appoint Roland Resavit, who was actually a descendant of the Tamkiell line of Kings, as King of Galion to give Galion a central figure to rally behind. That same year, King Resavit named me as Steward of Galion. I had been the Assembly's record and history keeper, so I assume the King thought my knowledge would be useful.

"In 1076 AD, King Resavit and his wife were killed and their children went missing. All of Erith mourned for weeks, assuming the worst for the children of the King. By the end of the year our forces were under siege throughout Camledor and the people began to push for me to take the throne. I refused, attempting to build up faith that the royal line was not, as they believed, gone. In the twenty years that followed I gathered a small Guard together, and then this year I finally succeeded in finding someone worthy of taking the throne."

Utherrian looked up at the Resavit family portrait again. "I can only hope that I have done right by Roland, he was a true friend."

The Steward fell silent. Joshua looked up at the painting as well, trying to keep track of all the dates and information that Utherrian had just given him. Finally, Joshua said "I think that you've done well, Utherrian. Galion is still standing, and the Light in Chapel Lux seems to remain hopeful."

Utherrian chuckled. "Thank you, my King. I hope that you are right." Utherrian stood from the chair and walked towards the door. He turned and pointed at the journal in Joshua's lap. "You really should read that, I think that you will like Roland Resavit almost as much as I do by the end."

With that the Steward left the room, closing the door behind him. Joshua looked down at the book, then set it aside, too tired to begin reading. Instead he stripped off his clothing and crawled into his bed, falling asleep the moment his head hit the pillow.

43
Death or Service

When Joshua woke the next day the sun was already climbing in the sky. He slid from the bed and dressed. He grabbed King Resavit's journal and left his room, heading directly towards the dining hall. On his way he passed Martin in the entry hall.

"Good morning, my King," Martin said.

"Good morning Martin, how are you?" Joshua responded.

"As well as can be expected. Will today be the day you finally take the throne, my King?"

Joshua looked at his feet and sighed. "I don't think so Martin, I don't think I'm ready yet."

Martin made no effort to hide his exasperation. "What will it take for you to *be* ready then?" he spat. Noticing his tone, he bowed his head and added, "my King."

Joshua thought about it. "I honestly don't know. For now it just seems like the moment I sit on the throne, everything becomes real."

"Everything is already very real, my King. It does no one any good to delay." Martin walked into the throne room without giving Joshua a chance to respond. Joshua watched him go, shocked by the abrupt departure. Shaking his head, Joshua continued on his way to the dining hall.

When Joshua entered he thought the hall was empty, but then he spotted Ryland sitting alone near the kitchens. Joshua walked to the table and gestured to one of the empty chairs.

"Do you mind some company, Ryland?" Joshua asked.

Ryland looked up. "Not at all my King!" he said jovially. "Sit, sit, let me go tell Megno to make you something."

Joshua began to protest, but Ryland was already gone through the kitchen door. Joshua noticed that the large man was stumbling a bit.

Ryland returned quickly, carrying two bowls of steaming oatmeal and two large tankards. He sat and slid one of the bowls and tankards to Joshua. Joshua lifted the tankard to his mouth and caught the strong scent of alcohol. He set the tankard back down and pushed it away.

"I think it's a bit early for drinking," Joshua said. "Thank you though."

Ryland laughed. "Never too early for that, my King, especially when one is fighting a wicked hangover. More for me I suppose." He reached over and took the tankard, lifting it to his mouth and drinking the booze in one gulp. He slammed it back to the table and let out a loud belch that filled the hall.

Joshua turned back to his bowl and began to eat the oatmeal, its heat warming him. He watched as Ryland picked at his meal, paying more attention to the second tankard in front of him. This one he drank more slowly, but still at a voracious pace for the early time of day.

"Ryland," Joshua said.

"Yes, my King?"

"I just realized that I don't really know much about you. The rest of the Guard has told me their stories, but I don't know yours."

Ryland laughed loudly, letting out another strong belch in the process. "There is not much to know, my King, but go ahead and ask anything. What is it you would like to know?"

Joshua thought for a moment. "How did you join the Guard?"

"I was a drunk!" Ryland said, a bit too loud. He drank deeply from the tankard and seemed to think about the statement. "Still am, I guess. Anyhow, Utherrian found me in the streets of Erith after a particularly fine week of drinking. As it turned out, I must have killed a man in my drunken haze, and Utherrian brought me to Eringhal to charge me. He got me here, dried me out, and when it came time for the sentencing he said that I was to serve life as one of the Steward's Guard. I thought that he was joking, but he said that as long as I stayed sober in the field I would be allowed to serve. If I got drunk in the field, he said he would execute me himself. Been a little over a decade now, and I have held up my end of the bargain, just as Utherrian has. Proud to do it too, it has been good for me."

Joshua nodded, returning to his meal. When he finished he took the empty dishes back into the kitchen and when he returned to Ryland he found the large man passed out on the table. Joshua checked to make sure he was still breathing, grabbed the journal, and left.

Not knowing where else to go, Joshua returned to his room. He sat by the window, opened King Resavit's journal, and began to read.

44

King Resavit's Journal

1071 AD

The war continues to get worse. Lacrym has been sending forces into Galion for over a month, but the attacks do not seem to be any real attempt to conquer us. I fear that he is teasing us, testing us, finding our weak points. Thus far we have held the attacks back without much problem, though we have lost a few men along the way. Good men, strong, the kind we will need in order to win this war. Perhaps Lacrym is merely trying to wear us down...

Joshua continued to read. The entries weren't marked with the days or months, but there were breaks between each entry, and it didn't take Joshua long to realize that each empty line between entries noted the passing of a day. There were times when an entire page would be left blank, usually after an entry detailing some expedition or another that the King was leaving on.

The entries were very scattered, switching topics randomly. Most days the King wrote about the war, about reports that had come in or battles that had been described to him. Other days he would write about his family, the Queen and their daughter. As Joshua worked his way through 1072 AD he came across an entry that was a single line:

Susan has given birth, and it is a boy! Thank the Light, the Resavit line will continue!

Joshua smiled, looking across the room at the young boy in

the painting, trying to imagine what Roland must have felt. Joshua continued reading through the day, skipping lunch and forgetting dinner. As the sun began to set there was a knock on his door.

"Come in!" Joshua called.

Rainira walked into the room carrying a tray. The smell of food hit Joshua's nostrils and his stomach rumbled. Rainira laughed. "It would seem that I came just in time," she said. She set the tray down on the table in front of the fire. "When I did not see you in the dining hall at lunch or dinner I assumed that you must be busy with something, so I thought that I would bring you some food."

"Thank you Rainira," Joshua said, eyeing the plate.

"What is that?" Rainira asked, pointing to the book in Joshua's hand.

"King Resavit's last journal," Joshua responded, picking up a roll from the tray and biting into it. "Utherrian thought that I should read it, and so far it's been fascinating."

Rainira looked out the window, then to the fireplace. "Well, if you are going to continue reading you will need light. Would you like me to light a fire?"

Joshua was shoving food into his mouth and swallowed hard. He gasped for air and said, "That would be great. I've never been very good at getting them lit."

Rainira smiled and began to pile logs in the fireplace. She worked quickly, and within minutes she had a roaring fire going.

"Thank you, Rainira, I really appreciate that. And the food."

"You are welcome, my King. Unless you need anything else, I should be going, there is much to do."

Joshua nodded, a bit sad that she was leaving so quickly. "I understand. I should get back to reading anyway. Thank you again."

"Good night, my King," Rainira said. She bowed her head and smiled before leaving the room.

Joshua sat and ate the rest of the food that she had brought before opening the journal again and picking up where he had left off. He read until the fire had burned itself out, too caught up in the journal to notice the dying flames. With the light gone and the sun set, Joshua marked his place in the journal and set it aside. He stripped and crawled into bed, thinking of Roland's writings and the royal family as he fell asleep.

45

Awakened Memories

Joshua woke early the next morning. Rather than getting right into the journal, he left the room and made his way to the dining hall, intent on not forgetting to eat. The hall was empty when he arrived, and he was unable to find anyone in the kitchen, so Joshua took a couple of rolls and left the castle. He found a tree on the grounds and sat beneath it to eat, watching the sun rise over the castle walls and listening to the city come alive beyond them.

Joshua stayed outside that morning, watching the people coming and going through the castle doors. He was far enough away from the main path that no one noticed him, but he had a feeling like he was being watched. He scanned the courtyard carefully, finally spotting Nitika sitting on top of one of the small buildings, her back to the castle's walls. He raised a hand in the air and waved to her. In the distance he could see her wave back, though she made no move to join him.

As he began to feel hungry again Joshua stood and walked back to the dining hall. Most of the Guard was present, and Joshua joined them to eat. Ryland was in the middle of telling a long drinking story, and Joshua was content to eat in silence and listen, happily joining the Guard in laughter.

When the meal was finished Joshua helped take the dishes into the kitchen. On their way out of the hall, Ryland caught Joshua's hand and stopped him.

"My King," he said softly. "I wanted to apologize for my behavior yesterday morning. Sometimes I get a little too into the drink when we are in Eringhal. I hope I said nothing to offend you."

"You didn't," Joshua said with a smile. "I enjoyed hearing your story, and I hope to hear more of it someday."

"Well, ask away! I am an open book for the King!"

Joshua laughed. "Not today, Ryland, I have a lot of reading to get done. Thank you though, I will take you up on that soon."

Ryland clapped Joshua on the back and left the hall. Alone, Joshua walked through the halls across the castle and back into his room. He settled into one of the chairs in front of the fireplace and opened Roland's journal to the place he had left off. He was a little more than halfway through the large book, but had already begun reading about 1075 AD.

Things still seemed to be pretty much the same in Eringhal during that year. The gaps between days were shorter than before, Roland leaving the castle less frequently. Most of the pages were a recounting of reports being sent to the castle during the day. The sun was beginning to set as Joshua reached the final section of the journal.

1076 AD, the year that Roland Resavit died. A chill ran down Joshua's spine at the realization that he was reading a first-hand account of a man's last year alive. The year started off similar to the others: reports came in, Roland sent units out to meet Lacrym's forces, and there were the occasional accounts of the royal family, though those were becoming more and more scarce.

The sun set as he was reading, and Rainira came in to build him a fire again before heading off to bed. Joshua wished her a good night, then settled in to continue reading. When the fire finally began to burn low, Joshua flipped through the pages until he found the last page with writing, then paged backwards to the beginning of the section, not wanting to wait another day to read the end.

I have come to the end. There is little left for me to do to face the coming Darkness. Logan Lacrym wields Dark magic the likes of which I have never heard. There are rumors that Droven, an obsidian dragon, possibly the last, is with Lacrym, though which one is the master is beyond me. Either way, it is a threat that must be dealt with before too long. I can only hope that I have heard of the news early enough to quash this uprising.

In any case, I take joy in the knowledge that my son is already showing signs of aptitude for rule. Just today he helped a young girl in the street, and the boy is only four! The young girl had fallen down, and he brought her into the castle to have her skinned knees treated. I am constantly in awe of the boy's kind heart.

My daughter, on the other hand, is as stubborn and defiant as always. She disappears most nights, heading into the city to cavort with the less savory folk who occupy Erith's streets in the dark. I can only hope that the Darkness has not already begun to take her.

Joshua reached the last page, the handwriting growing a bit sloppier as the King wrote faster.

My heart is heavy in these dark times. We have enjoyed generations of peace under the Assembly, but the growing Darkness in the west gives me pause. I can only hope that I can end this war before too long. If I do not return it will mean that I have fallen, for I will not leave this throne, or this world, voluntarily with the Darkness still spreading.

If I should fall to the forces of Darkness, it will be left to my son to take up the crown and finish the war. I only hope that the Light will guide him. I have already instructed Utherrian to watch after the boy no matter what. I've ordered the Steward to protect him until the time is right to take the fight to Lacrym. I can only hope that Utherrian has taken the request to heart. Please, Utherrian, watch over him, watch over my Joshua...

As he read his own name a bolt of pain shot through Joshua's head and he fell from the chair, the journal tumbling to the floor. He reached up and dug his fingers into his hair, screaming as pain ripped through his mind. Flashes came to him, memories, threatening to tear him apart. He screwed his eyes shut as he fell forward onto his knees with his forehead against the floor, his fingers still digging into his scalp.

A young boy, maybe two years old, ran through the stone halls of the castle, his arm outstretched and holding a long silver ribbon that gleamed despite the lack of light through the windows.

Joshua realized that it was him. The memory disappeared in a flash, only to be replaced by another.

The same boy, now three, stood outside the dirt training grounds and swung a long, thin wooden sword, pretending to fight like the men in the circle. He laughed as he thrust forward, then clumsily danced around in a circle, slashing again before falling to the ground, dirt puffing up around him. His laughter echoed through the afternoon sky.

Flash.

The same boy, now four, terrified. He stood trembling against the stone walls of his parent's room. His mother had been reading to him moments ago, but now she was laying before him in a pool of her own blood. Monsters stood above her, and they were looking at him. Their mouths dripped with his mother's blood, and the boy began to cry, Joshua began to cry. He looked past the monsters and saw Utherrian burst into the room. In a blink Joshua was surrounded by bright light, and when he was able to see again he was in the middle of a forest.

Four days passed, and Joshua was scared. He had found water and some berries, but he was feeling sick. He fell into a troubled sleep amongst the trees. On the fifth day he was awoken by Utherrian. He cried as he threw his arms around the man's neck. Utherrian held him close, offering what comfort he could to the small boy.

"You are going to have to go away for a while," Utherrian whispered.

"Where am I going?" Joshua asked.

"To a place far from here. A place where you will be safe."

"Will mother and father be coming?"

A tear fell from Utherrian's eye as he looked at the small child. "I am sorry Joshua, but they cannot come with you. You have to be brave. I will come back for you when the time is right, I promise."

With that Utherrian led Joshua into a clearing in the forest and drew a circle around him and the boy. He raised his staff into the air and brought it down in the center of the circle. An orb of light burst out around them, and as Utherrian muttered something under his breath the orb closed in. Joshua was once again blinded by the light, and when he opened his eyes he found himself in a strange bed.

He looked around but was unable to recognize anything. Despite his terrified state, he felt a heavy weariness fall over him and he fell asleep. When he woke in the morning he had no memory of his family...no memory of Galion or Camledor...no memory of the life that had been taken from him...

As the memory faded the pain in Joshua's head subsided. He

raised his head and looked up at the painting above the fireplace again.

"Mother," he whispered. "Father..."

"Yes," Joshua heard from behind him. He turned to see Utherrian.

Before Joshua could say anything Nitika appeared behind Utherrian, her eyes wide. She looked at Joshua and rushed into the room, throwing herself to her knees and wrapping her arms around Joshua.

Joshua looked at the painting behind him, then embraced Nitika tightly, pulling her close.

"Brother," Nitika sobbed.

"Yes," Joshua responded, his voice choked with emotion, tears rolling down his face. Another memory consumed him for a moment, a vision of himself at three with his then teenage older sister playing with him out on the castle grounds. "Yes, Nitika, I am here."

They held each other for a long time, and when Joshua finally regained himself and stood he found that Utherrian was still standing in the doorway, watching them.

"I am relieved that it worked," Utherrian whispered.

"What worked?" Joshua demanded, his voice hot with anger.

"When I sent you away I locked the memory of the royal family's children away in that journal. Only when someone of royal blood read the final entry would the spell be broken."

"You stole my life," Joshua accused, straining to maintain a semblance of reason. "You stole seventeen years from me."

"No," Utherrian said. "I gave you the chance to grow in peace. Hate me if you must, but if I had not done what I chose to do, you would have died that night along with your mother, and the last of the Resavit line would have been consumed by Darkness."

Joshua looked down, and Nitika took his hand, squeezing it to reassure him. Joshua looked at Utherrian and frowned. He brushed past the Steward and out into the hall, still holding Nitika's hand. She followed willingly. The rest of the Guard were in the hall as Joshua entered, all of them looking confused, but he remained silent as he walked past them all. They shared a look before falling in behind Joshua. Utherrian and Martin followed behind the group.

Joshua made his way through the halls easily, almost as if

guided by some force outside of himself. He went through the entry hall and threw the doors open to the throne room. He walked straight up the center aisle towards the throne, finally stopping when he reached the foot of the stairs leading upwards.

Joshua stopped and turned. Nitika had stopped a couple paces behind, and the Guard was formed around her. They moved aside to let Utherrian and Martin through as they came up the aisle.

"Joshua, please, talk to me," Utherrian pleaded.

Joshua glared at Utherrian. "No," he said, his voice stern, more confident than ever. "You and I have much to talk about, but not now." He took a step backwards towards the throne.

"As you wish, Joshua," Utherrian said. "Just tell us, what is going on?"

Joshua took two more steps upwards. He turned and looked up at the Crest of Light, flanked by the Seal of Galion. He took the final few steps towards the throne and went to one knee before the banners, bowing his head for a moment, letting his memories flood through him. He stood and turned to the Guard.

"Utherrian took something from all of us. He stole memories that we all had. He locked away the memory of my sister and of myself from the entire world," Joshua said. The Guard looked at Utherrian, confused. Joshua drew their attention back to him. "While his actions are questionable, his intentions were pure. There will be much to discuss in the coming year, but for now let it be known that I can forgive him."

"Thank you Joshua," Utherrian said, bowing his head.

Rainira looked around at the Guard, "What is going on? My King...Steward...what is this?" She reached up and rubbed her temples. "What are these thoughts running through my head?"

"I am confused as well, Rainira, but I am sure that there is an explanation," Alaric added.

The Guard began to mumble amongst themselves, trying to understand what was happening to them. Little did they know that the same thing was happening throughout Camledor. People woke from their beds in the night, their minds reeling. Across the ocean, deep in the halls of Karanlik, Logan Lacrym sat straight up in bed, a cold sweat covering him as he screamed in rage. Everywhere, everyone's mind was spinning with memories of a royal family long thought deceased.

"I am Joshua Resavit," Joshua said from the throne room of Eringhal. The Guard fell silent at once. "I am the chosen servant of the Light, and the last living male heir of the Resavit line," his voice boomed through the stone hall. Joshua looked down at the Guard as he slowly sat on the throne. "I am your true King."

Alaric was the first to step forward. He walked to the base of the throne and knelt, lowering his head. Nitika was next, followed by Rainira. Corwin and Ryland took a knee next. Martin and Utherrian approached the throne last. They looked at each other, and Joshua noticed that Utherrian was smiling as they both took a knee together.

In one voice, the Guard said "All hail the King!"

"I am Joshua Resavit, your King," Joshua said. "Rise, and prepare yourselves for tomorrow."

The Guard rose and Utherrian asked "What happens tomorrow, my King?"

Joshua looked over all of them slowly, his gaze coming to rest on Utherrian. He met the Steward's silver eyes and held them for a long time before answering.

"Tomorrow we begin preparations for war."

END OF BOOK ONE

Author's Note

This book was first written during NaNoWriMo 2016. The idea had been swimming around in my head for a couple of years at that point, and the event helped me to get everything on paper. Books two and three in this series were written during NaNoWriMo 2017 and 2018, so the conclusion of Joshua's story is already on the page, it just needs to be cleaned up.

The books sat on my shelf for a couple of years while I tried to figure out what to do with them. Publication became more difficult during and after the COVID pandemic, so eventually I decided to publish the first part myself, which is what you hold in your hand.

I did not get here alone though. Special thanks to:

- Jamie Benn for proofreading and editing the final draft, her input was invaluable,
- Mike Lees for the amazing cover art, he nailed Utherrian (and put up with my constant requests for tweaks),
- Sonny Onderwater and Nemesea, who allowed me to use quotes from their music, which was inspirational for many scenes throughout the trilogy, and
- Most of all to my wife, Brittanie Lewis, who helped throughout the process. She gave me space to write, helped polish the final draft, helped with the jacket blurb, and overall just supported the hell out of this project.

Finally, thank you for giving a new author a chance. I hope to see you again when Lillith, book two of the Blood & Dragons trilogy, comes out.

-M. S. Lewis

About the Author

M. S. Lewis lives in Pennsylvania with his wife, daughter, and nineteen animals. While not writing, he passes the time playing board games, painting tiny figures, or relaxing with his cats.

He has always loved the escapism of books, and hopes to give his readers the gift that so many authors have already given him: a bit of peace within the pages.